A Better Next

A Better Next

A Novel

Maren Cooper

SHE WRITES PRESS

Published May 2019
Printed in the United States of America
Print ISBN: 978-1-63152-493-6
E-ISBN: 978-1-63152-494-3
Library of Congress Control Number: 2018965117

For information, address:
She Writes Press
1569 Solano Ave #546
Berkeley, CA 94707

Interior design by Tabitha Lahr

She Writes Press is a division of SparkPoint Studio, LLC.

This is a work of fiction. Names, characters, places, and incidents either are the product of the author's imagination or are used fictitiously. Any resemblance to actual persons, living or dead, is entirely coincidental.

Epigraph

◇◇◇◇◇◇◇◇◇◇◇◇◇◇◇◇◇◇◇◇◇◇

And the day came when the risk to remain tight in a bud
was more painful than the risk it took to blossom.

—Anaïs Nin

Chapter 1

◇◇◇◇◇◇◇◇◇◇◇◇◇◇◇◇◇◇◇

An errant breeze unfurled her loosely belted robe as Jess dipped down to pick up the newspaper snagged between budding azalea branches near the front step. She savored the touch of her nakedness as she retied her robe and smiled, rested after the deep sleep that always followed making love with Arthur. His arrival in the early-morning hours after a late flight home had been a surprise. She remembered how her skin had tingled as she'd woken to his touch, their bodies instantly aroused, hungry to satisfy themselves and each other. It had been awhile but worth the wait. She pondered the possibility that the sex had been good because no words had been spoken, body language all they had needed. Of late, that was the safest communication between them.

She went back inside, started coffee, and considered the rare luxury of the Saturday ahead: their son, Tom, away at baseball camp; their daughter, Beth, off at Stanford; and Arthur in town. She carried the newspaper to the bedroom, shivering as she dropped her robe on the floor near her nightgown, and slipped back into bed to spoon Arthur and extend the mood.

"Your feet are cold."

"Exactly why I'm here." She giggled and planted baby kisses on his shoulders, still youthful from years of hockey, now some thirty years earlier.

"Paper here?" Arthur sat up and pulled it from the middle of the bed, forcing Jess to adjust her position. "And did I hear you start coffee?" He yawned, looked past her at the bedside clock, and flinched. "Is it really ten fifteen? I've got to get to the lab." He gave her the briefest of kisses and hightailed it to the shower.

She followed him into the bathroom, already losing hope. "You know, you just flew into town. Maybe you could take the day off, for a change, and spend some time with your wife?"

"Can't hear you. Can I have coffee ready to go in a thermal mug?"

And that was that. No surprise to Jess. They again went their separate ways, she to the grocery store and dry cleaner, and Arthur to the lab for a few hours. After a midafternoon lunch together in the kitchen, Jess saw the opportunity to nail down the family calendar for the next few months. It was always complicated, and as Beth neared the end of her sophomore year and her upcoming theater performance and Tom approached his senior year of high school, they had important dates to prioritize that spring.

"Aha! Gotcha. You're here, so let's do this thing." Jess grabbed the calendar posted on the bulletin board above the kitchen-corner office with an eye on Arthur.

"I've gotta go in a minute. Can this wait?" he groaned, taking his lunch dishes to the sink and dropping them in noisily.

"It will take only five minutes, and no, it can't wait. Your haircut isn't until four."

"Can't you just do it?" He was backing out of the kitchen.

"Nope. This is *our* family, not *my* family, and if I schedule something that doesn't work for you . . . well, we know how that ends." She feigned pulling her hair out and put her arms around him to corral him back to the kitchen work island, placing the calendar in the center. His body was rigid as he perched on the lip of a stool. Exhaling loudly, he went through the mail stacked on the island and responded in monosyllables when prodded. Jess kept her eyes on the calendar, quickly transcribing the decisions, as she knew he would not indulge her for long.

They made plans to meet at Stanford for Beth's play in April; Arthur would fly in from a meeting, Jess from their home in St. Louis. Tom's baseball games and prom night were still not sorted properly, but they had some luck with Arthur's schedule around their son's debate tournament. Jess wondered how they had ever been able to work any adults-only time into their schedule.

She turned the page to July and pointed at the big circle in the middle. "I guess we'll have a major celebration when the merger actually happens."

"You mean, *if* it happens," Arthur challenged, a hard edge in his voice. Jess knew he was concerned his academic career would lose its luster when a large private health care system took over his university hospital. And the fact that Jess worked as a consultant representing Midwest Health, the very system in question, certainly didn't help matters.

"Don't be silly. There's no stopping it now," Jess said, sorting through Tom's college application papers to check fall deadlines.

"You sound sure of yourself." Arthur's voice rose. "And you don't have a clue how wrong it is, do you?" He threw the sorted mail down in a huff, empty envelopes scattering onto the floor.

"Arthur, calm down. We don't have to go to any celebration if you don't want to go. I just thought it might be . . ." Jess reached for his hand, but he went for the envelopes.

"Might be what—fun for you and your friends to have a victory party?" His face was growing red.

"Arthur, you know that's not the way anyone looks at this." But Jess's words rang hollow, even to her. She knew mergers were always tough, even when both parties got something they wanted; people always needed a winning side. This one was particularly challenging. Protecting a university's mission of medical education and research while pursuing Midwest Health's business need to drive patient volume was akin to walking a tightrope.

Suddenly, Arthur's face became a mask of anger. "It doesn't matter. I'll be gone once the new regime is in charge!" he blustered as he shot off his stool so quickly, it rocked back and forth precariously. He stormed out of the room, leaving Jess open-mouthed, holding the family calendar. She jumped up, steadied the stool, and followed him.

"Arthur, why are you so upset? Let's discuss this." Arthur dodged her, and seeing that he intended to leave the room, she quickened her pace. Her anger finally matched his. "What are you talking about?" she yelled at him. "Come back here! What are you saying?"

He rounded the corner from the kitchen, beelining for the door to the garage, and said, "I've had enough! I'm taking my research to Portland, where I'll be appreciated." Behind him a step or two, she opened the just-slammed door to the garage in time to see his body turn to drive out. With no chance to make eye contact or be heard, she screamed, "Arthur! Arthur! What are you saying? Come back here!"

Her heart beating out of her chest and her fists closed tightly, she watched the door move down its track, looking like a willing prizefighter with no ready opponent.

She slammed the same door almost as hard as Arthur, but failed and then tried again and succeeded. She backed herself against it and lowered herself to the floor. Her breathing slowed. She saw Tom's missing sock under the bench in the entry and reached for it. It reminded her that she had laundry to fold. She pulled herself up and sleepwalked to the laundry room. She took out the fluffy and fresh-smelling clothes and swaddled herself with a still-warm towel while she stood at the utility room table, sorting and folding. Lots of men's briefs and T-shirts—nothing of Beth's. She missed having her daughter's girlie clothes around.

She climbed the stairs to put it all away, finally taking the towel from her shoulders, and peeked into Beth's room. The stuffed animals were still in order. She reached for her daughter's favorite dog-eared teddy bear and hugged it tightly to her chest, closing her eyes. After a moment, she repositioned the bear on the bed and returned to the kitchen.

The damn calendar had landed on a stool, pages aflutter. She picked it up and threw it back on the island. It landed, face up to June, that month now undone from its spiral tether.

As she threaded it back into place, she thought, *I can't even breathe. I have to get some air before I explode,* and pictured the welcome feel of pavement under her feet. She walked through the house twice before she found her running shoes, and searched three closets for a waterproof jacket. She fiddled with the stuck zipper until it unlocked so suddenly that the rapid motion got away from her and nearly pinched her neck. She looked at the ceiling and held her breath for five beats before leaving the house.

The wind whipped the patio furniture covers as she set out for her jog. It was starting to rain—not the best conditions for running. But nothing could stop her from finding a way to rebalance, maybe just go numb for a bit, not overthink anything.

After a block or two, she stopped gulping for air and breathed more steadily. She settled enough to take a quick inventory of her body and confirm that she was sure-footed as she navigated the slippery pavement. She was already getting wet, but her slicker would keep her upper body dry, so she was good to go the distance without turning back and facing Arthur too soon. She had to be calm before she could see him again.

Jess hoped her forty-five-year-old legs wouldn't give out as she rounded the first mile, past the nearby college campus buildings, noticing lights on inside and out. Dusk was falling, and the rain was coming down harder. Not many people around. Spring was unpredictable and could range from snow and sleet to early heat all in one week. She watched a couple run for their car, laughing as they tried to share an umbrella.

During the second mile, she tried to collect her thoughts, and on the third mile challenged herself to close off all emotion and focus on her next steps. She would not give up on this relationship. Too much at stake, too much pain for the people she loved to consider that.

Her mind darted wildly to an assortment of theories for Arthur's outburst. She had felt him pulling away for months. She couldn't remember the last time they had taken an evening stroll through their neighborhood or shared an intimate dinner out. She knew their work situation was part of the problem. It was bound to be difficult for them to be involved in opposing sides of a health care merger, but she had thought her twenty-plus-year marriage could survive the temporary strain.

All the principals at her firm who were working on the merger had had to disclose any real or potential conflicts of interest, and of course Jess had done so. She stated that she was married to a professor of surgery whose interest would lie with the university and not with Midwest Health, run by Dick Morrison, her client. Paperwork filed, she and Arthur had agreed not to discuss business at home during this time. But that wasn't a real change. Although he appreciated the sizable salary she brought in, he had never considered her health care consulting work particularly important. Not like curing cancer—which was, of course, what he was attempting to do.

But what would picking up his research and moving to Portland mean? It was an announcement, not up for discussion. Arthur was a gifted scientist with intellectual interests ranging far and wide. She had never known him to get overwrought about any business aspects of health care. Did the merger with his beloved university really make him feel this distraught? Was he that worried his research would be compromised in the new system?

The fourth and last mile was a struggle. The wind grew stronger and the rain even heavier. Her lower body was soaked through. And even though she was not ready to go home, she needed to deal with whatever came next. Her pace slowed considerably. One of her laces had come loose, and her socks had disappeared into the heels of her shoes, but she had made it. Only one light was on, in the living room.

As Jess came up the stairs after shedding her wet clothes, Arthur called to her from the lit corner of the room, using his dismissive voice: "You have forty-five minutes to get ready for the concert. We're picking up the Myerlys at seven fifteen."

She considered storming in and yelling her head off, but she was so bedraggled that she didn't have it in her to grasp the moment, so she merely whispered, "OK." She finally released tears of hurt and confusion in the sanctuary of a hot shower. Ever the well-preserved doctor's wife, she was ready for the concert in forty minutes flat, but not for the conversation now looming ahead of them.

Chapter 2

◊◊◊◊◊◊◊◊◊◊◊◊◊◊◊◊◊◊◊◊◊◊◊

No time for chatting on Sunday. The usual blur of catching up on laundry and household tasks and planning for the week occupied Jess, who barely saw Arthur, out somewhere until dinner. Sunday evening was always reserved for family and real conversation with the kids, now just Tom, at home. She was tired but put some effort into making chicken marsala, one of Tom's favorite dishes. He was full of fun stories about the baseball camp and hungry for home cooking. Arthur went to his home office after dinner cleanup, and Jess went to bed. She chalked up Saturday's drama to his letting off steam, something he could do safely with her. She was glad the merger would be finished soon—they needed to get back on the same team.

She overslept and got to work after nine a.m. on Monday. A scrawled note from Dan taped to her door and a blinking message light on her phone greeted her as she walked into her roomy space in the law offices of Getz and Braun. A floor-to-ceiling window facing north toward the Mississippi River gave her light without the blinding sun of an east or west orientation. A sitting area for casual meetings and a small conference table for work sessions allowed her to get most of her office work done right here.

Dan had offered her a corner office opposite his, but that wasn't her style. She much preferred being in the middle of things, able to watch people traffic up and down the corridor through the glass door. She had given up the freedom of her private consulting practice to bring her staff in-house with his law firm three years before. She had tired of the marketing part of her business, and Dan had the infrastructure she needed to tap into. She found she no longer craved the ego boost of finding new business in the complicated world of health care. Her clients followed her, and Dan seemed to love having her business skill set readily available to his legal clients.

They had a good working relationship, based on mutual respect and a shared moral code honed by having faced similar family dysfunction as children. But it was rare for him to summon her this way. What could be so urgent?

"Ah, Jess, good. You're here," Dan said as he motioned for her to take a seat in his grand corner office, with a panoramic view of downtown St. Louis. The skyline had grown more impressive over the past few years, new towers having diminished the size of the US Bank Plaza and One Metropolitan Square. The Gateway Arch remained the breathtaking structural statement among them all.

"Of course," she responded, still curious about why he had hunted her down early this Monday morning, when she wanted to do nothing more than put the surreal events of the weekend behind her and delve into work.

"What's this about Arthur leaving the university?" Dan asked her.

Her head jerked up so suddenly that she was sure her glasses moved. She looked at him straight on and noticed he seemed uncharacteristically flustered. Buying time, she asked, "Excuse me? Who told you that?"

"Dick called me this morning and asked me about it. He's concerned that any departure by a senior university doctor will cause a morale problem and wondered if I had heard. Frankly, he was ticked that I hadn't given him a heads-up." Dan stood against the sunlit window, causing her to squint up at him. She couldn't see his eyes, but his crossed arms and stiff posture told her he was annoyed. If that annoyance was directed at her, she was about to let him know he was wrong.

She slowly stood up and moved behind his desk to face him directly. Nose to nose, they were the same height when Jess wore heels. "Dan, whose business is this, may I ask?"

He moved back slightly, shrinking into a more conciliatory pose. "Jess, you know how this looks to Dick."

"How about you, Dan? How does 'this' look to you? What is this anyway?" She held her ground, glad that she had taken the time to dress in an elegant brown-and-cream business suit that helped her pull off her steely tone. Her career depended on being impeccably groomed and ready to exert personal power at a moment's notice. After the ragged weekend she'd had, she had a reserve of anger that she could access easily.

Just then, Amy, Dan's assistant, brought coffee in and set it on the table near the sitting area, picking up on the thick tension in the room. Amy was new to the job but a pro in knowing when to listen in on conversations and when to make a quick departure, which she did now, taking some of the battle out with her.

"Jess, listen. Let's have some coffee." Dan touched her shoulder lightly and guided her back to the table. "I apologize. But Dick has a way of getting me irked more than I should let him."

They sat. Dan poured her coffee, his voice softening. "So, how do you think Amy is doing so far? Her first performance check-in is next week. Any input for me?"

Not about to let him off the hook so easily, Jess straightened her glasses and took a sip of coffee, returning a tight smile. "She seems very competent. But let's finish the other conversation. What exactly does Dick think he needs to know about my personal life?"

"He must be worried that Arthur is a lynchpin. I can see you're going to make me say it, so I will." His voice rose a tad, his facial muscles tightening so his handsome face seemed a bit too rigid for morning-coffee conversation. "He's worried that you know all about it and are keeping it from him."

Jess, sitting ramrod straight, paused to let Dan regain his composure and smiled with a bit more warmth. "Well, you know how these academic doctors are—they get recruited all the time. And this is a time of change at the university. Ripe for recruiters, I would think. Arthur has had other lucrative offers thrown at him over the years." She spoke slowly so Dan could repeat her, word for word, back to Dick; she also ensured that she did not say anything untrue, trying to minimize the issue into a normal occurrence. Whether it was real or not, she was careful to stop short of dismissing Dan's claim entirely, even as her mind raced with the question *What in the hell* is *Arthur doing?*

Jess looked Dan directly in the eye and added, "You and I both know how important family is, and this is my family. Dick doesn't own us." She held his eyes as she stood up and said, "Now, I have a ten o'clock meeting. Is that it?"

Chapter 3

◇◇◇◇◇◇◇◇◇◇◇◇◇◇◇◇◇◇◇◇◇

L ater that day, Jess dashed from her office to the yoga studio. She felt as fragile as a baby bird and knew time with Diane would give her a much-needed lift. She quickly changed into her sneakers, gently placed her Dolce & Gabbana heels in the shoebox she kept in her car, and dodged several manhole-size puddles while navigating the sidewalk.

She peeked into the studio; when she spotted Diane doing warm-up stretches, Jess felt her body ease. She waved to her friend and quickly ducked into the locker room to change.

Diane was immaculately put together in bright pink yoga pants and a fitted top. With her long blonde hair pulled back in a ponytail, she looked twenty-five, except for the well-deserved smile lines around her mouth and eyes.

"It's about time. I was thinking I might have to take this class without you." Diane was new to yoga and had embraced both the practice and all of its trappings: trendy outfits, the most expensive mat and blocks, and an enthusiasm that Jess hoped would last beyond the next few months.

Friends since second grade, Jess and Diane had always made time to nurture their relationship. Over the past several years, their twosome had grown to include Jess's newer friend

Claire, and the three of them were now as close as sisters. A fast-track executive working for a firm based in St. Louis, Claire was often out of town on business and preferred competitive sports and her company's fully equipped gym to the slower pace of yoga.

"I think you still need me around to model the perfect downward dog!" Jess challenged Diane now with a bravado that she didn't feel. "Do you have time to grab juice after?" she asked, hearing her too-eager voice.

Diane nodded after pointing out that Jess's tank top was on inside out. When meditative music signaled the start of class, Jess tried to lose herself in the flow of the moves and the slight hint of lavender in the air. Sixty minutes later, she felt more flexible and relaxed.

They headed to the juice bar beyond the yoga space, where appetizing bottles of all types of juice and enhancements sat atop a carved-wood bar. The combination of mirrored shelves reflecting flattering, low light and the sounds of smooth jazz created an oasis of calm.

After Jess ordered a papaya smoothie, she grinned at Diane and said, "You have a glow to you today. Something exciting going on?"

Diane couldn't keep much from Jess, and vice versa; they knew almost everything about each other. Diane fiddled with her ponytail as she answered, "Well, I've been seeing someone who may be interesting." Still single at forty-five, she was ambivalent about her status. She had tried dating many times and had had a few serious relationships. She hadn't found the right guy yet, but she was always looking for him.

"Oh? Interesting how?" Jess encouraged her.

"Well, George is the architect my nonprofit commissioned for the new community center we're finally able to start. We've hit it off and are having fun getting to know each other. He's a landscape guy, so we've been sharing ideas about how we might get a healing garden on the site as well."

Jess nodded and leaned in as she let her senses absorb the music, the warmth of the small space, and the comfort of Diane's soothing voice. She needed this reprieve from her own situation, and Diane was so excited; it was like free therapy. Seeing her friend's twinkle as she spoke about George, Jess rallied.

"Sounds like this one might be a keeper. You haven't scared him away yet?"

"Not yet." Diane smiled, then slowly added, "We're going to drive home to Goodrich on Sunday."

Jess stopped sipping her smoothie and pulled herself up tall in her chair. "What? He's made it across the first hurdle?" Diane had a rule that if she didn't want to introduce a man to her parents, then he wasn't someone to date for more than a month. This didn't happen very often. The mention of Goodrich took Jess back to the warmth and love of Diane's home, in which she had frequently found refuge as a child. She could almost smell the combined aromas of Murphy Oil Soap and just-baked cookies wafting from the kitchen.

It was so different from her own family's house, where tension hung like draperies, and accusations and melodrama were as common as support and affection were rare. After Jess had refused to take sides in her parents' bitter divorce battle, Diane's parents had welcomed her to spend the last few months of her senior year of high school living with them. She had bolted to Boston after graduation with a full scholarship to Harvard and hadn't looked back until she'd had several years of therapy. By then, her family had scattered, but Diane had remained constant. Jess's move back to St. Louis for Arthur's career had only further invigorated their friendship.

"This is exciting!" Jess started sipping again, taking a good look at her smitten friend. "Oh, happy day!" She laughed. "I knew it *could* happen; I just wondered if it *would*."

"Yes, it's a surprise to me, too. I feel different than I have with any other guy I've dated." Diane gazed beyond Jess.

"Uh-oh . . . I think you're a goner, Miss Diane."

"Hey, don't get ahead of yourself. It's still early days." Diane looked slyly at her friend. "Did you know right away with Arthur?"

"Oh my God, that's ancient history. Where did that come from?" Jess shivered. She fumbled in her bag, pulled out her cover-up, and slowly put it on over her head, knocking her glasses off onto Diane's lap.

"Well, remember, you were out East, and I wasn't close enough to hear about all the romantic twists and turns of your early courtship." Diane reached over, tucked the still-visible tag into Jess's cover-up, and straightened her friend's glasses, taking a long look at her.

"Boy, I must have since I married the man in six months!" Jess surprised herself with her best available laugh as she tightened her cover-up around her. "But I do regret eloping and not having my best friend with me. Gosh, I'm chilly. Must have been that smoothie. Ready to go?"

They stood and gathered their gear. Jess caught a flash of Diane's bright image in the mirror and looked away before she could study her own reflection. She didn't want to see herself disheveled and far from the "perfect" person she needed to be to keep her life under control. Diane's question echoed. She wondered if things might have been different if she'd had her friend in Boston during those heady days of falling in love with Arthur.

They opened the studio doors to fast-fading light. Diane hesitated, then turned to Jess. "Hey, are you OK? You look . . . distracted. I didn't really ask about what's going on with you."

Jess was glad for the dark as she wavered briefly. "I'm just a little tired. Lots going on at work."

"Are you sure that's all it is?" Diane didn't move.

"Of course. I'm so happy for you. This guy sounds terrific."

"Beth and Tom?" Diane probed.

"The kids are great, as always." Jess smiled, noting that Diane didn't inquire about Arthur, not her favorite guy. Jess recalled the night a year earlier when Diane had shared her real thoughts about him, after a rare overindulgence in wine, and she doubted now that Diane would even remember how she had spilled her guts on the subject. "A supreme ass, king of the castle" was how she had described Arthur, lambasting him for assuming that Jess would manage the household and the children while he presented himself to the world as a lifesaving hero.

But Diane didn't know Arthur the way Jess did. She gave her friend a warm hug. This was clearly not the day to share any marital drama. "Have a great trip, and hug your parents for me, please."

She drove home slowly, hoping to extend the reprieve until morning. She needed to think. Talk to Arthur. Yell at Arthur. Demand an explanation. They were a team, and they needed a plan. He was out of town at a meeting until Friday. What rumors were out there? What had he started with his wild talk?

Chapter 4

Jess had back-to-back meetings the next morning at the university hospital, so she left her downtown office and raced over to make the first one on time. Rounding the corner of the last corridor, she had just enough time to slip into the bathroom before the meeting. Coming in a little too fast, she practically ran into Joan, Arthur's longtime research technician, a salt-of-the earth woman whom Jess loved.

"Uh . . . oh, hey, Joan. So nice to run into you—but not literally!" Both women laughed after shifting from their awkward body blow into a hug.

"Same to you. How are you? Arthur tells me Beth is doing well at Stanford. Are you expecting her back for the summer?" Joan asked.

"Gosh, I hope so," Jess responded. "Is it wrong to want my girl home? Tom will be going away next fall, and I'm already missing him."

"No, keep them home as long as possible," Joan offered wistfully. "Family dynamics change when they leave. Empty nests aren't what they're cracked up to be. I sure miss the chaos of my three coming and going. Speaking of transitions, how are you feeling about the Portland thing? Arthur has asked me to go with him to set up his research lab there."

Jess collapsed against the tile wall, her knees shaking. Her reaction must have frightened Joan, who started backpedaling, literally, out of the bathroom.

Before she could leave, Jess grabbed her arm and, after taking a deep breath, managed to ask, "Is it real?"

A new arrival into the public restroom allowed Joan to brush off the question—"Oh, you know him; could just be a whim"—and then scramble out before Jess could get the answer she needed.

Chapter 5

◇◇◇◇◇◇◇◇◇◇◇◇◇◇◇◇◇◇◇◇

In their quick phone call the night before, Jess had found out that Arthur's flight would come in around six o'clock that evening. She was startled to realize he was no longer in the practice of e-mailing her his itinerary, then admitted to herself she might have told him to stop doing it. She wondered what other common courtesies of their relationship had fallen by the wayside.

She told him she'd like to pick him up at the airport and grab a bite afterward, as they needed to talk.

"Good. I need an update on the kids. See you then."

Typical of him to assume the only thing on her mind was a child-related issue. She didn't correct him but wondered now if they could actually engage in an adult conversation about what was really going on, since she could no longer dismiss his behavior as simply letting off steam.

Traffic was light, and she arrived at the pickup spot early. The usual patrol of security police loomed, so she went around the airport loop again, then hovered and watched people coming and going. Lots of business travelers. Not a life she would choose. She opened the car window to get some fresh air.

She recalled the excitement of her international trips to scientific meetings with Arthur early in their relationship. But once the children had come, she had put a stop to accompanying him to serve as a supportive appendage in his rarefied world. Keeping her career going while raising children was challenging enough, especially as he traveled so often. These days, she didn't confide in Arthur about what she did in her own demanding profession, and he no doubt realized that stories of his globe-trotting no longer mesmerized her. And now that the two of them were doing this strained merger tango, she wondered how they could ever find their old rhythm.

Her mind drifted to an earlier, pivotal moment in their marriage, another dangerous time. It seemed like yesterday, even though it had been almost fifteen years since then.

◇◇◇◇◇◇◇◇◇◇◇◇◇◇◇◇◇

"I can't believe you're unwilling to go to this with me. I shouldn't even have to ask you!" Arthur's voice was barely shy of shouting.

"Shh, you'll wake the kids!" Jess had turned on him. "Don't you dare tell me I'm 'unwilling' to see you receive the European Award for Cancer Research, for God's sake. I just can't go that week, which, you know full well, is the week I'm closing out the Darnell deal. I need to be there. That's just how it is!"

Tom started wailing then, giving Jess one more line. "And I suppose you think the children will just take care of themselves while we're off partying in Amsterdam?"

She stalked off to her son's room to coax him back to sleep. His warm toddler body against hers calmed her. How could Arthur be so obtuse? She was terribly proud of him, but the sheer logistical nightmare of juggling kids and work was more than she could face.

The next day, as she waited for her stylist at the hair salon, she had picked up a magazine and noticed an article about how to prevent the seven-year itch in a marriage. It spoke to her. Was she making time for her husband? Did she prioritize her children over him? How often did they have sex? Had they tried anything new lately? Did they discuss anything other than children and household matters? As the stylist came for her, she put the magazine down, but not before she saw a photo of a woman in a bustier and fishnet stockings, with the caption "Spice up your marriage before it's too late."

She then had returned to her office and gotten busy. She still wouldn't go to Amsterdam, but Arthur had agreed to fly to Chicago one night earlier than his departure to the Netherlands to speak at a fund-raiser for the cancer charity that supported some of his research. She would surprise him there.

Three tense days later, she was in Chicago, executing her plan. Her damn stilettos were killing her, but she was able to navigate to her hotel's bar directly across the street from the Drake Hotel.

In her mind's eye, she saw Arthur charming the two hundred people in the Drake ballroom, as she had watched him do with so many similar groups in the past. Handsome and charismatic in his tux, he would be seated at the head table with the chair of the gala. He would make witty conversation so every guest would be able to recall a personal exchange he or she had had with this brilliant scientist. His talk would be short but would make an impact. His favorite device was to tell a story about one of his pediatric patients, using the child's words to relate a conversation Arthur had had with him or her, describing the parents' angst and dire situation. Careful not to overplay the drama, he would simply describe the treatment required and the research process, and how important it was to get to the clinical-trials phase so Johnny or Susie would have a chance at survival. By the end of his talk, his voice would be a whisper, and everyone would be listening intently. As he closed and thanked the audience, the table captains would be asked to hand out pens and envelopes to accept a flood of generous donations.

That should happen at about 8:35 p.m. When he returned to his seat, he would find a note at his place allowing him to make his excuses for an early departure from the event.

Jess had wanted to see him walk into the bar to gauge his response. But now that all was ready, she had stage fright. *What if he doesn't get the note or is angry that I've come?* At eight thirty p.m., she positioned herself at a corner table opposite the door and ordered scotch—not her usual drink, but there was nothing usual about this. She had flown into Chicago in the late afternoon and spent two hours at the salon in her boutique hotel. She'd asked for upswept hair, smoky eyes, and red nails. She had ordered champagne to be delivered to their suite by nine p.m.

She sipped her drink and took a deep breath, then looked down at her cleavage and closed her satin evening coat a bit. Her push-up corset was working wonders. After two babies, it helped. Luckily, the elegant coat concealed it well. Nobody would guess she wore a short, slit skirt and a black lace garter belt. She carefully crossed her legs so her spike heels could work their magic.

She only wished she could see. But she refused to spoil the look by putting on her glasses. After the fourth sip of her cocktail, she saw a blurry man in a tux at the door searching the bar, then coming her way. From five feet away, she locked eyes with the love of her life. Her anxiety had melted as she saw his look of relief, then desire.

"Jessica."

"Arthur."

"I can't believe you came."

"I can't believe I did either. Is it OK?" She trembled in response to his slow appraisal of her.

"OK? Are you kidding? It's incredible. Thank you."

"Arthur, I'm sorry to disappoint you and not go to Amsterdam."

"And I'm sorry I pushed. I do get it, most of the time. I just miss you. I love you."

"I know." She took his hand.

He touched her leg. "What are you drinking?"

"Scotch."

"Really? That's different." His hand stroked her thigh.

"Yes." She closed her eyes. "Arthur?"

"Yes, Jess."

"Would you like a drink here, or . . ." She hesitated, suddenly shy. "I have a room upstairs. Would you like to go up with me?"

He smiled and held out his hand. "I'd love to go upstairs with you. Shall we?"

As she moved to rise, her coat opened a bit. He stood in appreciation, then watched her walk to the door. Once they were alone in the elevator, she managed to get the room key from her bag and hand it to him.

He pulled her close and studied the bright blue eyes he knew so well, striking amid the dark makeup, then giggled and nuzzled her ear. "I see you didn't go so far as to get contacts. So you can't see much, can you, my love?"

She laughed then and kissed him lightly on the lips. "Lucky I recognized you!"

They had arrived at the suite to find champagne, strawberries, and whipped cream on ice, and the lights down low.

"Wow. Jess, you're amazing! I can't believe you did all this."

As he looked around the suite, Jess dropped her coat on the chair and stood before him in her skirt and black silk corset.

"Va-va-voom. Look at you." He started for her. "You're gorgeous, Jess."

She moved away but did kick off her stilettos. "Let's have some champagne and play, shall we?" She glanced at her bag. "I even brought your camera . . ."

◇◇◇◇◇◇◇◇◇◇◇◇◇◇◇◇

An airport security guard waving a hand at her window broke her reverie, so she drove the loop one more time. She smiled as she remembered that crazy, fun night and the sexy pictures Arthur had taken of her dressed that way. That night had brought them back together. She wondered what it would take this time.

Arthur was at the curb as she returned. They exchanged polite pecks on the cheek, their normal greeting, and then were off to dinner. She had chosen the Worthington, an old-fashioned, white-tablecloth restaurant with a marvelous secluded bar that always seemed perfect for quiet conversations and excellent food. Arthur loved this cozy spot; they had come here often when they had first moved to St. Louis. Not so much anymore, though, which was why it seemed the perfect place to conjure up a mood of intimacy and sharing. As she drove, she found herself replaying the memory tape of their sexy getaway and reminded herself again that the marriage was worth saving.

Arthur was chatty. He told her about the scientific conference, what it meant to his research, people he had seen whom she might know, and how great the food was in Quebec. He seemed to be in a good mood, and Jess wanted to forget her worries and tune in to him but found herself barely able to swallow her wine one minute and then succumbing to the ease of their shared history the next. They chatted happily about Vincente, a scientist from Italy and frequent houseguest, whose daughter, Liliana, was newly engaged to be married.

"Do you remember when Liliana nannied that summer when the kids were little? She loved taking them down to the park all the time, and then we finally discovered why," Jess said, while she thought about all the childcare, summer help, and after-school support she'd needed over these past years to keep things working at home.

"You mean when it led up to some guy coming to the house one night and Tom getting to the door first and saying, 'Oh, hi, Sean. Come on in. My mom and dad are here, but you can still see Liliana'? How old was Tom then? So cute the way he took charge of the situation." Arthur laughed, and Jess joined him. Along with that sweet glimpse of the man she had married, she felt a glimmer of hope.

When the food came, Jess forced herself to face the issue, straightened her spine, and calmly told him that Dick Morrison, Midwest Health's CEO, had questioned Dan about Arthur's plans and caused her own awkward interaction with Dan. "So, Arthur, what's going on? What tale are you telling?"

He wasn't as steamed up as she'd expected he would be to hear that their mutual colleagues were talking about his career plan with her and not him.

"Really? That's interesting. Good old Dick is worried about his standing if faculty start to leave. Hmm. I didn't think he had that much insight into how he was perceived in this whole mess. Maybe I should organize a revolt, have everyone threaten to leave, and see how that goes over." He chuckled at his own musing, totally missing her body language, which forecast stormy weather ahead.

She waited for him to deny the fact of the story—that there was no serious move under consideration, that he was just shaking things up. She waited for the denial that she wanted to believe and the apology she deserved.

Years earlier, they had considered a move. Arthur had been actively recruited to take a special position at Johns Hopkins that would have been good for both his academic and his research careers. Jess had been encouraging. They had gone together to visit Baltimore, where the recruiting committee had wined and dined them. Jess had gotten excited. Arthur had not. "Too many elites—not enough room for me," he had said. To her knowledge, no one since then had made any other serious attempt to recruit her husband away, or he'd put out the right signals that he could not be recruited. They then built their life in St. Louis and were happy there. Or were they?

"Arthur," she finally repeated, her head beginning to ache in the face of his continued light mood and his avoidance of her question, "please tell me what's happening. Are you being recruited? Are you interested in the job? What are you thinking?"

He finally looked at her and then away. "I may go. It's a good place. My research would be well funded, and I wouldn't have to deal with the Dicks of the world."

She heard only his first words and barely registered his reasons. She dropped her fork with such force that it ricocheted off her plate and onto the floor. "What do you mean, 'I may go'? Need I remind you that you're not a free agent? What about your family? What about me? Have you no sense that you can't just leave?"

The older couple at the next table turned to look as Jess raised her voice. Arthur reached down to retrieve her fork but did not look at her.

How can he stay so calm when I'm reeling? What's going on with him? She couldn't continue the conversation. She crumpled in her chair and started crying quietly. Arthur signed the bill, and she handed him the keys. She was in no shape to drive home.

As the adjacent couple looked on, Arthur took her by the arm and led her to the door, carefully putting her sweater around her shoulders.

It was a quiet drive home, interrupted only by Jess's involuntary sobs and the classical music Arthur chose whenever he drove. "Calming," he always explained, "to face the idiots on the road." But it grated now.

Jess's only thought as the car stopped was *escape.* She bounded out of her seat, slammed the door, and dropped her sweater in the street. She leaned down to retrieve it and realized Arthur had just dropped her off and was already driving away. Still in the street, she threw her sweater toward the car and spat out, "Where are you going?"

But Arthur had already tuned her out.

Chapter 6

After Arthur's evasiveness, Jess realized how serious the situation was. He might have become distant and moody of late—indeed, their marriage had cooled a bit over the past year or so—but he wasn't usually this secretive. His withdrawal, added to his unwillingness to comfort her and tell her all was well, left her unable to sleep.

The next morning, she rearranged her schedule to work from her downtown office to avoid going over to the campus. She changed a couple of meetings to conference calls and kept her door closed to focus without interruption.

There were no tears today. She needed to regroup and fight back. She wouldn't give up on this marriage, not because of a merger. If Arthur's sulking was the result of his worrying about his research in the new world order, then she had other cards to play.

She realized now that their own ground rule of not talking about work at home during this merger was a mistake. She recalled her relief when she had no longer had to listen to all his talk about work; as busy as she was herself, it had seemed like a bonus. How stupid she had been! And now it might be too late.

An elevator speech. She needed one and needed it now—
something quick and easy that would quickly silence the curious
and discourteous but perhaps well-meaning people who would
be all over her when she went to campus the next day. She would
be ready, she would be rested, and she would be motivated by
her number-one goal: saving her marriage. Loyalty to Arthur
was how she would play this for onlookers.

And she needed a sounding board. She e-mailed her friend
Claire and made a lunch date for the next day.

◇◇◇◇◇◇◇◇◇◇◇◇◇◇◇◇◇

"This table isn't right. We need one that's not so close to the
kitchen," Claire commanded the restaurant host once she saw
where they would be sitting. All five feet of her were in hyper-
drive. No matter that there seemed to be no tables open and
they had no reservation. Sure enough, Claire noticed a table in
a quiet corner, overlooked by the flustered host, as she scanned
the restaurant with her X-ray vision. "There—thank you. This
is so much better. You're a dear to find this for us." She fawned
over the host now that he was under her control, a flash of her
green eyes and brilliant smile his reward.

She caught Jess's raised eyebrow and defended herself.
"Hey, my East Coast aggressiveness is part of my charm. And
besides, we now have a great private little spot. So don't give me
that look." She smiled. "You know you love me just the way I
am." Claire waited for Jess's smile of approval and then started in.

"OK, what gives? You don't usually give me only twenty-four
hours to clear my calendar to meet with you. You know I always
will, but out with it. What's up?" Claire's over-the-top personality
always took over a room, but she also had an uncanny ability to
zero in on the person to whom she was speaking. She silenced her
phone and put her bag under the table. "I'm all yours."

Jess was unbeatable once she focused her thinking and
was now in full combat readiness. She just needed someone to

help her with strategy. Claire was an excellent strategist, and she knew Arthur. Actually, not only did she know him, but she also had his number.

Jess remembered the first time Claire had come to dinner and met Arthur. In his usual manner, he had tested her intellect before making any effort to try to impress her. After thirty minutes of listening to him talk about the intricacies of his research, Claire had rolled her eyes and made a funny face to Jess behind his back. She asked lots of questions about the scientists involved and found it humorous that world-renowned researchers were fraught with the usual human flaws. She told Jess later that Arthur puzzled her: He was bright and charming when he wanted to be, but seemed to always know something nobody else did, and liked it that way.

Claire was a realist and would call it as she saw it. That above all else was why Jess needed her—someone to check her thinking and keep her in the game, which she was determined to win.

Jess distilled the story to its essence. Claire knew about the challenges Jess faced in her marriage, given the merger situation, so much could be omitted. "Arthur has evidently announced to some that he's moving his research and himself to Portland. Dan and others are questioning my loyalty for not having told them this was happening, or for preventing it if it's a real threat."

"Ooh, that's rich. I didn't see this one coming," Claire offered. "There are so many dimensions to this, I don't even know where to start."

She hesitated for a few beats and then asked quietly, "How do you feel about this? Do you want him to stay?"

Jess avoided her eyes. "I can't go there. I can't even consider my emotions. This is business, and I need your help to make sure that my marriage remains intact. What are my options?" She could hear that her tone was off—she was speaking as if she were trying to close a business deal—but she knew Claire would understand how much she needed her as a friend right now.

The waiter came to take their order. "Your best mixed green salad with grilled chicken, please," Claire said without taking time to look at the menu. "Chef's choice vinaigrette on the side, times two." Jess didn't protest.

Claire played twenty questions about the offer, the institution, the prestige-factor comparison of the two universities, the players at each, and how the research would be funded at the new place.

Jess hid her eyes behind her water glass as she drank.

Claire's beautifully arched brows lowered with concern. "Honey, how can you be worried about something that's so unformed? Is it a real offer? How come you don't know more about it if it's serious?"

Jess didn't flinch. "He's not speaking to me about any of this. So let's just deal with it theoretically, as a competitive offer."

Claire looked directly at Jess until she had no choice but to respond. "I just thought he was ticked about the merger and acting out."

Claire went on to ask more about what was on the grapevine, who knew, and how the Midwest Health people, the medical school people, and Jess had all responded.

Suddenly, a matronly woman wearing too much jewelry appeared noisily at their table, her eyes drilling into Jess. After she and Jess exchanged air kisses and warm greetings and Jess introduced Claire, the woman jumped in: "Jessica, what's going on? Is Arthur really leaving for Portland?"

Jess laughed easily and responded brightly, "Deanna, I've always admired your ability to steer clear of these rumors that come out of the blue."

Fortunately, their food was just being served, and the jostling helped move Deanna along. But not before she could whisper, "Call me, Jess" as her parting words.

Once Deanna was no longer within earshot, Claire asked, "So, you're basically dismissing the speculation as rumor?"

"Yes, but you can imagine how long that will last." Although Jess had not lost her nerve in the interaction, she could feel her cheeks flushing from the adrenaline rush.

"And who was that again?" Claire started on her salad.

"That was Deanna Miles, wife of the medical school dean, and I will not be calling her—"

"Unless you want a megaphone for your elevator speech," Claire quipped, and Jess couldn't help but chuckle.

"Frankly, I can understand how the Midwest Health people feel, as unfair as that may seem. You're a trusted member of their team, and they have a right to expect an oath of loyalty from you." Claire looked back over at Deanna, who had joined two other bejeweled matrons across the room.

"Of course, your husband and his career aspirations are complicating things, but I don't think you can keep this situation on hold for long. And as your friend, and someone who knows and admires Arthur, I urge you to talk this out with him. Like it or not, you two are in this together. Honey, you can't afford to let him be evasive at this point."

Chapter 7

◇◇◇◇◇◇◇◇◇◇◇◇◇◇◇◇◇◇◇◇◇◇

Jess was scheduled for meetings at Midwest Health that afternoon, and she couldn't go ten feet without bumping into somebody who wanted to talk to her about Arthur's plans. She was leaning against a wall with her eyes closed, catching her breath, when Nate Michaels, a hospital administrator Jess had worked with on a clinic purchase, turned the corner of a wide hospital corridor and came upon her. He approached her with a gentle tap on the shoulder and ducked his head down to meet her eyes. He gave her a quick smile, took hold of her elbow, and said, "Let's get out of here" as he escorted her out of the hallway and toward his office nearby.

Once he had closed the door, he said, "My God, Jess. What's happening? You look awful. Are you OK? I usually see you cool, calm, and collected." He gave her a half hug before he lowered her into a chair and handed her a bottle of water. "What's gotten you so rattled?"

She could feel his eyes studying her closely as she tried to calm down. She hadn't seen Nate for several months and could see his concern reflecting her stressed image back at her.

Jess caught a stray strand of hair and tucked it behind her ear before glancing up at him. *My God, I must look a mess,* she thought. She measured her words as she said, "Oh, Nate, it's so good to see you. I just need a moment. There was a virtual feeding frenzy going this morning. Everyone seems to be rushing to be my friend in order to warn me of rumors going around about Arthur." *How much does Nate know?* she wondered. *Is he already aware of what's really going on?*

"Oh, that—yeah. That rumor has been around since last week. I actually dismissed it, as I figured you'd tell me personally if there was something to it. You know how merger gossip is. For some reason, people have to sort themselves into winners and losers and choose sides. And when they hear a tidbit to strengthen one side or the other, they're all over themselves to spread it like wildfire. Human nature, I guess. Fear can make even decent people act without thinking."

She felt her face relax as he went on: "As you yourself told me many months ago when this assignment came your way, it would be good and bad to be involved in this transaction, as it's so close to Arthur's professional life. But you believed it would be better to be a part of it and help make it go right than to be on the sidelines, watching it go wrong. Remember?"

Jess straightened up, feeling her shoulders drop away from her neck. "I did? That's right—I did." She took a drink of water and smiled warmly at him.

"It's not too surprising that two members of a power couple involved in this crazy deal would be the focus of wild rumors. I said as much to Dick when he asked me about it the other day."

At the mention of Dick, Jess blanched. "Dick asked you about it?"

Just then, her beeper went off, and she realized she was late for her next meeting. She gave him a quick hug, said quick thank yous, and dashed out the door, grateful that she had not had to deny the rumors this time.

But for how long would she be able to keep that up?

◇◇◇◇◇◇◇◇◇◇◇◇◇◇◇◇

Over the next ten days, Arthur stonewalled Jess, and she stone-walled everyone else. It became easier every day, and Jess let herself be lulled into disbelief that there was a true threat. *The tension of the situation just has him saying things he doesn't mean.*

As they gave each other room to breathe, life went on. Tom needed a normal household, and they both went out of their way to remain civil and polite to each other, avoiding any real conversation. *If I'm honest with myself,* she thought, *we've been living this way for a while already, so why not wait it out?* Besides, she had an idea brewing.

Chapter 8

ⵔⵔⵔⵔⵔⵔⵔⵔⵔⵔⵔⵔ

Jess woke up the morning of her flight to Stanford with puffy eyes and heavy limbs—inevitable side effects of her underlying anxiety. But the prospect of spending that weekend in Palo Alto for Beth's theater performance gave her the motivation she needed to pop out of bed. Arthur was flying in from a meeting in Phoenix, and Jess planned to meet him and Beth on campus after her late-day trip from St. Louis.

The taxi dropped her at the student commons. A soft breeze swished through the palm trees around the campus buildings. Jess removed her sweater and swung it over her shoulders. She looked up to a sea of young people and rolled her small carry-on bag to the door of the two-story stone building.

She entered to a cacophony of young voices against a background hum of elevator dings and electronics. She smiled ruefully as she thought, *Make way for the dinosaur, kids*, but she didn't have much time to dwell on self-pity, for the youth surrounding her swept her right up with their energy and into the open expanse of the crowded, noisy main room. Time to find Beth.

It didn't take long to spot them. Father and daughter were huddled together in an island unto themselves. Arthur's briefcase and overnight bag were holding a soft-cushioned chair for Jess. When they looked up, she recognized the deep-set blue eyes of her husband repeated so beautifully in their child. She teared up suddenly as she realized how much love she had to protect.

"Mom! So happy you're here." Beth jumped up to hug her close. Jess melted into her and closed her eyes. Yes, whatever else she was concerned about in her marriage, she would never regret having had her two beautiful kids with Arthur.

"You made good time. Flight OK?" Arthur stood and kissed her on the cheek.

"Yes, easy flight." Jess leaned in and gave him a full kiss on the mouth. "Love you."

Arthur, surprised, responded quickly, "Love you too," and moved his bag from the chair he had saved for her.

"I'm so glad we figured out how to make this work!" Jess settled into her seat and beamed at both of them. "So, what are you two conspiring about?"

"Oh, you know Dad. He's giving me an update on his stash of miles. He made some breakthrough on categories or something." Beth rolled her eyes.

"Oh, I see." Jess also rolled her eyes. Arthur loved to play games with airline rewards programs in order to maximize his free miles, and he loved to talk about it.

"Tease me if you want, but the whole family benefits from my strategic calculations!" Arthur boasted. "How do you think we got here to visit you, dear Beth?"

Beth's eyes shone as she filled them in on the weekend schedule and choices to be made beyond the play. She particularly wanted them to meet her friends and see her dorm room.

"Just remember, I'll be spending tomorrow morning through lunch with the Stanford medical people. They have me giving a talk during rounds." Arthur directed his comment at Beth.

"Remember? I didn't know you scheduled something," Jess quickly cut in. "When did you do that?"

"Hmm. Thought I told you." He was looking at his daughter. "Beth already forgave me. This way, you two can have some girl time without old dad hanging around. Right, Beth?"

Beth looked adoringly back at her father. "Well, I didn't think you'd be too excited about spending time in the dorm and meeting my girlfriends. It's OK, Dad." She turned her attention to her mother and continued, "Mom, I hit the jackpot with my roommate this year. I already know Lucy and I will be friends forever, and you have to see how we fixed up our room—it's so cool. It's much better than last year's."

Jess smiled. "Excellent. I'm very excited to meet her and your theater friends. And, darling girl, have you cut your hair a bit? I just have to look at you for a while. I've missed you so much!" She reached over for another hug, grateful that her daughter was beyond the stage where public displays of affection were forbidden.

"Gosh, this is a big space." She let Beth loose and took in the surroundings. The sandstone arches from the exterior were repeated in the entryway. She marveled at how well the original Romanesque style had been preserved in this student-friendly building, clearly modernized for technology. Off in one corner, she saw the inevitable coffee shop. Overflow seating was filled to capacity. Students sat or slept on the scattered furniture or sprawled on the floor, looking quite comfortable. She noted the location of the gift shop. "Beth, let's make sure we make time for me to stop and pick up a Stanford sweatshirt for Tom in the morning."

"Sure, Mom. We can do that. By the way, as long as you're so good at the miles game, Dad, do you think you and Mom could come to a couple of my touring performances next year? I know for sure there will be one in Portland, and they're still trying to make arrangements for Chicago." Beth looked eagerly at her father.

Arthur's and Jess's eyes locked with more intimacy than they had shared in months. He broke his gaze first.

Jess held her breath and watched him squirm. Her first thought was, *I hope now isn't the moment he chooses to announce an impending move to our daughter.* But when he replied only, "Which of these acts are you in, Beth?" she added silently to herself, *Why can't he just say, "We'll be there"?*

Beth sprang out of her chair as she spotted her roommate. "Mom, Dad, Lucy's here!" Beth ran off to meet her, and Arthur popped up to follow, leaving Jess with the luggage.

The girls approached her, arm in arm. "Welcome to Stanford! Beth has been so excited to see you, Mrs. Steele." Lucy pivoted to include Arthur, who was a step outside of the circle. "And Dr. Steele."

Jess pulled Lucy in for a hug, and Beth piled on. "We're so delighted that you and Beth are having so much fun together. I hear I'm in for a treat when I see your dorm room tomorrow. We'd love for you to join us for dinner?"

Jess turned to her husband, taking control quickly. "Arthur, where are we staying? Have you already been to the hotel? Have you made a dinner reservation? Make sure to include a seat for Lucy at our table."

Beth pulled herself away from Lucy long enough to have the last word with her father. "And, Dad, don't think you're off the hook. Those airline miles can get you and Mom to at least one of my performances."

⋄⋄⋄⋄⋄⋄⋄⋄⋄⋄⋄⋄⋄⋄⋄⋄

Jess left the happy dinner party as dessert arrived to take a phone call she was expecting. She needed to go back to the beginning to save her marriage. She was hoping Hazel, and Los Amigos, could help.

Jess and Arthur had originally met in Boston, where they had been paired to lead a medical-aid team to Colombia for a two-week service trip. At the time, Jess was a rising star at a big consulting firm, working eighty hours a week. Her organizational skills were requested to manage the annual pro bono project, and Arthur was the charismatic doctor chosen to recruit the medical personnel. Thrown together in a strange land with primitive conditions to handle, they at first admired each other's professional acumen. Then the long nights and close quarters threw them together romantically.

Jess considered it a two-week fling that would conclude naturally after the Colombia trip was over. Her preference was to date someone for a few months and leave when things got heavy or the guy got clingy. It was a pattern she was comfortable with, as the notion of getting close to someone seemed too dangerous to contemplate.

She was surprised when Arthur pursued her back in Boston, but she enjoyed his world. Playing supporting cast member to his starring role worked for her. Arthur was growing tired of his playboy lifestyle, and, as Jess didn't require much of his attention, they settled in.

Hazel, the executive director of the Los Amigos program, had been after them to serve again in the first few years after that initial trip, but careers and then family always seemed to keep them from it. Now, Jess was willing to drop everything if she could present Arthur with the hook of a service trip.

"Hazel, thanks so much for getting back to me so quickly. I was so happy to hear you're still at Los Amigos."

"So lovely to get your note. I can't believe you two are soon to be empty nesters."

"Time goes so fast. But yes, our youngest, Tom, leaves for college in the fall."

"Jess, I'm going to send you some material by e-mail and a packet to your home address. We do get people coming back to us after a lifestyle change, and we would welcome you and Arthur whenever you can find the time. The need continues, as you might know."

◇◇◇◇◇◇◇◇◇◇◇◇◇◇◇◇◇◇

Arthur and Jess walked the girls back to their dorm, and after they were alone, she reached out for his hand. He seemed startled but did take it, after a slight hesitation, and they strolled through campus back to their hotel.

"We have great kids, don't we?" He smiled warmly. "Beth seems to be in her element out here."

"And Tom will find his way as well. Pretty soon, too." *Take advantage of his good mood,* Jess told herself as she stopped and turned to face him. "Arthur, I think we should go back to Colombia this fall for a medical tour with Los Amigos. I've been in contact with Hazel just tonight. She's sending us some information."

"Wow. When did you think this up?" He seemed bemused.

"Well, I think it would be exactly the right trip to celebrate the end-of-merger strain. What do you think?" Jess immediately regretted having mentioned the merger when she saw Arthur's eyes darken and he dropped her hand.

"We'll see." He started walking again, ahead of her.

Chapter 9

✧✧✧✧✧✧✧✧✧✧✧✧✧✧✧✧✧✧✧✧✧

Jess took her relaxing route to the office. She loved meandering into downtown and watching the sun start to move up over the Mississippi River. It was a breezy day, and she could feel the brisk wind buffeting the car as she drove slowly past the Missouri Botanical Garden. *It'll be nice to get back to my regular routine*, she thought as she approached the elevator from the parking ramp at work.

As she walked out of the elevator into the offices, she instantly caught a whiff of freshly baked cinnamon rolls. She saw a handful of her colleagues in the conference room, enjoying an early-morning birthday celebration for Cindy, one of the attorneys, who was also very pregnant.

Someone called out, "Hey, Lawson—just in time to lead us in 'Happy Birthday.'"

Jess obliged happily and gave Cindy a hug. "Wow, there's a lot of you to squeeze! Not to worry—that will change in, what, about a month?" Jess chuckled as Cindy sighed and pulled her aside.

"This last month is a trial. I can't sleep, can't wear heels, and can't wait to meet this little person! But I'm so glad you advised me to work through. If I were at home, the waiting would be making me crazy."

"And you'd be invisible here. If you want to stay on that partner track, and you should, plan your time off carefully. Take a few months when the baby comes, hire a nanny, and organize your household to work for you. You can do it, and you'll be glad you did." Jess winked at her while eyeing the cinnamon rolls on the table.

"You know, it helps to know you did it, and your kids are great. You and Arthur are both at the top of your careers, rock-solid marriage, the whole deal."

Jess rolled her eyes at that description. They both laughed, and as she maneuvered her way to the table and scooped up a roll, Dan walked up to the conference room glass and gestured for her to come with him.

"Oops. I guess I'll have to take this with me and enjoy it later." She smiled and followed him back to his office.

"Good morning, Dan. Did you get your own sweet treat? Aren't we lucky to be officed so close to the best bakery in downtown St. Louis? These rolls are so good. I only let myself have one when there's a birthday." She was chattering while negotiating the door to Dan's office, her briefcase, her coat, and the roll, and she didn't notice until she turned to face him that he had a stony look and was not about to enter into any casual conversation about bakeries with her.

"Dan, what is it? I know you wanted to see me this morning, and here I am. Has something happened? You look very serious. What's going on?"

He took a breath and motioned for her to sit. "I wish I knew, Jess. I can't figure out what's going on, and I hope you can shed some light on it. I'm not quite sure how to tell you this, but I trust you know me to be straightforward and honest, so please bear with me as I struggle through."

He looked so forsaken that she smiled at him, dropped her briefcase and coat in a chair, and settled herself in the other. "Dan, it can't be all that bad. Take a minute, and then tell me." When she struggled to figure out where to put the cinnamon roll, they both broke the tension with a laugh, and she placed it on his desk. She pushed it forward to him as an offering.

"Jess, I've known you for fifteen years, worked with you for twelve, and always found you to be the absolute picture of integrity. You're a role model to professional women here and in the field, and I know you're beyond reproach. So I'm beside myself trying to figure out why Dick has asked that you be taken off the merger project."

"What?" It took her a moment or two to even form her words, beyond repeating the obvious question several times. She finally managed to ask, "Do you know why, Dan?"

Dan told her that Dick had called him up over the weekend and demanded that she be removed, with no explanation. Dan had talked to him again briefly that morning and firmly asked why, but Dick had given him the runaround and shut down with, "Don't you think the client can choose which senior people can be trusted with such a monumental project?" Then he'd lowered the boom: "Maybe I should reconsider the firm itself if you can't oblige me."

Dan went on to tell Jess that he had worked on his contacts on the Midwest Health team and not gotten anywhere. "It's as if there's an understanding that no more discussion is necessary, now that this decision has been made."

After ten minutes, Dan started repeating himself. Jess was surprised by how calm she felt when she asked, "What does this mean, Dan?"

"I don't know, Jess. I don't want to go there yet. Can you think of any reason why Dick would take this position?"

"Yes, I can. But I don't want to believe it. I think it might be because he can't control what Arthur does, or might do, and he's using it as leverage. Let's both think about this and talk later." Jess picked up her coat and briefcase, reclaimed her cinnamon roll, and walked out of the office.

At least they had not wasted time discussing whether her work had been subpar; Dan had saved her from that insult, if nothing else.

Jess went to her office, closed the door, checked e-mail, and distracted herself by tying up some loose ends. She put a call in to Claire, whose assistant said she would be free in about an hour, and then went to the break room to get coffee.

Claire called back, and Jess quickly brought her up to date. Claire's reaction was immediate. "That bastard! How can he hold you accountable for something Arthur is doing?" Although Claire had apparently reached the same conclusion Jess had, that this was all about loyalty and sending a message to Jess that she needed to put the brakes on any possible move her husband was considering, she added, "Can you think of anything else it might have been? You know I think you're brilliant and can do no wrong, but I don't have context for you here and wonder if there is something that may have . . . I know you've been distracted about this whole thing over the past several weeks."

Suddenly, Claire's voice escalated with emotion. "Wait a minute. Why are you so damn calm? I'd be sticking pins in a voodoo doll by now. What are you thinking?"

"I'm thinking about what a lovely family I have and how much fun our weekend was with Beth, and that this is only a job." Jess laughed. "I'm sure I'll be outraged soon. But you know how important family is to me. And, frankly, I think the whole Portland thing was just a threat. All is back to normal, and I am not going to let this get to me."

"So, Arthur has categorically denied that there's anything serious about this Portland thing?"

"Not in so many words, but we have so much going for us right now that I just don't think it's a worry," Jess said, willing herself onto the road back to normal.

"Jess." Claire sounded worried.

"So this is what I'm going to do, and I need you to critique my plan." Jess described her strategy and heard Claire out on some of the finer points. She knew her idea would disappoint some people; she hoped she wouldn't regret what she was about to do.

Chapter 10

Jess left work on the early side and was able to get a run in before meeting Arthur and Vincente at Forest Park Bistro for dinner. Vincente was a visiting professor from Italy, staying with them for the week while he worked with Arthur and his lab team on some joint research that had been underway for years.

"Jess, Arthur has promised that I can cook for you tomorrow night. I'm thinking pasta and veal. Is that little market on the corner still the place to find a good cut of meat?" Vincente had stayed with them many times and always cooked for them at least one night, which Jess loved almost as much as she loved having him visit.

"Vincente, you know I love it when you cook, and yes, the corner market is still reliable. But you have me wondering how often you cook at home for Sylvia."

"Ahhh, you have found me out. Sylvia is a much better cook than I am, and very, how you say, territorial of her kitchen, so when I am here . . ."

"You practice?" Jess caught him in the truth and laughed. "Well, your practice is *perfecto* for me, and you're a dear to do it. Any chance we could eat a bit later, like you Italians do? I have a late meeting tomorrow that I'd like to keep."

"For you, my dear Jess, anything." He kissed her hand—another reason she loved having him as a houseguest.

After he gave them some welcome updates about his family, including Liliana's wedding plans, they chatted about other characters they had all come to know in the international-research community—whose star was rising, who was moving, whose marriage was faltering, and other tidbits of interest. Jess was relieved that there was no mention of Portland, and took note that Arthur was as charming with his longtime friend as he could possibly be.

The two men battled over the bill, and Arthur won. Vincente put his wallet away and said, "So, how's it going with the merger? You two still getting along?"

Arthur lost himself in conversation with the server, who had come to retrieve the check. After an awkward fifteen seconds of ignoring the question, Jess smiled tightly and answered, "Of course."

The next morning, Jess found Dan alone in the break room and described her plan. She was prepared to be forceful about it but didn't think he would resist her. Why should he? She would be fighting her own battle, and he would be able to stay above the fray. She knew he was supportive of her, but he had a business to run. He seemed relieved, and she fought her initial fear that he might distance himself from her, as if she were yesterday's problem.

First, she formally asked for a meeting with Dick. She wasn't sure he would meet with her, but there was no way she wasn't going to push hard for a face-to-face with the man who was determined to cut her out of the merger. His assistant, Laura, sounding bored, offered the routine, "May I tell him what this is regarding?" followed by the usual stale excuse, "He's really booked up, and I can't make any promises for the next several days."

But Laura perked up when Jess said, "Tell him this is about a personal matter that I would like to clarify. Dan Getz knows that I'm asking for the meeting. Just give him my name and my reason, and I'm sure he'll be willing to see me in the next few days." She left it at that. Jess thought again how useful it was that she had not taken Arthur's name when they'd married. The assistant might not put her together with her husband, but clearly Dick had done that and more.

Jess knew it would take a day or so to hear back from Dick, so she sought Nate out for drinks in the meantime. She hoped that, having worked on Dick's Midwest Health team and having denied the rumor once on her behalf, he could give her some idea of what she would be walking into. He agreed to meet her not far from the Midwest Health corporate offices, but at a less-traveled neighborhood bar that she liked for quiet conversations.

"You look good—certainly a hundred times better than the last time I saw you, being hounded in the hallway." Nate smiled as he slid into the booth next to her and sighed deeply. "What a long day. I'm glad to see you. The tension around the office is so thick. A year ago, I had a big job. But with the merger added to it, it's almost too much."

He was the rare man who could allow himself to sound vulnerable about the grinding workload of health care and what it meant to him personally. He was now on his second marriage and trying to make sure he carved out the time it took to keep his relationship working. There had been a time, after his first marriage ended, when he had made some transparent hints that he was interested in Jess and wondered about the health of her own relationship. Jess had been taken aback, but, knowing he was a friend going through a bad time, she had set him straight and they hadn't spoken of it again.

"Nate, I'm sorry things are so complicated for you right now. Don't you just hate it that we live in such interesting times and that the accelerating changes are almost too much for mere mortals to handle?" She tried to tease him a bit as she saw him rub his temples with his fingers. "I can listen if you want to unburden yourself. I'm all ears. It's the least I can do after you rescued me the other day. What a friend you are."

They ordered and caught up a bit, and then Nate turned to her. "So, how's the battle against the rumor mill going? I haven't seen you on campus for a while. Are you staying away from the rumor mongers?"

"Actually, I wanted to ask you if you know anything about what the grapevine is saying now, and if Dick has asked you anything more about it."

"Dick hasn't asked me anything else, but I don't know if he's done with it. He may just not be talking to me about it because I was so certain it wasn't true. Dick is under a lot of stress, and you know what it means to him to get this merger sorted." He looked at Jess. "He needs the proverbial 'closed deal' on his résumé before he can move on to his next big job. It's something he's been pretty open about since he came five years ago."

Nate had never been a fan of Dick's, and he suspected Dick would be long gone by the time the hard work of actually effecting the merger was left to the minions who'd have to carry it out.

"So, you aren't hearing anything more about it? It's cooled off?"

"Nope, I haven't heard anything else. But I've been pretty deep in the weeds with my own team, working on the operational plans for combining the laboratories. I've heard that Sam Hirsch is pretty worried about some departures from the brain trust at the U but that there's some big plan to keep that from happening. I haven't heard any names or any details, though." He paused. "Actually, now that I think about it, it's pretty hush-hush, and I don't know what that means."

"Well, at least Arthur isn't still hot news. That's something." Nate reported directly to Dick, and the leadership team was pretty close, so if Arthur's pending departure was an issue, Nate likely knew about it. She smiled at him and finished her drink. "Thanks, Nate."

"Jess, you look so much less stressed than you did before. Tell me everything is going OK for you." Nate smiled at her so empathetically that she almost missed the fact that he didn't say "going OK for you *and Arthur.*" She hoped his own marriage was still solid.

The fact that Nate hadn't heard any concerns about Arthur should be good news, but it didn't ring true. She had to put on a brave face for him as they parted with a hug. As she went home to try to enjoy Vincente's meal, she couldn't help but feel something gnawing at her.

Chapter 11

<><><><><><><><><><><><><><><><><><><><>

"**G**ood morning. This is Jess Lawson."

"This is Laura, Dick Morrison's assistant. There's been a cancellation in his calendar for this afternoon. I know this isn't much notice, but does four thirty work for you?"

"Yes, that will work. Thank you."

"And, Ms. Lawson, Mr. Morrison is off campus earlier in the p.m. Could you possibly meet him at the Bellrive Country Club?"

"Of course. That's fine." Jess had to smile. Nobody losing face here. Dick's assistant had found some time due to a cancellation, even though he had no free time. And Dick could hide the fact of the meeting by holding it off campus. *Hmm . . . Works for me.*

Jess had delegated the most pressing work on the merger to others, so she left for a late lunch and a run. As she jogged, Jess thought about what she knew of Dick Morrison and how he might approach her. She appreciated his rise to power and influence in health care and knew that he was at the height of his career right now as CEO of Midwest Health. She had not personally seen him lose his temper but had heard from Dan that he could be harsh and sarcastic with those he saw as not bright enough to do his bidding. She didn't know much about his personal life, other than that he was long married to his college sweetheart and that they had grown children. His wife, who didn't work outside the home, devoted herself to charity causes in each of the communities to which her husband's career had taken them.

The run gave her a great adrenaline rush, and she stopped at home to shower and change before driving out to Bellrive. When she arrived, Jess was happy to see eager golf and tennis players out and about, taking advantage of the weather. She didn't know this club well, but her impression as she drove through the grounds was that it was a bit pretentious. She got out of her car, welcoming the late-afternoon sun on her back. Strolling from the parking lot, she felt just charged enough to be eager for the meeting.

The host ushered her to a corner table. "Mr. Morrison is running a bit late. May I bring you a beverage?"

As the waiter delivered her glass of merlot, Dick arrived. "I see you've started early." He glanced at her wine and then turned to the waiter. "I'll just have a cup of coffee, James. Thank you."

The waiter left and dimmed the lights to signal that the evening had begun, and Dick sat down. He was a good-looking man in any light, blessed with that graying-at-the-temples feature that worked so well for men.

"I appreciate the meeting. I wasn't sure you'd agree to it. Thank you." She gave him a warm smile. She didn't need chill; she needed him flexible.

"I'm a reasonable man. What exactly did you want to talk to me about?" Dick smiled back. "I believe Dan has relayed my wish that you no longer work on the merger as a consultant for Midwest Health."

His voice was firm, and she intuitively identified the style he had honed over thirty-five years of executive leadership: When heading into a meeting after a decision has been made, be firm and resolute, get the objective out immediately, and hold. There it was. Jess gave him credit for getting right to the point.

"Yes," she countered, taking her time. "Dan did relay that to me. However, he wasn't clear on the reason. So I was hoping you'd tell me why you no longer want me working on the team. Surely you can give me that. I like to think I try to continually improve and can take honest criticism of my work. What is it I can do to bring more value to a project as complex as this one?" Guessing he wouldn't come up with much detail and that he was barely aware of what she did, she was curious to see how he would handle her request.

"You're a very bright woman. Nobody would ever mistake you for a naive schoolgirl. I understand you were a smart one, graduating second in your business-school class at Tufts. Is that where you met Arthur?" Dick asked, a smirk threatening.

Now they were getting someplace. She met his gaze and responded with a coy smile. "Oh, no, no. Arthur is my senior by almost ten years. He was already through Harvard Medical by the time we met in Boston. He was recruited here to the U after we married and has remained here for, let me think, almost twenty years now."

"Happily?"

"Excuse me?" Jess wasn't going to make this easy. She sipped her wine.

"You said Arthur has been here twenty years. Have those been satisfying years here at the U?"

"For the most part." Jess hesitated, then moved ahead sharply. "But, Dick, I'm sure you could have that conversation with Arthur directly. I asked for this meeting to find out why you're cutting me out of my role on the merger team. Is there something I've done to harm the project? Why are you dissatisfied with my work?"

Dick leaned back, took a sip of coffee, and casually put his arm over the side of his chair. "Jess, I'd love to keep you on the team. But you need to show your ultimate loyalty to us. You need to remember that the objective of Midwest Health's successful merger with the university hospital requires an intact faculty. You need to keep Arthur in St. Louis."

Jess was so surprised by the direct order that she barked out a laugh, causing a few patrons to turn their way. She looked around and saw that the place was getting busier. The waiter stopped by to refill her wineglass and Dick's coffee cup. She scanned the room once more, but the people who'd been staring were once again involved in their own conversations.

She took a deep breath, trying to relax her shoulders. Leaning in closer to him, she said in a low voice, "You can't be serious. Do you honestly think you can threaten my job unless I prevent Arthur from taking a position elsewhere? Do you have so little faith in the merits of your merger proposal that one faculty defection, if it was real, could destroy your plan? What about the Midwest Health board, the university's board, all the employees and patients of both institutions? All that, yet the merger could be foiled by one potential departure? You've got to be kidding me."

"Jessica." Dick picked up his coffee cup, slowly took a swallow, and then shifted his posture closer to her. "Arthur is a leader among the faculty. If he left, taking his research and its significant dollars, he could open that possibility to others. We just can't let that happen. I would expect that if you were thinking as a team member, you'd see that. You yourself just mentioned all those who would be hurt if this didn't work."

Jess just looked at him, wondering how he could be so sure of his position and not have any sense of how off it was. Her mind was ready to burst. *Is he really saying this out loud?* Beyond the raw sexism of his thinking, he was ignoring any of the conflict-of-interest barriers.

The smirk was now in evidence. "I can see that you're thinking about this, and that makes me happy," he said. "I hope you're beginning to understand my position and will consider this as the serious matter that it is. We need Arthur to stay, for everyone's sake. Please take the rest of the week to think about it, and then let me know what you decide." He leaned back in his chair and finished his coffee.

After he motioned for the bill, he stood up and said to Jess, with more warmth than he had shown so far, "Have a good evening." He stopped to greet a few patrons on his way out and to give the signed bill to James. His commanding presence and warm chitchat turned many heads as he left.

Jess slowly finished her glass of wine, taking time to process the conversation. She knew Dick believed he had won and that she would fall in line. "Let him think so," she whispered, and willed herself to move beyond the meeting.

Looking out the windows at the spring green of the golf course and a spectacular setting sun, she realized how hungry she was. She looked at her watch and jumped up. As she left the bar, she walked by the kitchen and caught the wonderful aroma of roasting meat. As good as it smelled, it reminded her of the treat she anticipated at home. Tom was making homemade pizza that night, as a way to thank Vincente for the cooking lessons Vincente had been giving him. She could almost taste it now.

She was halfway across the lobby when she heard a familiar voice. "Jess, how wonderful to see you." Charlie Williams, university board member and fellow homeowner in Jess and Arthur's lake association, was just turning away from a conversation with Dick.

She approached to accept a warm hug from Charlie and caught a glimpse of Dick's face as it flushed.

Charlie started to ask about her family and then found his manners and swiveled around to include Dick in the conversation. "Dick Morrison, this is—"

"Charlie, Dick and I are acquainted," Jess interrupted.

"Yes, Jess is on the merger team representing Midwest Health," Dick added quickly.

"Really? I didn't know that. Well, I'm feeling better already. Jess's negotiation skills are top-notch—I can attest to that." Charlie's eyes twinkled, hinting at shared experiences, as he smiled at her.

"Thanks for the update, Dick. I'll be in touch. Jess, can you spare five minutes for a quick catch-up?"

She couldn't help but enjoy watching Dick walk away, dismissed.

Chapter 12

∞∞∞∞∞∞∞∞∞∞∞∞∞∞∞∞∞∞∞∞∞

Jess entered the house to the unmistakable smell of pancetta and basil. Warm male laughter in the kitchen pulled her away from any further thought of Dick's obvious attempt at a power play. She joined the happy men in her kitchen, their mood infectious.

"That smells so good! I'm absolutely famished." She greeted both Tom and Vincente with a kiss and a hug.

"Hey, Mom, perfect timing. The pizza is just coming out of the oven. Vincente helped me improve my crust technique, and I don't want you to miss out on how it looks when it's piping hot." Tom gave Vincente plates to set the table.

"Jess, your son is a natural. My work with him is almost done!" Vincente took the plates from Tom.

"And I'm very grateful." Jess found a stray bit of cheese on the counter and popped it into her mouth. "How many years have you two been on this cooking adventure together?"

"Well, Tom, how old were you when we started this—nine, maybe?" Vincente's eyes crinkled as he looked fondly at his protégé.

Tom chuckled as he caught his mother's knowing smile. "Mom, don't tell the story again—I know, I know. We had quite a mess that first time we made sauce, but that's only because Vincente let me mash and taste everything."

Jess squeezed by them and put her briefcase down in the corner office space. "And it was delicious. Once Vincente also taught you the virtues of keeping a clean kitchen, everybody was happy!" They shared a laugh, and Jess realized how fortunate Tom was to have Vincente in his life. Vincente not only was far more patient than Arthur but also genuinely appreciated spending time with Tom, the son he'd never had.

"Where's Arthur? Vincente, you know your job while you stay here with us is to make sure Arthur is home for dinner every night. Did you let us down?"

Vincente looked so upset, Jess wished she hadn't teased him, and quickly added, "Hey, I'm joking. Tom and I both have experience in how tough it can be to get him home. Right, Tom?" He shrugged.

She trotted out of the kitchen to wash up before eating and was surprised to find Vincente hot on her heels. He pulled her into the den and put his finger up to his lips, signaling her to be quiet. "Jess, I don't know if it's my place to say any-thing"—he hesitated, then went on—"but I've known you for many, many years now, and I do not like what I'm hearing during this trip."

"What exactly are you hearing, Vincente?" Jess could see alarm in his expressive eyes.

"Arthur's going to Portland."

"Oh, that." Jess's shoulders relaxed. "That's not likely." She took his hand. "You don't have to worry about that."

He stood looking at her, as if he were trying to put the puzzle pieces together. "But I heard him on the phone today with the Portland people, talking about moving his research labs. And you do not know this?"

"Oh, Vincente, there must be something lost in translation here. That's absolutely not happening." Her mind caught up to his words, and she felt a chill. No researcher she had ever known was casual about the location of his or her labs. Was Arthur really on this road, without her?

As they stood looking at each other, more questions looming, Tom rang the dinner bell. "Get it while it's hot: pizza pie, fresh from the oven."

The moment passed. They put on their game faces and rallied for Tom's dinner, although now Jess wasn't quite so hungry.

◇◇◇◇◇◇◇◇◇◇◇◇◇◇◇◇

After Tom left to study with a classmate, Jess and Vincente had a long conversation over a bottle of wine. He told her more about what he had heard and said it was an open discussion among Arthur's lab staff.

In a broken whisper, she asked, "Then why isn't it an open discussion with me, Vincente?" As her tears began to fall in the darkened room, she added, "Why not talk to me?"

"My dear Jess, I do not know," he said, taking her hand in his. "I can tell you what I do know: Arthur's not happy right now. He seems distracted to me, and perhaps a bit down. Is that how you say 'depressed'? Not his usual self. You must know this, yes?"

"Yes, down and moody, too. I didn't know it was evident at work, though. Of course, he may be letting you in a little, as you're such a good friend. Is he this way in the lab as well?"

"Not so much with everyone. I think Joan, his research assistant, sees it. But, Jess, I need to tell you that I've asked him questions about this and do not believe he's thinking very clearly about this move. When I asked him why, he said he's tired of the political mess of the merger. He wants a new start, with people he can trust. When I asked him about what this means for your family, he would not talk. He would not say anything. He just looked very sad."

"How can he be anything but sad when he's keeping this secret from us, from me?" She sobbed. "It's all my fault. I never should have agreed to work on this merger. What was I thinking? How could I put that much pressure on both of us?"

"Long marriages survive many obstacles, and you and Arthur have a strong one. I'm sure when you talk together, you will figure this out."

"Thank you, Vincente. I have to believe that. But I fear it's too late . . ."

"Ah, Jess, it's never too late when the heart is involved. Sylvia and I have been married for thirty-one years and have been through some, how can I say, difficulties. She left me for a time." When Jess looked up in surprise, he said, "You did not know that. So I am able to speak to you from experience. It's not too late. When I leave tomorrow, you will no longer have a houseguest in your way. Go to Arthur, and have the conversation you need to have. Will you do that for me?"

"No, dear Vincente, I'll do that for *me!*" Jess rose from the chair, leaning on him to keep her balance. She was so sleepy from all the emotions and the wine that she barely made it to her bed before she fell fast asleep. She awoke just enough when Arthur came home to peek at the clock and wonder where he had been until one a.m.

Chapter 13

Arthur looked up at her sheepishly the next morning as Jess came down for coffee, feeling drained after the night before.

"Did you get any sleep? You came to bed very late. What were you up to?" She went to hug him, but he was stiff like a board and didn't respond.

"Can we have a check-in tonight?" she asked. She was still attempting the awkward hug, not giving him an inch to move into that untouchable place he liked to hide of late. The one conscious thought she'd had before she'd fallen asleep the previous night was that she could no longer let him go there.

Vincente came into the room, took in the scene, and said, "Yes, yes. You should catch up tonight. Your guest is finally leaving you. Jess, I believe we had too much wine last night." He touched his temples and asked, "Do you have some aspirin around here somewhere?" He grabbed a cup and got some coffee.

Arthur came to, as if from a trance, and was all charm. "You two—a *bit* too much wine? And you ate almost all the pizza! Fortunately, Tom hid a piece for me with exact instructions for warming it up, and I just had it for breakfast. It was really delicious. Vincente, you're making a proper cook of him.

And I get the benefit. Seems a good trade-off for a guest stay once a year or so. You know we love having you. When is your flight, again? Can I give you a lift to the airport?"

"I wouldn't think of imposing on you in the middle of the day, Arthur. You are too gracious. I'll arrange for a taxi. No problem at all." Vincente took the two aspirin Jess proffered. "And I'm all packed and ready to go into the lab with you whenever you are." He gave Jess a warm hug and a wink and said his goodbyes.

Before they left, Jess said, "Arthur, I think Tom has to stay late at school tonight. Are you willing to let me cook? I know it's a comedown after both Vincente and Tom have spoiled us this week, but I feel like making something. Can I entice you home by six for a good meal?"

It took him a bit too long to respond. She detected a mix of sheepishness and suspicion in his glance toward Vincente. "Of course. You know I love your cooking. I'll absolutely be home by six. See you then." He gave her a quick kiss and headed out with Vincente in tow.

Jess took a pork tenderloin out of the freezer and made sure she had cream, dried apricots, and quinoa. She whispered a quick prayer of thanks that she didn't have to try to fit shopping into her day. It was not a running day, but she needed to talk to Claire. And today she really did have meetings to see to and deadlines to meet, and oh my God, she really had a hangover. Fortunately, she had made a decision that she thought would make things easier.

◇◇◇◇◇◇◇◇◇◇◇◇◇◇◇◇◇◇

After a busy morning, she ran over to Claire's office with takeout salads during her only open slot that day and filled Claire in on the strange meeting with Dick. She knew that Claire would find it interesting, so she exaggerated the putdowns and the ultimatum a bit, but not too much. Dick really did fit the stereotype of a sexist male.

Claire guffawed at the demand he had made. "That's unbelievable. Does he think you, the little woman, can just put her foot down and keep her man from making Dick's life difficult, and by doing so keep her job? My God, he didn't even offer you something! And you don't work for him; you work for Dan. What a blatant power play!"

Claire pulled open a drawer from her credenza, pulled out fancy napkins and real cutlery, and put the plastic forks back in the takeout bag. "These salads look good. Let's sit over here so we can have some privacy." She gestured toward the corner conference area, which was less visible from the busy corridor outside her office.

"It really is a crazy, wrongheaded power play. I knew you'd enjoy hearing about it. But, Claire, I've reached a decision. I'm going to let it go and work on my marriage. I know this whole thing has gotten out of whack; I set up these barriers between Arthur and me because of the conflicts, and that isn't fair to him." Jess picked at her salad. "I know now how large this merger looms in his mind, and depriving him of the chance to talk to me about it has been totally unfair of me. I so regret it."

"Are you sure that's what you want to do?" Claire stopped eating and looked directly at her friend. "I think there's a way you could call Dick's bluff and embarrass him enough to continue. It would be a tough game to play, but I hate to see him getting away with something so outrageous."

"You're right. I know I could get Dick to back down, and it would be fun to see him squirm a bit. But just because I could doesn't mean I should. And the bottom line is, I need to get out of my current role and be Arthur's wife. That's what he needs right now. So why play the game to win and then lose everything anyway?" Jess finished her water and pushed her half-eaten salad away.

"I knew there was a reason I never married. I'm way too self-centered. I appreciate your position, Jess, and if that's what your heart is telling you to do, I applaud you for your sacrifice.

But it makes me damn mad. You shouldn't have to do that. You *don't* have to do that."

"Claire, I've made up my mind. Please don't be disappointed in me. My family is what matters most. Keeping it intact is my life's objective, not having a line or two on a résumé that I can brag about. This feels right, not just to my heart but to my head."

Jess thanked Claire for her support and left her office. She felt lighter now that she had made the decision and shared it out loud with someone she knew did not agree. Claire was driven, and so was Jess. But Jess was battle tested, after years of personal havoc. She knew when to fight and when to withdraw, and she intuitively felt that now was the time to regroup with her loved ones and be strong. She could fight other battles another day. She had been up against sexism in her career for so long that it didn't surprise her anymore. The blatant example—sleeping with the boss—was easily avoided under any circumstances. More subtle had been a situation when she'd discovered that one of her male colleagues had taken credit for her work and won a promotion for it. And then there was the female friend who'd elbowed Jess aside to get close to a powerful man and then used her sexuality for personal gain.

This standoff with Dick was just another chapter from the same book. When she had started her own consulting business, Jess had been able to control the environment from the top down, but she knew from Claire's and Diane's stories that this kind of bad behavior was still common.

She finished her day and went home to prepare dinner. She was drinking lots of water, and her hangover seemed to be subsiding. But no wine tonight! It was just as well. Arthur didn't drink much, and she needed to be clearheaded to determine what was going on with him and what that meant for them as a couple.

◇◇◇◇◇◇◇◇◇◇◇◇◇◇◇◇◇

He was home by five forty-five, and, since the tenderloin was still roasting, she invited him to take a short walk around the neighborhood. Although it was nearly dark, the weather was mild as they strolled through the streets, watching all the lights in the houses go on while families gathered for the evening. He still felt distant, and so, although she wanted to take his hand, she held herself back and focused instead on trying to relax. "It's been awhile since we took an evening walk. Nice, isn't it?" she said.

"You've been just as busy as I have."

"Hey, I know. It's just nice, that's all. Nice to spend time together. We should do it more often." She was about to raise the question of the mission trip together, when a neighbor pulled into the driveway in front of them and they stopped to talk a bit.

When they got home, she lit the patio lanterns and served dinner outside. They chatted about the kids over dinner. Arthur was still somewhat distracted, but she needed to get the conversation started, so she said, "Vincente told me that you talked with the Portland people yesterday about specs for your new lab. That really surprised me. I thought that was off the table." Jess kept her voice light and passed him the vegetables.

He didn't say anything, so she went on. "I want you to know that if you want to go to Portland, we'll make it work. Now that Tom is so close to graduating and going off to college, there's no reason you and I couldn't make a move. Actually, it would be fun to start a new chapter in a new place. I've always loved the Pacific Northwest. Depending on when you had to go, I could stay here with Tom until he's settled at college, and then we could sell here and buy there." She kept looking at Arthur as she rambled on, but he still didn't respond, just looked at her with a sad face. She put her fork down, pushed her chair back, and pulled herself up tall.

"Arthur, I'm quitting the merger." She didn't go into the ultimatum story; she said simply, "I've decided it's too much. So from now on, I'll just be working with my own clients and on other projects for Dan. I don't like what it's done to us, and

I'm sorry that I've not been here for you as you've needed me. I know that it's been impossible to talk to me about work, and I want to be available to support you as we move forward, wherever that is."

He had stopped eating and wasn't even looking at her anymore but staring into some foreign space. "What are you thinking? Talk to me, Arthur."

"I don't want to talk about this now."

"But we *need* to. It's driving a wedge between us. I realize now that I should never have agreed to work on this merger. Things will be different if I'm not working on it like before, don't you see?"

"I really don't want to talk about this now," he repeated. He stood up and started putting dishes on a tray. And, raising his voice, he added, "It's really best if we don't talk about this now."

She stood, too, grabbing his arm, and said, "Dick wants me to influence you to stay here. Tomorrow I'm going to tell him to go to hell. My personal life is not negotiable."

With that, Arthur shook her off and turned on her. "I don't really care what you do, Jess. If I decide to go to Portland, I plan to go alone."

She barely noticed him leave the patio, and this time, she didn't call after him. She simply went into the den, folded herself into her favorite chair, closed her eyes, and thought, *After all these years, is it really going to end like this? And over a merger? It has to be about more than that.*

Chapter 14

◇◇◇◇◇◇◇◇◇◇◇◇◇◇◇◇◇◇◇◇◇◇◇◇◇◇

Jess caught Dan early the next morning and beckoned him into her office before the day got lost. "I wanted to let you know that I met with Dick."

"Oh." His eyebrows shot up. "How did it go?"

"Well, no surprise to me, he was pressuring you to keep me off the merger. He wants me to influence Arthur against taking a position elsewhere. The surprise is that he was so blatant about it."

"What do you mean? What did he say to you?" Dan leaned toward her.

"He told me he can't count on my loyalty unless I do what I can to keep Arthur in St. Louis."

Jess watched Dan carefully to see what his reaction would be. She wanted to believe he was one of the good guys and that he'd been honest about not knowing what Dick was up to. But she'd been around awhile and knew how some business deals got done.

"What a bastard that guy is," he responded quickly, pounding his fist on the table. "You know, when we initially talked about this and you commented that you thought that might be the reason, I hadn't given that any thought. It's so overtly sexist. Unbelievable!"

Dan fixed his gaze on the cityscape for a moment, then looked back at Jess. "Are you sure? Is there any way you could be mistaken about his intent?"

"No. He put it in very plain language. I even challenged his thinking a bit by pointing out that one physician didn't make or break a major deal like this. But Dick said that since Arthur is a leading influencer, he could start something that might snowball."

"Good God. How much research support does Arthur bring in anyway—millions?" Dan asked. "Is it a National Institutes of Health grant, or where's it coming from?"

They discussed the arcane business of haves and have-nots in academic-research circles. How once someone was established, it was so much easier to draw in new money. This made things hard for young scientists, even if they had brilliant ideas. It was as limiting a bureaucracy as any, amid all the political jockeying that occurred.

Dan sighed deeply. "It's a stretch, but I guess I can see where the guy is coming from. Dick has bet the farm on the merger coming together and must want to make sure there are no loose ends. But this seems a bit desperate, and it's clearly unfair. Unfortunately, I don't think it's illegal." Dan was gazing out the window again, seeming to gather his thoughts. "I can't approach him about it from that angle, but I *can* call him out for being an ass, and I will." He straightened up and looked directly at Jess.

She smiled warmly at him. "You know the client does get to have the team he wants, and he's the client." She paused, then added slowly, "I really don't have the energy to fight this now, although I appreciate that you're in my corner."

She looked down at her hands, playing with her wedding ring. "You may not want to hear all of this, but this whole merger project, and my involvement, and Arthur's position—it's been difficult for us as a couple. At this point, I want to leave the project. It's best for me personally."

She paused to clear her throat and control her emotions. When she looked up, Dan's face was rigid. He picked up his office phone and dialed a number. "Amy, get Dick Morrison on the phone ASAP."

Jess joined him at her desk. "Please don't. You're a good friend, but I don't want you to take a bullet for me. Don't risk the project. Besides, it's late to be making too many changes. My lead people know what they're doing. The plan is all laid out, and I know they'll do well."

Just then, Dan's cell phone dinged with an incoming-text alert, and they both looked out the glass doorway to see the leadership team gathering in the conference room across the hall.

"Looks like it's time for the meeting," Dan said. "But, Jess, please don't be too hasty in making your decision. Now that we know what Dick is up to, let him wait; I can put him off for a while." He stood up to switch gears and looked around the office. "Is there potpourri or something in here? I smell something I can't quite identify, something really good."

"Uh, that would be the lingering aroma of the cinnamon roll I inhaled before you walked in."

"Oh, I remember how you love your cinnamon rolls!" They both laughed.

As they neared the door, Dan hesitated until Jess looked directly at him. "Please take some time with this. Whatever your decision is, I'll support you. Your clients need you. The firm needs you." He paused at the door, his voice quieting to little more than a whisper. "But I understand how you feel about family. So do what you feel you must do. There will always be work for you to do here. You know that."

She would do almost anything to keep her own family together, but she wouldn't allow Dan to put the merger at risk because of her.

Her phone rang. "Jess, it's Amy. I have Dick Morrison for Dan. Is he there?"

Jess didn't flinch. "No, Amy, he's already in the meeting. Tell Dick to disregard the call."

Chapter 15

◇◇◇◇◇◇◇◇◇◇◇◇◇◇◇◇◇◇◇◇◇◇◇

As soon as Jess decided not to play Dick's game, she felt lighter, as if she could float through any situation anyone could throw at her. She would wind down her work and delegate it to her colleagues over time, making sure they could use her as a resource as needed. No big drama. To prepare them for the transition, Dan simply announced, "As Jess has done a tremendous job of building the architecture that we needed to have in place to assure that human resources issues were addressed in the best business interests of our clients, and has built an excellent team capable of executing on that plan, she will now move on to a new assignment that needs her executive leadership." If there were questions, she didn't get any, and she didn't ask Dan what he'd had to field.

Once her path had been cleared, Jess decided to work on her marriage slowly. She hoped things with Arthur would normalize if she relaxed and waited. If not, at least they had a definitive timeline to work with. Arthur was committed to his faculty position until the merger date. He could close her out for only so long. In the meantime, she committed to fully enjoying Tom's senior-year family activities.

Tom's baseball team was in the school conference playoffs that spring, and Jess found welcome distraction in cheering them on at their games. On prom night, all the parents gathered at the school to take pictures of their beautiful children looking grown-up and glowing. When Tom realized his father would be out of town for the dance, he volunteered Jess's services as a chaperone.

They all gathered for Tom's graduation. Arthur might still have been avoiding Jess, but she knew he loved having both children home. Beth had just returned from Stanford for the summer. Tom was in his element, enjoying all the attention. Diane made him a scrapbook of all the artwork he had sent to her on her birthdays. She told him he couldn't keep it, since it was too dear to her, but that she wanted him to savor it for the summer.

Diane was nervous about introducing George to Jess and her family, but she shouldn't have been. He was a hit with the kids, who immediately responded to his humor and obvious affection for their mother's dear friend. It helped that George and Tom found a common language in their love of baseball.

Several people from Arthur's lab and from Jess's office came to celebrate as well. The weather was St. Louis May beautiful, the food and drinks were delectable, and several people made a point of seeking out Jess to tell her what a beautiful family she had. Pictures of the day recorded two joyful children, a proud and happy mother, and a distracted but affectionate father.

Dan pulled her aside and gave her a warm hug. "This is what it's all about, right? I'm so happy for you, and so happy to see you all looking, looking . . ." He seemed to be searching for the right word. "Looking so intact!"

Before she could respond that "intact" might be too certain a choice, Arthur came by with Joan, his research assistant. "Dan, could you spare a minute to help us understand something about the faculty's legal obligations to the hospital as far as surgical pathology revenue goes?"

"This sounds like merger talk, so I'm out of here." Jess raised her eyebrows to exaggerate her point and squeezed Dan's elbow as she left. "I'll leave you to it. But do remember that this is a party, not a business meeting!" She turned toward the entry just as Claire arrived and immediately grabbed Tom.

"Tom, you're way too much fun to leave for college. Can't you stay here with us?" Claire hugged him more tightly than anyone else would have dared to, Jess noted out of the corner of her eye. Finally releasing him, she turned toward Jess and said, "What're we going to do without him around?"

When Diane and George joined them, the group laughed and watched the blushing Tom scurry off to find his friends. As he walked away, Jess noticed uncharacteristic tears streaking down Claire's cheeks. When George excused himself to get drinks for the women, Jess declared, "Claire, we'll all miss him, but it's the way things go. How does that saying go? Raise them with wings to fly away from you?"

That didn't seem to stop the tears, so Jess whispered to Claire, "Hey, are you OK?" Diane leaned in to hear the response, as Claire straightened her posture, smiled bravely, and wiped at her eyes.

"Sorry. I don't usually get this emotional. Of course I'm fine, but are you two free for a bit tomorrow morning? Maybe coffee at my place? I think I need some advice."

After agreeing to Claire's request, Jess moved on to take care of her other party guests. When she joined Beth and her friends in the backyard, Beth said, "Mom, guess what Jen is doing this summer? Jen, tell her," Beth urged her friend.

"Well, my parents haven't exactly agreed to it yet." Jen looked around to see who might be lurking as she shared her news. "But I'll be working wardrobe for a small off-Broadway theater!"

Jess noticed that the quartet of twenty-year-olds didn't squeal, as they might have a few years earlier, but seemed to be going for a certain detachment. Until Jen added, "And I get to share a flat with some actors in the play!" That brought the squeals. As they all talked over one another, offering to come visit her in New York City, Jess asked if her parents knew about the living arrangements.

"Not exactly, Mrs. Steele—oops, I mean Ms. Lawson." Jen pulled Jess aside. "Actually, they don't know I'm even thinking about it. Would you please not—"

"Jen, of course. I wouldn't dream of upstaging you. This is your conversation to have with them. Good luck!" She gave Jen a quick wink and moved on. Beth followed.

"Mom—I mean, Mrs. Steele." Beth giggled. "Seems so 'high school' to hear my friends call you that." She looked up at Jess with a pleading expression. "So, if she does go to New York City, do you think Dad can free up some miles for a trip for me?"

Just then, Arthur moved in on them. "Did I hear my name mentioned?" He put his arm around his daughter and surveyed the party. "Are you having a good time, baby? What were you going to ask Dad about?"

Jess laughed lightly and left them to their discussion. "Go for it, Beth. You're on your own with this one." Not to worry. Jen's parents would never agree to this summer plan. Once she had checked on the beverage supply, she glanced back to the patio and saw that Beth was back hanging with her friends and Arthur was nowhere to be seen.

Later, putting the fine crystal away, Jess wondered what was going on with Claire. Jess had been so preoccupied with her own issues that she hadn't been as attuned to her friend recently. Claire conquered most professional challenges, but maybe something was going on with the new project she had started. She recalled some problem with Claire's newly hired project director. Was that it?

∘∘∘∘∘∘∘∘∘∘∘∘∘∘∘∘∘∘

The next morning, Diane and Jess arrived simultaneously, in their running gear, having decided it was too nice a Saturday, and Claire's house in the Soulard neighborhood too enticing, not to take advantage of a jog after their coffee. As they walked up to the house, Diane said, "So, do you know what's up? I've never seen her so shaky. Any idea?"

Jess shook her head. "I don't have a clue, but I hope it's not because I've been so self-involved in the midst of all my merger drama."

They went around to the porch entrance to find Claire, curly black hair in a loose chignon, ensconced on her wicker sofa, with coffee and fruit set out on a tray. "Thank you both for coming. I feel so foolish for making a scene yesterday. How embarrassing." Jess noticed that Claire's face was drawn and tight around the eyes, and that she didn't seem to know what to do with her hands, which were flitting around almost beyond her control as she served coffee.

"Not to worry. Tom loved the attention and asked if you were up for a tennis game with him soon. I think he's a bit nostalgic about leaving us. It's an emotional time, for sure." Jess sat, took a sip of her coffee, and said, "Ah, this porch—so peaceful and homey," in light and high tones, to see if she could comfort her friend.

Diane caught Jess's eye and, seeming to confirm her intuition, decided on small talk until Claire was ready to share. "It was a lovely party, Jess. George was totally taken in by your and Tom's hospitality. He said he didn't get to talk to Arthur much . . ."

Claire hugged herself and looked from Diane to Jess and back again. "OK, OK, I'm ready. And I'm so confused about what I'm about to tell you. I feel so dumb . . ."

"Well, we all know you're not dumb, so just let it out. I'm sure it's not so bad. We'll be here for you whatever it is." Jess looked at Diane for confirmation, and then both leaned in to coax Claire into unburdening herself.

Claire closed her eyes and spoke in a whisper. "I'm pregnant!" As she opened her eyes, Jess tried not to stare at her with her mouth hanging open, but she couldn't help it. Finally, she said, "What?" and Diane said, "How?"

Claire's body remained so rigid that Jess moved to join her on the couch and touched her arm. "Claire? How are you feeling about this? Are you sure?"

The human touch seemed to start the tears, as Claire finally softened her posture and exhaled deeply. The words rushed out. "Confused is how I feel, and totally silly that it happened at all without trying for it. And now that it's happened, I don't know if I want to undo it." She stopped to catch a breath. "Those pregnancy tests are pretty good, and eight of them say I'm pregnant. Not one of them said negative." She stopped again to grab a tissue and blow her nose.

"You tried *eight* pregnancy tests?" Diane inquired softly, stifling a giggle that turned into a belly laugh as both Jess and Claire finally relaxed into the joke.

The tension broken, Diane continued the humor by adding, "I bet you went to eight different pharmacies and not one in your own neighborhood, right?"

"How did you know?" Claire said, looking up and smiling coyly.

"We know you, my friend." Diane got up to hug her too, and then she and Jess returned to their original seats to give Claire space to explain.

"At first I thought it was just the beginning of changes for me. I'm forty-three, and I know that's not very young. But then I started feeling nauseous in the mornings, and picky about food, which is really not me. Then I remembered a lovely fling I had with this visiting Belgian who was here on business . . ." Claire looked up to check her two friends' reaction.

Both Jess and Diane knew that Claire had a colorful dating history but never let a relationship get too serious. She had been in love once, but it had ended badly, so she didn't focus on that part of her life anymore.

"Go on. What will happen if a doctor, not just eight pregnancy tests, confirms this news?" Jess smiled encouragingly.

"Well, that's why I was so emotional yesterday with Tom. I never dreamed of a family. But now that the possibility is here, I'm thrilled and petrified at the same time. I have lists of pros and cons, and the cons are rational and the pros are emotional. And I never make decisions based on emotion." She stopped, tears threatening again, and searched her friends' faces.

There wouldn't be any happy grandparents to visit this child. Claire's mother had died years earlier. Claire felt certain that the lingering effects of having lost her only son, Peter, to suicide, were what had ruined her mother's health. Once that event had torn through the family, nothing had seemed to work anymore. Her father was now in a memory care unit out east and wasn't even aware that he had a daughter. She had needed to raise herself after her brother's death, and she had done it well. The strength of character needed to do so was a bond that Claire and Jess had identified early on in each other and that had become a source of their shared loyalty. There was a cost for each of them, of course: Claire's independence was a wall against the danger of intimacy, and Jess's pursuit of the illusion of perfection was her weapon of choice to protect her family.

While Jess struggled to intuit Claire's true desires, Diane seemed to have no such qualms. "This is a gift. Accept it. You are fully capable of raising a child with or without a father, although you may have some complications there." Diane looked off in the distance for a moment, then said, "Claire, are you going to let the father know? And what if he wants to play a role in raising the child?"

Claire looked down at her hands. "It's hard to admit that I don't know enough about him to know how he'll react, but yes, I don't think I could live with myself if I didn't let him know. Then I'll just have to let it play out."

"I think that's the right way to go, Claire. I'll help you any way I can." Diane reached out to squeeze her friend's hand and then stood up and danced a little jig. "We're going to have a baby! This is so exciting!"

Claire giggled with relief at Diane's antics but then calmly looked back to Jess and waited. "Jess?"

"You know me. I'm still on the pros and cons." She spoke slowly and clearly, awaiting Claire's response. "I have no doubt about your abilities, and you have, I'm sure, a good understanding of the unforgiving culture for single mothers in the workplace, even in the corner offices. But if anyone can fight through that hypocrisy with style, it's you." Jess smiled. "Motherhood is wonderful and challenging, and you never know how you're going to get through each stage." She paused and took a breath. "And then they grow up and go off to college!" She laughed, and Claire joined in.

"Seriously, it's a big responsibility to take on alone." Jess grew solemn again. "But you, my dear, will not be alone!"

With that, they all spent their remaining nerves on barely controlled giggles. Finally, all the tension left the porch and they were able to relax in the sweet reverie of their friendship.

Chapter 16

◇◇◇◇◇◇◇◇◇◇◇◇◇◇◇◇◇◇◇◇◇◇◇◇◇◇

Some days, Jess swore she could feel the house vibrate with the buzz of youthful energy: both kids busy with their summer jobs and their friends hanging out at their house at all hours; the sound of laughter everywhere—she wanted to bottle it.

Even Arthur seemed to relax a bit. He took a rare day off to play a round of golf. "It's only nine holes. I'll just go in after lunch, instead of at the crack of dawn."

"I love it." She smiled warmly and approached him to give him a hug. "You should do it more often. It's good for you." He still wasn't reciprocating her attempts to show affection, but she hoped if she kept at it, he would thaw.

"Remember, I'll be out late tonight and won't be around for dinner." He brushed her off and moved on to get his clubs from the garage.

"Yup, I remember. I'm running with Diane late this afternoon, and then the kids and I are meeting up with her here for takeout." Diane loved Jess's children and seemed as aware as Jess was that this summer was the last of its kind, that the inevitable empty nest was upon them. Tom and Beth loved Diane too, and were as enthusiastic as Jess was to spend as much time together as possible.

◇◇◇◇◇◇◇◇◇◇◇◇◇◇◇◇◇◇

Jess had just enough time to get home, change for running, and start a load of laundry before Diane arrived. "I'm here, and the door's open," she sang as she walked in.

"Hey, girlfriend. Nice to see you." Jess grabbed her for a hug. Then Diane handed her a small piece of paper, all folded up, and said, "I just found this on your floor."

"Oh, it must have fallen out of someone's pocket. Thanks." She took the paper from Diane and put it on the entry table. "One of the usual suspects will claim it if it's important. Ready to run?"

"Ready."

They headed out, and as they neared the parkway, Jess tried to pry open a door into Diane's new relationship: "So, tell me again how long it's been since you and George started going out."

"You know perfectly well how long it's been. You're beginning to sound like my mother, not my best friend," Diane laughed.

"OK, OK. I'll let you off the hook, as long as you tell me all the good stuff." Jess laughed. "I just like to get a glimpse of romance now and then. You're as bad as my kids; they don't want to tell me anything interesting."

They both laughed at that, but then Diane asked, "So, how are things going with Arthur? Less stressful now that you aren't working on the merger?"

"Fine, but our progress is slower than I thought it would be. I could just kick myself for putting my marriage at risk because of a professional move. I think he sees it as a real breach of trust, and I don't know how long it'll take to undo the damage."

"Don't be so hard on yourself," Diane said. "As I remember it, you didn't make this decision without him. He thought it was a good thing to involve someone like you, someone who understands the intersection between research and medical care, since he didn't think much of the others. Don't let him blame you for his discomfort. It goes with the territory of such a huge change. He's a grown-up; he should be able to figure this out. You can't protect him from the big, bad world any more than you can protect Tom or Beth. Mainly, I worry that you're not protecting *yourself* as much as you should."

Diane slowed her pace and put her arm out to slow her friend down to a walk. "Jessica, this is your marriage, not your parents'. You are not a guilty party here."

She held Jess's arm until Jess turned to her and nodded, tears close to the surface. Jess hugged Diane and took a few moments to regroup before they continued their run. She had heard this from Diane before and appreciated the concern. But Diane couldn't grasp how far Jess would go to keep her family intact. Diane had the core strength of the daughter of two parents who loved her and each other well. They taught her right from wrong and always made her feel secure. They challenged her to get out in the world and do her best but comforted her anytime she fell down. Diane's parents were not the drama in her life; they were the backdrop. She was whole. Jess understood that Diane took all that for granted.

But Jess didn't.

She was cleaning up her kitchen later that night, when she flashed back to her fifteen-year-old self, doing her homework at her parents' kitchen table. Her mother, dressed to go out, patted her shoulder as she walked by; her father, dark with rage, walked into the kitchen.

"Where the hell do you think you're going?" These were the first words he'd spoken in days.

"Out. What does it look like?" her mother taunted as she blotted her lipstick.

"Well, you're not."

"Who's stopping me?"

Jess could read the signs and was up with her books in her arms and out of the room before the first blow landed—removed from the fray, but not from the guilt that followed, nor from the constant search for self-perfection that she was convinced would keep her parents together.

Chapter 17

◇◇◇◇◇◇◇◇◇◇◇◇◇◇◇◇◇◇◇◇◇◇◇◇◇◇◇◇

The next morning, Jess noticed that the crumpled note was still on the hall table. Nobody had picked it up as a lost item. She unrolled it and saw that it was a golf scorecard for two people. Maybe it was Arthur's, but hadn't he gone golfing with Luke and David? This was a tally for just two: Arthur and Jennifer. Who the hell was Jennifer? Did they know a Jennifer? Did Arthur know a Jennifer? Her mind seized on the inexplicable tally and reminded her of his recent late night out. She quickly crumpled it up and threw it in the trash. *Whatever this is, I don't want to know*, she told herself.

She was folding the laundry later that day, when Arthur came looking for the shorts he had worn golfing the day before. "Oh, I washed those. They're in the dryer. But if you're looking for the golf tally, I threw it away. Who was it you were golfing with again?"

"It was just a pickup round. I went over and joined three guys who needed a fourth. Worked out pretty well." He grabbed his keys from the kitchen counter, and he and Tom left to pick up the lawn mower from the shop.

Jess got another load of laundry to fold and took the discarded note out of the trash. She looked at it again. *"Three guys who needed a fourth"? This scorecard has two names on it, and one of them is a woman's name. How does this make any sense?*

She mulled it over while she put the laundry away, went out to the garden and pulled weeds, and then watered the flowers. She was still mulling it over when the guys came home with the mower. Arthur dropped Tom off and went to the lab. Tom cut the grass. She made a light marinade for chicken, prepared vegetables for grilling, and went for a run, mulling all the while.

They had a family dinner on the deck. The weather was perfect. Her family was together. The kids were healthy and happy, playful with their dad. "So, Dad, how was your golf game yesterday? Are you getting back into the swing of it?"

"Tom, you know even if I haven't golfed for a year, I could still outplay you. Maybe we should go out this summer. You still have a couple of weeks left before you leave for school—what do you say?"

"Oh, you two." Beth sighed. "I can see it now: you'll keep golfing until you fall over if you can't determine a clear winner. By the way, Dad, who did you golf with yesterday, anyway?"

"Just some guys who needed a fourth," Arthur responded, suddenly turning his gaze to the backyard to point out a section that Tom had forgotten to trim.

"That is so strange," Jess said, looking straight at him. "The golf scorecard that fell from your shorts had only two names on it. Beth, could you go get the ice cream and berries and some bowls, please?"

Arthur continued to focus on the lawn, but the wave of surprise that came over him was unmistakable. After pointing out his son's deficiency, he finally turned to the magnetic force of her eyes, only to quickly look away again and say, "So, Tom, what do you say? A golf game in the near future?"

Jess might have imagined it, but Arthur sounded a little less sure of himself than he had a moment earlier.

"Kids, could you clean up? Your father and I are going to take a walk," Jess said. Arthur opened his mouth to voice a contrary opinion but, after looking at his wife once more, decided to fall in line.

"Mom, remember you said I could take your car over to Kim's? I'm leaving right after we finish cleaning up. I won't be out late. I have to work an early shift tomorrow. Love you guys. Have a good night." Beth embraced each of her parents as they left the house. Jess held on to the warmth for as long as she could.

It was a quiet walk. Jess was determined that Arthur feel her silence and not just respond to any conversation she made.

He finally started chattering about how good dinner was, and how the marinade for the chicken was new, wasn't it, and had she used fresh mint, and weren't they lucky that the farmers' market was so handy, and wasn't it nice that their children were so helpful, and had she noticed that the neighbors had put up a new fence, and did she have any idea why? Anything besides the issue at hand.

When she was sure that he was going to talk to her about world hunger, rather than the home front, she made a direct inquiry in a soft, low voice. "Arthur, tell me about golfing yesterday, please. Who is Jennifer?"

"She's a cardiologist from St. Claire's. We've been working on a project together and just took a little break."

"So why did you say you were golfing with three guys who needed a fourth?"

"Because I didn't want to have this conversation right now." He looked away.

"What conversation is 'this'?" Jess asked in a near whisper. She wasn't sure she had the energy to speak out loud. She felt like she was floating and would soon fall to earth and shatter. Her pace slowed. Three steps later, Arthur noticed and paused.

"The conversation we need to have," he said. "You know I'm not happy. I haven't been happy for a long time. I don't think you're happy, either. We haven't been happy together for a long time. We need to face the facts. Our marriage is over." He spoke so evenly and clearly that he could have been in a business meeting with his accountant, rather than with his wife, who was reeling from this revelation.

"Are you having an affair with Jennifer?" Jess struggled to get the question out and wondered if it was even audible.

"Not currently, no. But we were involved."

Jess gasped and stifled a sob, then turned around to walk the other way, without breaking stride. After a moment, she sensed that Arthur had stopped. She glanced back and saw him head toward home.

When her tears finally stopped, she looked up and realized it was dark and she was not in her neighborhood. It took her a minute to orient herself. She realized she had walked several miles and should start home before the kids worried. As she looked up at the full moon, wiping her eyes, her mind finally seemed to click on the fact that Arthur had just admitted to an affair. And he had done so in a manner that was so matter-of-fact that he obviously hadn't even thought about how devastating that news might be to her. In fact, he'd been so cavalier about it, she could only assume it was because he was no longer involved with the woman and must not think of it as a big deal.

But also, he had admitted it on the heels of declaring that their marriage was over.

She started to tremble, so much so that she had to focus to put one foot in front of the other. All this time, she had assumed that his despondency was due to the merger and that she was responsible for it. Had she been so blind as to read this inaccurately? Had he left her in the marriage alone while he started his own new path? How stupid could she be?

She beat herself up the whole time she walked home, then sat out on the deck in the dark and was still there when Beth returned. "Mom, what are you doing out here? Are you OK?"

"Just looking at the moon. Isn't it beautiful?" An idea popped into her head. "Do you want to go to the lake this week?"

"I'd love that, Mom."

"When could you go?"

"I have three days open this week. Can I invite Kim?"

"Yes, do." She would need some space as she thought through what her next steps should be. The kids would be going to school in a couple of weeks. She needed to hold herself together until then.

Arthur was sleeping soundly when she finally went to bed in the wee hours of the morning. Fortunately, their king-size bed allowed her a huge, neutral space. She was exhausted and not willing to leave her bedroom. She put a long, decorative pillow sham between them and curled up on her side of the bed. She refused to let him cheat her out of her sleep, when he had cheated her out of so much already.

∞∞∞∞∞∞∞∞∞∞

Home after three nights at the lake, Jess chose to confront Arthur when Beth and Tom were at a birthday party for one of Tom's friends. She was now ready to have the conversation that she realized she had enabled Arthur to avoid for months.

The grill cover was waving in the wind beyond the screened-in porch, where Jess and Arthur were sitting across from each other, bodies squared off and confrontational. The wind and rain were beginning to start some serious action, but neither of them moved to cover.

"I'm very fond of you. But no, I don't love you anymore." He had finally responded to the question she had vowed not to ask.

The answer provoked her anger. "You're *fond* of me?" She startled herself with her yelling. She didn't recognize her own voice. "One is *fond* of a pet. It's not a word used to describe a wife. Are you telling me you have no feelings for me at all? You're tired of me? You're no longer interested in me as a woman? What are you saying?"

"What I'm saying, Jess, and what I've been trying to tell you for the last hour, is that I no longer want to be married to you. I admitted that I've been unfaithful to you." His voice was as controlled as hers was wild.

"How many affairs have there been? Beyond this golfing person, how long has this been going on?"

"You really don't want to know. What I can tell you is that I am who I am, and I'm sorry for hurting you. And if we stay married, I'll just go on hurting you."

The tornado siren went off. Jess jumped. But they remained on the porch, until the phone rang and Arthur walked into the house to pick it up. She could hear enough to know it was Tom or Beth calling in from the party they were at. Arthur told them to stay there until the storm let up.

Jess tried to use the interruption to calm herself and connect with all the good they shared. When Arthur returned, she desperately sought to make eye contact to soften the tone of the conversation.

"Arthur, I'm trying to save our marriage. I hope you can see your way clear to thinking about how to do that yourself. I'm trying to ignore the fact that you're acting as if you have no desire to do anything to move us to a better place. You seem proud of the fact that you've been unfaithful and will continue to be." As Jess heard her own words, she registered the facts more emotionally and started sobbing loudly.

She stood up and, through ragged sobs and the whipping wind and rain, shouted to be heard. "Do you remember how carefully I asked you about whether you'd marry me for forever? Do you have any idea what your selfishness will do to our children? Have you no ability to put anyone else first? It's like you've resolved to be a bastard, and the rest of us be damned!"

"Jess, I'm very sorry to cause you pain. And of course I've thought about the kids. But I know how strong you are and they are. Everyone will be fine. And I have to take care of myself. Once you've calmed down, we can have another conversation, but right now we should both go in and get dry." He stood and left her wet and cold on the porch.

She hated herself for her emotional outburst and, for the first time, faced the reality that it took more than one person to save a marriage. She wasn't sure how much more effort she could or should make, even for her kids. She herself had never gotten to "fine" after her parents' divorce.

She carefully pulled the golf scorecard from her jeans pocket and checked to see whether it was still dry. Then she grabbed a slicker and drove to Diane's, where Diane and Claire were waiting for her.

The streets were slippery with rain, and when she slammed into a pool of water at a nearby intersection, she checked her speed and pulled over so she could calm down, dry her eyes, and take stock. Now she knew: Arthur had no interest in saving the marriage; he was just biding his time.

She turned onto Diane's street to find no lights on anywhere and a power line down just beyond Diane's house. She saw flickering lights in the living room, and as she approached the front door, Diane opened it, with Claire on her heels.

"Jess, come in out of this crazy weather. We weren't sure you could even make it in the storm, but then we saw your headlights. Claire, can you grab a towel?"

Only then did Jess consider that she must look a mess—wet and bedraggled. Moments later, her tears started. They took her slicker, toweled her off, and led her into a candlelit corner of the living room.

When Diane put an afghan around her shoulders and Claire brought her a cup of tea, Jess stopped crying long enough to blurt out, "You two are unbelievable. I've been so preoccupied with my own issues over the past several months, I've been a terrible friend to both of you, and here you are—here for me on this god-awful night, no questions asked. I don't deserve you, but boy, do I need you."

"Hey, it's OK. It's a good night for a slumber party, and we're here, so whenever you want to talk, we'll listen. And remember, you two were there for me not too long ago. That's what friends do." As Claire curled up on the couch opposite Jess, Jess noticed that her baby bump had become visible.

Jess took a deep breath and started. "I'm a fool. It's not the merger, it's me. Arthur doesn't love me anymore . . ."

Diane handed Jess a box of Kleenex and waited.

"And he's been cheating on me."

"What?" Claire leaned forward. "How do you know that?"

"He admitted it. Finally." Jess pulled the crumpled note from her jeans pocket and handed it to Diane. "Do you remember when you found this at my house?"

Diane opened the golf card and read the names: "Arthur and Jennifer. What does that mean?"

"It means that Arthur lied about who he golfed with, and when I confronted him, he admitted that he and this woman had been involved."

"He admitted that they had been *involved*, as in past tense?" Claire asked.

"Yes, but after I processed that for a while, I confronted him about other affairs." Jess wiped her eyes. "He spared me the details but implied that it's a long list—and that he wants out of our marriage."

"That bastard." Claire stood up, and both she and Diane went to sit on either side of Jess. "How long have you been aware of this?"

Jess sensed where Claire's head was going. "For a few days, but I just had it out with him tonight."

"It would have helped to know this when you were dealing with Dick." Claire's voice was bitter.

"Maybe, but maybe not. I'm not sure I wouldn't still have wanted to try to save my marriage. You know how I feel about keeping my family solid. I realize I'm a masochist, but I didn't want to quit on a marriage if I could help it."

"He certainly is a man of secrets. I'm so sorry he's treated you this way, Jess—you deserve so much better," Diane said. "So what now?"

"Now, I try to power through the next few weeks. I can tolerate almost anything to keep a sense of normalcy going until the kids go back to school."

"Oh, Jess, can you really stay in the house with Arthur after this?" Claire asked.

Jess shared a knowing look with Diane, who responded, "Jess has resilience that has seen her through difficult times before. If she believes this is best for her family, our job is to support her through it. Now, let me call your house, Jess, to let your family know you're sleeping over because of the power-line problem."

Chapter 18

◇◇◇◇◇◇◇◇◇◇◇◇◇◇◇◇◇◇◇◇◇◇

The last weeks of summer were a blur of activity. Beth left for Stanford early to start her campus job as a dorm assistant. Tom socialized with his friends right up to the end. Jess hosted a goodbye party for all of them and their parents to celebrate, and to hang on a little longer. Yet all of these emotional activities went on with little emotion from Jess. She knew she couldn't let herself go even a little, because if she did, she would break. She allowed herself to cry with Diane and Claire some nights, as they handed her tissues, but not at Tom's party.

"Jess, the garden looks lovely. Isn't this just the best time of year in St. Louis?" Martha, Zack's mom, pulled her aside to a private corner. She spoke low and fast. "I'm having a hard time with this. Are you? I feel silly, but this empty-nest thing has me so emotional. It's like I've been looking forward to having some 'me' time for years, and now it scares me to think of him gone. I'm worried I'm gonna go crazy." She laughed almost hysterically, holding Jess's arm tightly.

Jess pulled from a reserve she thought was nearly gone, laughed softly, and led her friend to the drinks table. "Martha, Martha, just think about not having to drive carpool or attend every baseball game or stay up worrying until your kids get home. And about being able to have a glass of wine before dinner because dinner doesn't have to be sandwiched between activities . . . Here, have some now." She handed Martha a glass and gave her an encouraging squeeze. "Just another transition. It will be fine," she soothed, trying to convince herself, or at least get through the evening.

And, of course, she did get through it. All of it. She counted the days until Tom was safely out of the house. By sheer force of will, she would not show any hint of trouble before both her kids were on their way. She told herself all would be well when they next came home. Just different.

Arthur attempted to engage her in a conversation about the future several times, but she wouldn't oblige. Finally, he cornered her in the laundry room. "Jess, we need to talk, now. Do you really want to hear news about me from a third party?"

Jess looked through him. "Well, if it were the truth, I guess it would be better than what you might tell me. Why are you so eager to share now, when I practically begged you to let me in not that long ago?"

"Jess, this is very painful for me."

Struggling to keep her cool, she pushed the basket of dirty clothes into his arms. "Why is this so painful for you, Arthur? Are you the injured party here? Are you the victim of betrayal? I can't feel your pain, because right now I'm trying to stay numb, just to function."

"I need to hear from you that you and the kids will be OK," he whispered.

"Well, I'm sorry, Arthur, but I don't know if we will. I can't comfort you. I'll talk with you more about this after I get Tom to school, but not before." She turned slowly and left him in the laundry room, holding the basket of dirty clothes.

◇◇◇◇◇◇◇◇◇◇◇◇◇◇◇◇

Travel day arrived. Jess and Tom flew to Boston to take in a Red
Sox game at Fenway, before driving to Brown in Providence to
settle him in the next day. Jess salvaged the remnants of a plan
that Arthur had mentioned to Tom earlier and then abandoned,
but not before buying three tickets to the game. Arthur went to
London for a meeting, possibly to avoid this last family outing.

"Mom, this is too cool. I've always wanted to see a game
at Fenway. I can't believe Dad is missing this." Tom pointed out
the long line of people waiting to buy tickets.

"Well, since he is, do you want to try your hand at scalping
his ticket?" Jess pulled out the extra ticket and scoured the area
to see where the stadium property started. She spotted some
likely ticket scalpers at the corner across the street and scanned
the crowd, looking for any police officers who might have opinions about her idea.

"Really?" Tom looked at his mom. She grinned at him and
cocked her head at the two guys they were now both watching
across the street. The men were standing about ten feet apart,
posted opposite incoming fan traffic and forcing groups to separate to get by them. Each in turn talked to a fan now and then.
Sure enough, Jess saw a pair of tickets change hands as one
of them palmed money. As the transaction was finalized, Tom
turned to his mother, a smile playing on his face. "You're really
gonna let me do this?"

"Go for it, before I change my mind." She handed him
the extra ticket.

Tom bolted across the street when he found a pause in
traffic, then assumed the pose of a casual, blending-into-the-
crowd local. He kept his distance from the two vendors already
in position but checked them out. They were clearly aware of
him. Jess could see him try out his moves with a couple of potential customers, keeping his head low and showing the ticket when
he had a true prospect. Fifteen minutes crawled by, and then the
transaction took place lightning fast. One of the veteran scalpers sent a singleton over to Tom. Jess didn't see any evidence of

communication between them, but, in an instant, Tom handed over the ticket and pocketed some money. He casually looked over at his mother. He walked back across the street with a bit of swagger and rejoined her, a more worldly boy.

"Hey, you did it! Good job!" She chuckled.

"Mom, that scalper sent me that sale. Did you see that? Not many people needed just one ticket. That's why he helped me out."

"That, and to get you off his patch, no doubt." Jess tousled her son's tawny hair. "Let's go use your earnings for a Red Sox cap."

Hat purchased, they headed into the stadium. It was August-in-Boston hot, and they melted while they ate hot dogs and drank beer. The Green Monster helped the Sox win, but when Arthur called later to hear how it had gone, the scalping episode was what won the day. As she heard Tom recount the experience to his father, she heard him say, "Yes, she surprised me too, Dad."

Jess had surprised everyone, including herself. She wondered what was next.

They drove out of Boston the next morning. Tom wore his Red Sox cap and listened to music with his headphones. Jess tried to avoid thinking too hard about anything, knowing time was running out on this trip. Her focus narrowed as she hit bad traffic on the entry ramp to the expressway. An emergency vehicle blocking an additional lane created a blind spot, making it hard for drivers to merge responsibly. The inevitable dance played out. Some drivers were polite and reluctant to pull out, others brazen and pushy as they all jerked ahead and braked hard until they passed the narrow spot. Jess's heart was in her throat by the time they made it. She missed the common-sense zipper merge from home. She missed home itself—until she realized "home" was about to undergo a radical change. She would be returning to an empty house. She looked over at Tom, who seemed oblivious to her white knuckles clenching the wheel. She exhaled slowly and loosened her grip, thankful that much of her world went unnoticed by her children.

Tom perked up when they arrived on campus and saw all the hubbub of parents and kids in clusters near the dorms. She lost him quickly to the activity of moving his luggage in and registering with his resident advisor. Fortunately, his stuff had arrived via UPS and been hauled to his room. They found his roommate and family already there.

"You must be Jake." Tom extended his hand to a slightly built young man with a tattoo on his forearm and an earring in one ear. "Nice to finally meet you in person." The boys had been in touch for a few weeks and already knew they were both tennis players and had similar taste in music.

Jess visited with Jake and his parents for a few minutes and then, as she and Tom had agreed earlier, was to make her exit. "No drama, OK, Mom?" had been Tom's precise words as they'd discussed the trip. He walked her back to the car, and they both kept it together, though Tom showed more affection than Jess expected. He watched her drive away and blew her kisses until she had turned out of the parking area.

◇◇◇◇◇◇◇◇◇◇◇◇◇◇◇◇

She settled into her hotel room and took a late-day run around the campus neighborhood, making sure she didn't go too close to Tom's dorm. It was one thing to have a loving mother, but she didn't want to embarrass him by clinging. The air was crisp, and the exercise helped her shed the unspent emotion from the hectic run-up of delivering Tom to his next phase. And, of course, now that he was settled, she realized she had to prepare emotionally for her next discussion with Arthur, which she could no longer postpone.

Brown University, located in the College Hill Historic District, was a beautiful campus surrounded by colonial architecture. Narrow streets gave way to lovely green boulevards as she ran toward the school. The grounds were flawless. Closely cropped grass impeccably edged the brick-and-cement walkways that seemed to crisscross the campus endlessly. *Not a bad place to spend the next four years*, she thought.

She ran past many family groupings in the midst of final goodbyes, hugs, and tears. She noticed how young and beautiful the children were, and how proud the parents. Many lingered to watch their children walk into a dorm before they headed off, some holding hands en route back to their cars. Farewells and fresh starts were in the air.

The academic year was always a new beginning for Jess, and she decided to own that theme. She knew it was better to embrace the future than to hide from it.

The crisp air and color of the light as dusk approached energized her, and she realized she was hungry. Rather than having a room-service dinner, she decided to go to the hotel dining room and eat a decent meal. She arrived with a book and was prepared to read if she needed to avoid the awkwardness of eating alone in a small dining room.

As it was, she was seated in a corner and had a good observation point from which to people watch. She wanted to get lost in the moment and not face the future before she had to. She was happy to sit and enjoy her wine and her meal, without worry.

It was early, just seven o'clock, so only a few tables were occupied. She noted most were tables for two, but there was one with two couples together and a party of six. She guessed it was a mom and dad with adult children and spouses celebrating an anniversary dinner. They were all dressed up, and the celebrated couple, in their seventies, were wearing a boutonniere and a corsage. The sweet looks they exchanged throughout their meal were adorable.

One pair near Jess seemed to be romantically involved, lost in their own world—lots of giggling, close conversation, and intimate looks. She saw no rings. She wondered if they were staying at the hotel. How long had they been together? Was it an assignation of people married to others, or a business-trip opportunity for them to be together, or were they single and just newly dating?

Another couple close by her bore the signs of the long married. They didn't talk to each other at all and had only limited conversations with the waitperson. They nursed their drinks for a long while before ordering food, and still no talking. How could this be? No smiling, no shared glances. It didn't bode well for their future, she thought.

Jess tried to keep her mind in forward mode but couldn't stop the invading thoughts about how often Arthur was away and how easy it was for him to stray. She had never worried about it—how stupid of her. How naive to think he was in love with her and that was enough. And even when he had still been in love with her, had that kept him faithful?

She tried to recall their last romantic dinner but couldn't. She thought about the long-married couple who didn't speak and looked miserable. Was that how she and Arthur would appear if they were here together?

She lingered with her coffee and a complimentary chocolate. The romantic couple made their exit in character. Sweet conversation wafted over to Jess. "Should we have room-service dessert and champagne sent up?" the man asked his lover as he motioned to the server.

The woman giggled softly. "Oh, what an idea! Yes, let's do."

When they left, Jess looked up and was startled by images reflected back at her in a wall mirror that the couple's bodies had previously concealed. Light danced around her own image from the table candles and wall sconces; she quickly looked down. She wondered if she was ready to focus on herself now.

She considered picking up her book, when one of the anniversary celebrants approached her to take a picture. "It's our parents' fifty-fifth wedding anniversary. Would you . . ."

"Of course. I'd be happy to." Jess made her way to the table and gamely suggested poses for a group shot. She took a few pictures.

The jovial husband scanned her face and ring finger. "How is a nice lady like you having dinner alone in this romantic hotel? Where's your husband?"

Jess's eyes followed his, and she promised herself to retire the ring when she got home. "Oh, well, he travels a lot. I'm here dropping our son at school." Jess smiled broadly and turned down an offer to join them for cake.

She returned to her table and started to collect her things. But the party group sent over a piece of anniversary cake, and the server freshened her coffee. They looked over at her as she raised her cup in a toast to the couple. The cake was delicious, and the irony made her smile. She slowly lifted her head, and this time, she actively sought her likeness in the glass. The flattering light helped obscure the dark circles under her eyes and any new frown lines she was sure she had developed. Slowly she focused, shakily at first, but then gave herself a full-blown smile as she toasted her image with decaffeinated coffee. Her auburn hair tucked behind her ears, she saw that she was overdue for a trim, but that was a minor adjustment. She felt ready to make some major adjustments as well.

She left the dining room with her book but found she didn't need to read to put herself to sleep. It was staying asleep that eluded her. Tomorrow she would start to clear the fog and begin the search for her future.

Chapter 19

◇◇◇◇◇◇◇◇◇◇◇◇◇◇◇◇◇◇◇◇◇◇◇

Jess returned home to an empty house but a glorious sunset. The view of Francis Park's trees showed red and orange as she walked into the living room and peered west out the picture window. She opened the side windows to freshen the air and take in the soft rustle of leaves through branches. It was dead silent in her house, and starting to get cold, almost time to turn the furnace on for the fall. She had begged off having company tonight. Both Claire and Diane had called her while she was in transit, but she needed some time alone.

And she needed some sleep. Most mornings, she awakened at three a.m. with an overall ache. Her physical self then alerted her emotional self to the hurt and fear that kicked in as she remembered her new reality. She wondered how long it would take to get through this wave of grief. She walked through the house, looking at all the lonely rooms, hearing squeaks and groans that seemed to bemoan emptiness.

She knew the grief would follow its own path, but she rallied to rid herself of the anxiety around putting Arthur off. She e-mailed him a time, in three days, when she would be available for their conversation. Finally, she lay down in Tom's bed for a nap that turned into her first full night's sleep in months.

In the morning, her mind started working on her behalf. A survival instinct, she supposed. Her immediate safety came to mind. She needed to be tested. She steeled herself not to hold back when she called for the appointment. "I need to see Dr. Scott in the next day or two."

She booked an appointment at the end of the day and attempted to hold her impatience in check until she got to the clinic.

The exam room had recently been redone in soothing green and blue coastal colors, with artwork and utilitarian chair cushions to match. Somehow, though, the colors didn't calm her. Rather, they seemed to be the perfect foil to her red-hot rage after she'd been humiliated into this situation. Her body was rigid, her breathing uneven, as she sat barefoot and naked under the wrap gown.

The exam table paper and vinyl cushion at the margins was cold, and she attempted to adjust her hot body to make direct contact with the chill. Just as she realized the gown was on backward, Dr. Valerie Scott hurried into the room, carrying Jess's chart. She made quite an entrance in her clicking four-inch heels, dangling earrings, and elegant silver bracelets peeking out the sleeve of her crisp white coat. Without looking up, she said, "Hello, Jess. I'm surprised to see you. What's up?"

Jess and Valerie had become acquainted while serving together on a hospital committee that addressed merger issues affecting the training programs at the university hospital. Jess had switched to Valerie a year before, when her previous primary-care physician had retired and moved to Florida.

"I got confused with my gown, like I haven't given birth or been in a gown countless times before . . ." Jess felt her face flush.

Valerie stood stock still, then quickly offered, "Oh, it happens all the time. Somebody should design a better gown. Let me help you." She placed a cool hand on Jess's shoulder while steadying her. "OK, now that we've gotten that done, let's relax a bit, and then you can tell me what's wrong."

Jess almost lost it. To have moved so quickly from an in-control professional woman to an emotional basket case who was not capable of getting herself into a patient gown was almost too much. Valerie's kind touch put her over the edge. She chose to avoid a total meltdown by blurting, "My husband has been cheating on me, and I need whatever STD tests you recommend."

Valerie stifled a gasp. "Dr. Steele?"

"Yes." Valerie's surprise gave Jess time to try to stop her body from shaking.

"I see." The doctor took both of Jess's hands. "I'm so sorry." She paused and took a couple of slow breaths before going on, as if to calm them both. "Can you tell me if this has been going on for a while, with one partner, or more?" Valerie asked in a soft voice.

"For a long time, and probably with various partners." Jess's voice was still emotional but stronger. The worst was over. For the first time, she had overcome her natural loyalty to her husband and given him up as the cad he was—and to a colleague of his.

"OK, then we'll need to take some blood and a vaginal swab to run some tests." Valerie started to describe the tests and the overall incidence statistics, but Jess interrupted.

"And I want you to send the tests out to a commercial lab." She forced the words out, knowing how they would be received.

"Oh, I don't think that's necessary," Valerie said in her doctor voice. Jess had chosen Valerie because she was smart, direct, younger than Jess by a decade, and a bright light in the U's academic leadership circles, which was rare for a woman. She was no pushover.

"OK, then I'll go elsewhere," Jess challenged, waiting for the expected confrontation.

But Valerie paused and said merely, "All right. I understand you're upset. I'll see what I can do."

Not yet satisfied, Jess pushed. "I'm asking you to take personal responsibility for this. Please?" She stared straight into Valerie's eyes until she received the consent she needed.

Valerie drew blood and took a vaginal swab while continuing to talk Jess through the incidence of any particular sexually transmitted disease. When she was finished, Jess scooted back into a seated position on the exam table.

"You were smart to take care of this. I'm glad you came in. Now that you're here, let me ask you, how are you sleeping?"

"Not very well, of course. But I'm getting by." Jess, now chilly, pulled the privacy blanket around her.

"Would you like something to help you get some rest?"

"No, I'll be fine."

"Do you think you need—"

"Please stop. I'm not going to harm myself or anybody else. I'll be OK. What I'm feeling is what I need to feel to move forward. But thank you for your concern." Jess sat up straighter and smiled at Dr. Scott, not her friend Valerie. "And thank you for sending these to an outside lab. I know it sounds crazy—it probably *is* crazy—but I have so little control right now."

"It's fine. I'll send them out and call you personally as soon as I get the results back. No lab personnel, no residents, no students. Just me." Valerie squeezed her hand.

Jess felt weightless as she walked to her car in the fading light. She tried not to think about the three days she would have to wait for the results. She opened the car window and felt the fresh air blowing on her face as she congratulated herself for trusting in Valerie.

Enough for this day, she thought as she drove to meet Diane and Claire at La Puesta del Sol, the tapas place in Diane's neighborhood.

Chapter 20

◇◇◇◇◇◇◇◇◇◇◇◇◇◇◇◇◇◇◇◇◇◇◇◇

That night, she awoke with an incredible thought. Pictures of her. Pictures of her taken by Arthur over the years. Pictures of her that he had convinced her he needed when he traveled without her. Pictures that should not be seen by anyone, ever. The memory of these pictures made her almost physically ill with regret and shame. What a fool she was. How could she have been so stupid?

She went through desk drawers and boxes, hiding places in the closet. Anywhere she thought he might have kept them. She looked through what remained of his travel gear, the pockets of his old jackets, then realized she would have been furious if they could be found so easily. Where were they?

"Damn, I'll have to ask him for them." She hated adding this to the conversation she already dreaded, but it couldn't be helped. By the time he called her from Portugal the next day, the delayed discussion was anticlimactic. Neither of them went through the charade of pretending there was a marriage left to save.

"It's an endowed chair with support for my lab and free rein to follow my research where it takes me." Arthur didn't try hard enough to keep the enthusiasm out of his voice. "The formal announcement will be coordinated between Midwest and the Portland people, but I wanted you to know before any of that happens." He went on to describe his new team and his hopes for his research in a more responsive academic environment.

Jess listened but couldn't emote. She recognized this as another in a long history of conversations centered on Arthur and his exploits, and on his expecting her to be supportive. Rather, she realized the end of her marriage had come and gone and she was well rid of him. It was the family unit she grieved.

"Jess, I've wanted to tell you all of this for a while now."

"Arthur, it feels like you want me to be happy for you. That's not where I am. But, out of respect for me and our twenty-two-year marriage, at least be honest with me. Tell me, are you leaving me or going to a new opportunity?" What she left unsaid was "or another woman?" She knew she couldn't handle that right now.

For once, Arthur was speechless.

She waited a full minute. "OK, so ponder that, then. It's a rhetorical question, really, for your contemplation, and will not hold us up from taking the necessary steps to end our marriage . . ." Her voice broke then, and she took a moment to collect herself, knowing she still needed to talk to him about the pictures.

Then she said, "The pictures of me that you took . . ."

The pause on the telephone line told her that he knew what she was referring to.

"They're in the safe deposit box."

"They're where?" She was so surprised that it took her a few moments to take it in.

"I wanted to avoid someone happening upon them."

Did that make sense? Was he being thoughtless or thoughtful?

Arthur quickly added, "I'll go to the bank when I'm back in town next week and get them."

"No," she said emphatically. "I'll go to the bank." Beyond her sense of humiliation, she realized that she didn't want him to see the pictures again, or have any further control over her body, or images thereof. Then it also dawned on her that she should go through the contents of the safety deposit box anyway. She wondered whether any further surprises awaited her there.

He challenged her a bit but backed down when he realized she would not allow him to win this battle. There was some confusion about where the key was, and she wondered why she didn't even know that. But he did tell her where to find it, in his desk, without any more discussion.

She found the key easily, but then, in her frenzied grab to do something, anything, to take control of her situation, she dropped it deep between the desk and the wall and had to crawl behind the desk to retrieve it. She had never been to the bank to deal with the safe deposit box. Not one of her jobs. Arthur's job. Why would she not have trusted him with that?

For a moment, she reflected on whether she had misplaced trust in him throughout their marriage. When had it eroded so badly? Had she missed some kind of signal? Still on the floor, she grabbed her phone to read an arriving text: "Lab tests clear, Jess. Let me know if you need anything else, my friend."

"Thank God for that." She quickly wrote a thank-you text back to Valerie, then checked the time. It was still early enough to get to the bank.

◇◇◇◇◇◇◇◇◇◇◇◇◇◇◇◇◇

Jess approached the clerk and said, "I'd like access to my safe deposit box, please." The twentysomething young man looked at her and said, "ID, please."

She dug in her purse, pulled out her driver's license, and handed it to him.

He scrutinized it and asked, "Are you Jess Steele?"

"No, Jess Lawson; my husband is Arthur Steele. I didn't change my name." She tried to peer across to see what he was looking at. She saw a card with typesetting and handwriting on it, but she couldn't make out the words.

"Just one minute. I'll need to consult with my manager. Your name isn't on the card."

"Wait. If you have Arthur Steele's name, you can look up our account, which has both of our names and should match this address." She pointed at her ID.

"I'll be just a moment." He disappeared.

An older woman came out from the back office and made quick eye contact with Jess. "I'm sorry about this, but I'm going to have to call Mr. Steele and make sure this is authorized by the safe deposit box owner. The number we have on file is this one." She showed Jess a slip of paper. "Is this where we can reach him?"

Jess felt herself filling up with raging mortification but managed to find her angry but controlled voice. "Unbelievable! We've had a mortgage and personal and professional accounts here for over twenty years. I can't believe this is an issue."

"Again, I'm sorry about this. But it's a safety precaution for our customers."

"Of which I am one—soon to be a very angry one."

"I'll make the call now and get this sorted out for you, Ms. Lawson, as quickly as I possibly can."

"Wait. You'll have to call his cell phone, not his office. He's out of the country," Jess managed to tell the manager before she disappeared into the back room again. She noted that it would be evening in Lisbon—too bad . . .

Jess's suppressed fury had overcome her fear, and now she absolutely would not leave the bank without seeing the contents of that box.

Five minutes later, the woman reappeared and apologized again. "Your husband confirmed that you should have access to the safe deposit box. And to avoid this in the future, I'd like to get your name and signature on this authorization card. Then you'll have full access to all of your accounts together, as well as the box." She handed Jess the card.

Relief kicked in. "Thank you. Of course." She signed the card and was escorted into the vault.

After signing in again in the vault, she asked to have a few minutes to go through the contents of the box. Was the clerk eyeing her with more curiosity than warranted a typical customer in this situation?

Tears of anger and humiliation threatened as she closed the door and sat in the cubicle. She took a few deep breaths and tried to get herself ready. *How could it all have come to this?* she wondered. She opened the box and began to sort through the contents. Stock certificates, Social Security cards, passports, deeds to the houses, and then, underneath everything else, an envelope. With pictures.

Waves of shame came over her as she looked through the photos. At least they were all there—as far as she could remember. Her heartbeat returned to a tamer rhythm, and her breathing evened out. She looked again at the images, more closely this time. She felt herself blush when she saw the one of her decked out in the corset and black lace. And even as she attempted to squint for a clearer look through her tearful eyes, she realized she didn't look half bad. Then, surprisingly, she started to laugh. Great guffaws came from her as she allowed her emotions to find release, followed by sheer joy when she realized that she had looked pretty good in all of the pictures. Oh, how ridiculous life could be at times.

It was then that she knew she would survive. The "how" part was what puzzled her.

Chapter 21

◇◇◇◇◇◇◇◇◇◇◇◇◇◇◇◇◇◇◇◇◇◇◇

Arthur and Jess moved forward on divorce arrangements, now all by telephone. Once he was in Portland and the kids were safely ensconced at their colleges, Jess started to breathe on her own and take care of the legal details. She retained an attorney, had their properties appraised and their finances reviewed, and made checklists of everything. No problem.

"How do you think we should tell the kids?" Arthur softened his voice to ask at the end of one of their calls.

This was a problem. For several moments, Jess said nothing. She knew they couldn't keep the charade going much longer, but she hated the thought of bursting the children's bubble.

"Jessica, I know this is hard to think about and will be even harder to do, but you know it needs to be done. They'll be——"

She broke in. She couldn't let him tell her they'd be fine. "Let's get them home for a weekend. We should both be here." She knew firsthand how much of an emotional whack this news would be, and how it would temper every move they made for the rest of their lives. There was no good way to do this.

When they ended the call, Jess was caught in her own memories. She knew how the conversation should *not* be done. Finding out from the school counselor that you were excused from classes the next day to testify at your parents' divorce hearing was not an option. Even though Jess had already begun living at Diane's and hadn't been returning calls from her parents by then, the public humiliation had still stung her.

"Your mother couldn't reach you at Diane's." At least Mrs. Busch, the school counselor, was a friend. Her help with securing Jess a college scholarship was a lifeline that Jess couldn't have found alone at that point.

But even Mrs. Busch couldn't cushion the blow when Jess learned that each parent expected her to sling dirt at the other.

◇◇◇◇◇◇◇◇◇◇◇◇◇◇◇◇◇◇

Arthur flew in from Portland, Beth from Palo Alto, and Tom from Boston. As Jess drove to the airport to pick them all up, she prepared for the performance ahead. They had used a false pretense to get the kids home, advertising the trip as an opportunity to enjoy a beautiful October weekend together, not to rattle their world. What a joke.

Beth and Tom were glowing, abuzz with chatter and light teasing. Arthur joined them at baggage claim. He gave each of the kids a hearty hug but approached Jess carefully, leaning in to kiss her on the cheek. *Sure*, she thought, *now that the kids are watching, you'll touch me to make it count.* She accepted the peck but turned away quickly. They got their luggage and followed Jess to the car.

"Hey, what's up with this, Dad? You're letting Mom drive?" Tom challenged as Jess headed to the driver's side. "Something's changed!"

Jess cringed but kept moving.

"Your mom's a fine driver." Arthur clipped his answer and saved himself. "So, Tom, are you still liking your roommate?"

They arrived home just after dusk. The red maple and gold birch leaves in the front yard swirled around the tree trunks, as if seeking a safe haven.

Dinner was festive enough. Jess thought how easy it was for parents to be subdued when kids were the focus. The plan was to tell them after the main course and before dessert.

Tom gave her a grateful squeeze as they walked to the living room. "Mom, I've smelled that apple cake since I walked in. Did you make it with your apple cider glaze on top? I can hardly wait. Nothing like that in the dorm. Right, Beth?"

The four of them sat in a small grouping, the kids in the love seat and Jess and Arthur in chairs facing them. Tom had brought a new CD and put it on. Tom and Beth sat close together, looking at the CD cover and enjoying each other's company. There was no hint of what was to come. Arthur fidgeted and left the room a couple of times, getting tea, fussing with the dishes.

While Arthur had agreed that both parents should talk, it appeared that Jess would need to take the lead. She swallowed hard. "I'm afraid we brought you home because we have something upsetting to tell you." She looked at each child in turn.

"Your mother and I are getting a divorce," Arthur blurted out. "We've been talking about it for a few months and have decided it's for the best."

Jess felt as if every responsible parenting moment of the past twenty years was wiped out in a flash right then. She watched her children fall into a vortex of pain, her own body's nerve endings instantly hotwired. Time seemed to stop.

Tom gasped. Beth collapsed into herself. Both made immediate eye contact with Jess that started all three crying. Tom blinked and looked away quickly. Beth looked from her mother to her father, tears streaming down her face. Jess leaped out of her seat and crouched between her children, embracing each of them as they leaned into her. Arthur hovered, then circled behind the love seat and patted Beth and Tom on their shoulders.

For several minutes, Jess watched the newsreel version of her family's life play in her head. She didn't want it to end. Tom cleared his throat and moved to Jess's chair. Beth didn't let go of her, so Jess sat next to her on the love seat.

Arthur sat back down across from them. "Of course, we both love you very much and are sorry that this will be hard on you, but we think this is the right thing for us."

Neither child spoke. Beth's face was still streaked with tears, but she managed to sit up straight and let go of her mother. Tom avoided looking at anyone but his father, who was blathering on and on about how he loved them and would always be there for them.

Finally, Tom said, "Mom?"

For the first time, Jess used words that would become a common refrain. "I'm so sorry—so, so sorry—that this is happening." She looked to her husband to continue the next chapter of the story, as promised: the why.

Instead, Arthur went to the kitchen to get tissues. No more discussion. Jess could only assume the kids were too shocked to get to questions.

Beth slept with Jess that night and cried herself to sleep, her mother at her side, repeating, "It'll be OK; we'll all be OK." Jess crept out of the bedroom briefly to check on Tom but heard Arthur leaving Tom's room after some muffled conversation, so decided against it. She returned to her bedroom to find Beth curled up in a ball on her side, sleeping soundly in the same position she had used since she was two years old.

Arthur slept in the guest room and left early in the morning to meet with someone at the lab about the research transition. Jess walked through her home like a zombie but felt the sad house reaching out to her as she noted floorboards creaking and a new wall crack in the corner of the den.

◇◇◇◇◇◇◇◇◇◇◇◇◇◇◇◇◇◇

The kids slept in. Each shuffled into the kitchen in turn with red, swollen eyes. Jess knew they would ask their questions in time, but for now, she served them untouched apple cake with breakfast.

"I'm scrambling some eggs. Who wants spinach and tomatoes added?" Jess peered over at Tom, who seemed very quiet. As she did so, she spilled some milk on the countertop and watched as it started dripping onto the floor. She grabbed the last paper towel and stopped the worst of it. "Tom, could you grab some more paper towels, please?" She pointed to the corner storage area.

When Tom went to retrieve a roll, she saw him glance at the family calendar. October was blank except for this weekend, circled in black Sharpie. He averted his eyes as he sat again, "Mom, what about Thanksgiving and Christmas?"

"We haven't thought that far ahead yet, love, but we will soon. I promise," Jess replied, feeling every maternal bone in her body revolt. "I do think you two should stick with your plans today. It will do you good to see your friends." She poured herself a fourth cup of coffee.

She instantly deciphered her children's body language. "And, yes, you can tell them. No need to keep secrets." She saw relief in their eyes.

They left to meet up with their various friends attending local colleges, and Beth called later to ask permission for her and Tom to go out together on their own Saturday night. Jess was glad they had a chance to huddle a bit and support each other.

Arthur called Jess when he couldn't reach the kids, and she told him of their plan. "I came all this way, and they go out? How did you allow this?"

She gave him a minute to cool off. She imagined the hard drive in his mind computing how far he could take this. Old habits died hard. She met him halfway. The cold silence on the phone told her he was fighting to control the urge to go after her for this decision their children had made. "Arthur, they need to process this. This is how they have chosen to do so." Her voice was even but weary.

"Fine."

She could imagine his exact expression and, with some unexpected relief, realized she wouldn't have to see it much more.

✺✺✺✺✺✺✺✺✺✺✺✺✺✺✺

Jess and Arthur took Beth and Tom to the airport Sunday morning, and there were tears and hugs all around. Nobody had slept well over the weekend, and Jess hoped the kids could nap on their flights.

They made the usual promises to call after safe arrivals, and then it was over. Jess felt numb as she and Arthur drove home one last time, in silence.

When they arrived at the house, Jess watched from the living room as he walked through each room, as if to check for forgotten items at a hotel. Finally, he approached her slowly—his final assignment. "Jess, I haven't forgotten your question 'Am I leaving you or going to a new opportunity?' As usual, you always get to the core of an issue." He smiled then and softened his tone. "It's a very good question, and you deserve an answer. The opportunity is one I feel I can't pass up. It's a perfect match for me right now." He looked away.

"And?" Jess whispered.

"And, yes, I'm leaving you. The marriage isn't working for me, and I've told you that. But, honestly, I think the two are interlinked. This just feels like the right thing to do."

"The right thing for *you* to do, Arthur, but is it the right thing for the rest of us?" Jess willed herself not to cry, and took a long, hard look at her husband, trying to find the man she had loved for so long.

"Someday, we'll look back and realize this was for the best." Arthur shifted his weight to stand taller, away from Jess. "It will all work out."

Jess thought how easy it was for him to say that. *Speak for yourself—we'll see how everyone else ends up feeling about it.*

Then Arthur called a taxi and left for good. His appointment in Portland had been formalized six weeks earlier. His final two suitcases, already packed and hidden away, were now gone.

And with that, Jess's golden family was no more.

∞∞∞∞∞∞∞∞∞∞

Claire and Diane arrived twenty minutes later.

"How are you holding up?" Claire asked, searching Jess's face while Diane hugged her tightly in greeting.

Jess broke free of her friend's embrace. "OK, OK. I promise we can talk about everything later, but right now I'm so tired, all I want to do is sleep."

They tucked her into her bed and announced that they would wake her in two hours. She heard the elves stripping bedding and starting laundry before she drifted off.

The clang of pots and pans woke her, and she found them making a mess of her kitchen. Grocery bags and foodstuffs lay helter-skelter on every countertop.

"What are you two doing to my kitchen?" Jess asked, hands on her hips, smiling slightly.

"Making a very complicated dinner. Where are your cutting boards?" Diane was opening cupboards.

"Osso bucco. You'll love it. How was your nap? You actually had ten minutes left." Claire shared a look with Diane. "Should we let her help?"

"I will be helping, thank you." Jess pulled open the sliding drawer for cutting boards and cookie sheets. "This is probably the only way I'll get to eat today." Her phone beeped from the charging station in the corner office. She walked over and quickly read a text from Beth, safe back at school, and saw that she had missed Tom's.

"Hang on, you two. Don't do anything complicated until I'm back." She stepped to her computer and composed a quick e-mail. She had started an e-mail loop with the kids at the beginning of the school year every Sunday night, and this was clearly not a night to miss.

Then, amid the comforting tasks of chopping vegetables and putting groceries away, the three women helped to restore some sense of order to Jess's life. After Claire handed her a glass of wine, Jess felt ready to talk about the weekend. "I think that may have been the hardest thing I've ever had to do."

"I'm sure you did it as well as anybody could, Jess. How did they take it?" Diane coaxed her friend.

"Hard to say. They were shocked, sad, confused, unsure of what it means—all to be expected. They wanted to spend some time together, just the two of them, which I think was a good thing."

"And Arthur?" Claire asked.

"He dropped the ball. He promised he would tell them there was another woman in the picture." Jess caught a stray onion wedge about to fall off the counter.

"And he didn't?" Diane asked.

"No, damn him. He defended himself to me later by saying, 'Nobody asked.'"

"Well, maybe that was more than they could take in right now." Diane collected the chopped veggies in a bowl.

"Maybe, but I know they'll both struggle with the why." Jess shrugged.

Claire sipped her wine. "It's really not part of Arthur, though, is it, to talk about real stuff that way?"

"It doesn't seem so. But I can see why you wouldn't want to be the messenger, Jess," Diane offered.

Jess walked over to turn on the gas stove in the family room. "The good news is, Stanford and Brown both have excellent student counseling services. I asked the kids to consider a visit or two so they can at least have a safe place to talk about their questions and worries. But I don't know that they'll do that."

As if I have the foggiest idea what any of us will do now, she thought.

Chapter 22

<small>◇◇◇◇◇◇◇◇◇◇◇◇◇◇◇◇◇◇◇◇◇◇◇◇◇◇◇◇</small>

Two weeks later, Jess woke with a shiver and sat bolt upright. She looked around to get her bearings. At least she no longer felt for Arthur's body for reassurance after a bad dream. That was progress. But she now slept in an empty house and needed lamplight in several rooms to keep her from feeling abandoned.

Trixie, her kitten houseguest, meowed in protest as she disrupted the warm spot she was molded to on top of the covers, nestled behind Jess's knees. She grabbed her cozy cashmere robe from the foot of the bed and felt for her slippers.

The day before, Jess's neighbor Dot had appeared at Jess's door in a panic. Her mother was in the final stage of an aggressive cancer, and she and her husband and their daughter, Mariel, had been called to the bedside, leaving Mariel's new kitten, Trixie, without care. "It will just be for a few days," Dot had assured Jess.

Cuddling Trixie, Jess made her way down to the den, turned on the gas fireplace, and arranged herself and the cat on the down-filled sofa. As she passed the clock, she was pleased to see that it was nearly five a.m. Another sign of progress—she had made it past three a.m.

Jess tried to focus on what had disrupted her sleep. She was dreaming about Arthur almost every night, and tonight was no exception. There didn't seem to be any particular theme to the dreams. There were dreams of Arthur when they'd first met. Dreams of Arthur as a new father. Dreams of Arthur playing with the children. Dreams of the family on special vacations. Pleasant dreams, actually, so they didn't disturb her. It was the fact that she had them that bothered her. He had certainly left behind any thoughts of her and moved on. She hated that he still filled her head, even if only in slumber.

She tried to remember tonight's dream. The lake house. Just the two of them. No one else around. Warm, beautiful night. Jess and Arthur were by the water. Lake of the Ozarks was still. No boats in sight. No competing city lights to dull the stars' shine. There was a fire in the stone fire-pit.

Suddenly, an image floated to her. Against her will, she smiled. They were making love, slowly and joyfully, by the light of the stars. She had never denied the good times, and she and Arthur had had many of them during their twenty-two-year marriage. They just hadn't lasted. She felt her eyes well up.

"Let it go," she said to herself, and let the tears fall. Her mind drifted back to the dream. She saw herself nude by the fire, and Arthur moving away to take a picture of her. A picture of her . . .

With a fury that suddenly engulfed her, Jess flew off the couch and ran to her desk across the room, flinging off the cat and moaning, "No, no, no, no," getting louder and angrier as she searched through the bottom desk drawer.

She found the envelope of pictures hidden in the tin behind her hanging files. She grabbed at it frantically and spilled them all on the desk. She ignored Trixie, now meowing loudly to be heard over Jess's commotion.

"Damn, damn, damn! I can't believe it! That bastard!" Jess was scattering the photos all over the desk and trying to recall the occasion of the dream more clearly.

She had been sure she had gotten all the pictures from the safe deposit box. But she had forgotten the night at the lake. An anniversary celebration. A romantic weekend away. It had been so lovely and warm that they had spent the evening on the deck that jutted out over the lake and enjoyed a bottle of wine, the night sky, and each other.

Jess let herself fold softly to the floor as her tears of nostalgia turned to tears of anger and shame. Trixie came close and sat near her on a picture that had fluttered to the floor, purring.

"Oh, you," Jess said. "You're going to keep me going, aren't you?" She pulled the kitty to her and heard the purring get louder. "OK, OK, now I just need to figure out if there are any others missing and where in the hell they might be." She lay down flat on the carpet and let Trixie walk all over her.

Finally, she was calm and ready to move forward with a plan.

Jess put the pictures back in their hiding place, showered and dressed, and was out of the house by seven a.m. She picked up coffee on the way and holed up behind her closed office door. She completed her mental inventory of pictures as she waited until West Coast time caught up with her.

At eight a.m. Portland time, she called Arthur and left a message on his cell phone. "Call me back ASAP if you don't want me to take a personal issue to the attorneys. And I'm not talking about your new roommate."

The other woman now had a name: Rebecca Spence. Jess's mailman had approached her to verify Arthur's forwarding address in Portland. It had taken only ten minutes of research for Jess to discover that Rebecca had completed a surgical residency at the university just the year before. She could connect the dots from there.

The divorce negotiations had been fairly straightforward. Arthur was so transparent in his motives to leave her that once he relocated to Portland and began cohabiting with the new love, he became distant to his children and more interested in limiting his financial obligations to them. Jess wouldn't let that happen and fought for tuition support for them, as planned. Fortunately, both kept any negotiation tension from Beth and Tom.

The kids kept the e-mail loop among the three of them going and checked in with her once or twice a week by phone. *How ironic that my empty nest comes with more, not less intimacy*, she thought. *I wish it weren't the result of the emotional upheaval we're all trying to avoid.*

Jess got the house, Arthur the lake house, and they split their savings. Not too complicated. That part had never been difficult. It was the emotional burden that she seemed to be carrying around that was taking a toll. And now, whenever she recalled a sweet, romantic, or lusty moment in their twenty-two years together, it was ruined when she had to wonder if there was a photograph that she had missed.

"Jess, what is it? Can we make this fast? I'm just stepping into a lecture." Arthur sounded rushed when he called back twenty minutes later.

"I hope we can make this fast. I'm not happy to be spending any time on this at all, so let's do that." Jess was crisp and determined not to feel guilty for prioritizing her needs over his. "The pictures that I pulled from the safety deposit box—I don't think they were all there. I recall an incident at the lake when we were outside." She faltered and took a breath. "Those pictures are missing."

Silence on the line for a moment. "Let me call you back from my office. I can't talk from here. Ten minutes." Arthur cut her off, and the line went dead.

He called back in eight. "OK, I can talk now, and I understand that you're upset about this. I'm sorry. What can I do?"

His voice was so soothing that it took the bite out of her approach, and she teared up. Her voice thicker and a bit unsteady, she replied, "I need to make sure I have all of the pictures."

"Yes, I can understand that," Arthur responded evenly. "I didn't see what you got from the bank that day, so can you tell me what you have? That's the only way I can give you any assurance that you have them all."

She wavered, swallowed hard, and looked at the family photos on her desk. Just Beth and Tom now.

"Jessica?" Arthur asked. "Do you know another way to do this?"

She breathed deeply and then charged on, as if reading from a shopping list. "No, I guess not. So here goes. I have an inventory of six episodes, and two to three poses from each episode. I'll go in chronological order: New house, wearing new lingerie. Painting nursery after debacle with the paint can." Jess heard a stifled laugh and stopped abruptly.

"Are you laughing? Arthur, how can you—"

"I apologize, but you have to remember the comedy of that scene. You had paint everywhere, and"—his voice was now an intimate whisper—"once we got you undressed, we made such sweet love. Do you remember?"

She gasped and replied sharply, "Of course I remember, but I'm trying very hard to forget!"

"Jess, we had some great times, and I, at least, have wonderful memories. I hope you do too." His voice was a caress.

She did not respond, and Arthur finally filled in the mutual silence. "OK, then two other 'episodes,' as you call them, that should have been at the bank were that wonderfully sexy surprise visit to Chicago, and one of you skinny-dipping at that secluded resort beach in Maui. Right?"

"Yes," Jess managed to respond.

"So I think the only other time was the night at the lake. And you say those photos were not at the bank?" Arthur asked.

"Yes, they were not at the bank, so where are they?" Jess found her words again.

"I know it's important for you to get these," he said. "The only other place I might have them would be at the lake, but I'm not sure. I know you're going up one more time to get your stuff, so maybe you can check then?"

"Where exactly would they be at the lake house?"

"If they're there, and I'm not sure they are, they would be in my desk, or in the closet somewhere. I'm sorry I can't be more certain, Jess."

"And, just to be clear, there were no more than two to three poses for each of those episodes, correct?" She pushed herself to finalize this conversation.

"Yes. That's correct," Arthur responded softly. "And, Jess, you're a beautiful woman now, and you were a beautiful woman in each of those pictures. If anyone came across—"

"That can't happen, Arthur." Jess hung up.

She walked around her office, stretched out her shoulders, did a few neck rolls, shook herself off, and picked up the phone.

First, she called her divorce lawyer and had his assistant call him out of a meeting.

"Is everything OK?" Mitchell asked. "Did you find something in the paperwork that didn't make sense with our plan?"

"No, the papers seem to be in order. But I need you to do one more thing for me."

"Sure. What is it?"

"Arthur has quite a number of rewards miles with two or three airlines, and I want them." Jess pulled a few dead fronds off the spider plant on her desk.

Earlier, Mitchell had advised her that she was being more than generous to Arthur in the proceedings, and that if she wanted to use his extramarital activity for alimony or a better settlement, it would not be difficult. But she hadn't wanted to take anything that wasn't hers. Until now. Now, she gave in to a base instinct to instill pain.

"That shouldn't be a problem, Jess. I'll bring it up with Arthur's counsel."

"Thanks, Mitchell. Arthur's not going to like this, by the way."

"OK. I'll see what I can do." Mitchell paused. "Is this about new discoveries of—"

Jess cut him off. "No. No women besides Jennifer and Rebecca, as far as I know."

"Then is there anything I should know?"

"Don't make me explain. I can't."

"No problem. You know where I am on this. You could . . ."

"I know, I know. But it's just this one thing I want . . ." Jess hesitated. "Actually, Mitchell, one more thing. It's non-negotiable." She pulled her wastebasket from under her desk and dropped the fronds into it.

"Consider it done."

Jess's next two calls were more pleasant. She left messages with both Diane and Claire, announcing a girls' trip to the lake house that coming weekend. If they could make the time, she needed help with a secret mission.

When Jess arrived home that night, she was relieved to see lights on at Dot's house and made a quick call to make sure they were ready to receive Trixie. "More than ready, Jess. Mariel has been watching your house. She's hurting from losing her grandmother and needs her kitty," Dot said. "Thanks so much for taking her so quickly. It meant a lot."

Mariel met Jess at the door as she arrived, carrying a very noisy Trixie in her crate. "I've missed you, Trix," she cooed to her pet.

"And she's missed you, Mariel. I'm afraid I'm a poor substitute for you. But if you need help with her again, I'm happy to do it."

As she walked back to her house, she mused, *First I'm suspicious that they chose me to care for their kitten out of pity*—poor Jess is all alone—*and now I'm offering to help again? Where's that coming from? I'm alone, but am I lonely?*

Chapter 23

Jess palmed the heart-shaped Lake of the Ozarks rock that she had found years earlier and that had graced each of her desks since. She had been putting off the last trip to the lake house and hadn't talked about it with Diane and Claire, so they were surprised at the invitation. Even now, with a reason that compelled her to get over there fast, she wasn't so sure the trip was a good idea. She would be losing the place in a few short months and wasn't sure she wanted to say goodbye to it with an audience. But more and more, Jess found it easier to ask for her friends' support and was able to admit to herself that she needed it.

"I call shotgun!" Claire called out as she headed for Jess's four-wheel drive vehicle ahead of Diane.

"There's nowhere else you'd fit!" Diane teased, catching up to her friend, clearly nearing the end of her pregnancy. "And I was going to insist on it anyway. So have at it. I imagine we'll be stopping every half hour for you to use the bathroom, too, and I'm not even going to complain."

"Am I going to have to be the parent with you two?" Jess asked.

"Nope, I need the practice!" Claire announced. "Should be me. I only have weeks before I hit the reality of motherhood."

They broke up the drive with a gas-and-bathroom break and reached the Lakeview Café in time for their reservation. Claire awoke from her second nap as the lights from the Lakeview appeared on the horizon. When they pulled into the restaurant parking lot, it had started to mist a bit, and the leaves underfoot everywhere were soggy. Situated just across the highway from Lake of the Ozarks, the Lakeview was a destination for anyone who valued fresh, tasty, healthy food—if there was a table available. Fortunately, that wasn't a problem in the late fall. The leaf peepers had already had their weekend getaways while the colors were at their peak.

They walked through the mist to the entrance, beckoned by the warm yellow light of landscape lamps. Jess smelled the familiar lake air mixed with the aromas coming from the open door of the restaurant: roasting pork, root vegetables, and the faint hint of baking apples and cinnamon. *Ah, it's so good to be here.* She allowed herself a moment to smile before a creeping feeling of loss swallowed her.

Diane took her aside as they waited for Claire to hit the restroom as soon as they walked in the door. "Jess, I need to tell you that this trip is hard for me. Saying goodbye to your place—so many happy memories. And if it's hard for me, I can only guess how tough this is for you. What can I do to help you through it?"

Jess instantly teared up at the show of concern and responded with a quick side hug. "You always come through for me, Diane, and I know you won't disappoint me this weekend. I'll make a deal with you: promise not to laugh at me when I explain the 'mission,' and you can be the designated driver for me tonight. I plan to drink some wine with dinner."

After her first swallow of a very good red, Jess laid out the plan. She would have preferred to drink more before she had to spill the story, but she had a sleepy pregnant woman who was eager for bed. Besides, she didn't think early-morning light would make this any easier.

"OK, ladies, good friends, friends who do not judge." Jess looked at each of them in turn, with just a hint of mirth in her eye. "I need your help this weekend on a kind of treasure hunt."

"I knew it," Claire jumped in. "Arthur has hidden gold up here, and you're going to find it and make sure it becomes the marital asset it should be!" She laughed giddily at her idea and looked to the others for their reaction.

Jess laughed too. "No, not quite, but that's a good one! *Treasure* may be a misnomer." She paused, taking a deep breath. "Oh, jeez, let me just explain it and get it over with." She exhaled and, looking at the fireplace in the corner, started talking.

"Over the years, Arthur took pictures of me that he wanted to have with him when he traveled. These pictures are not the kind of thing I want out there for anyone else to see. I believe I have recovered all but one or two photos, which may be at the lake place. Your mission, if you wish to accept it, is to help me find them." Jess's face felt hot when she finished. She picked up her wineglass before looking up at her friends.

"Oh my God," Claire said. "Arthur had naked pictures of you that he took all around the world with him? That is so romantic!"

"Hey, Jess, no biggie. We'll find them," Diane chirped.

"If they're here to be found, that is." Jess took a long drink of her wine.

The server came and mesmerized them with the offerings. They ordered four small plates to share and decided to save some room for the apple-ginger tart. The homey atmosphere, combined with the warmth from the fire, made them all want to keep chatting a little longer, even the yawning Claire.

"You know, honey," Claire said, "people are using their cell phones for this kind of thing all the time now, not to mention posting this information for all the world to see. Are these old-style photos, then?"

"Yes. They actually had to be developed! Way before the technology changed. I had forgotten about them until just recently. Arthur had them stashed in the safe deposit box, and I got them."

"He had them where?" Diane could not contain her amusement.

"He says he didn't want the kids to come across them." Jess shrugged. "I had a rather anxious trip down to the bank to get them." She raised her eyebrows, remembering her awkward encounter with the staff.

"Well, that makes sense, in an Arthur kind of way, I guess," Claire offered. "So, do we get to know what photos we're looking for?"

Jess poured herself a second glass of wine. "OK, you two. You've been good long enough. You can start to enjoy this now." She looked at both of them, feigning exasperation, and they giggled.

"You have to admit it's quite funny to think of Arthur carrying these photos around the world and then keeping them safe at the bank," Claire started, and they all laughed heartily.

"I can just see him taking them into the secure part of the bank," Diane offered, "kind of like a secret agent. Trench coat on, collar up . . ." And the giggles continued.

Their order arrived, and as they immersed themselves in the pleasure of the food, Jess felt herself slipping into the weekend, now that she had put the worst behind her.

As they finished off the tart, Claire asked, "So, Jess, is there a prize for whoever finds the photos? Also, you still haven't really described them."

"Hmm, well, I still co-own the place for a bit, so how about another weekend at the lake house for the winner? And the best description of the photo is 'love in open air.'" Jess, feeling the effect of her wine, smiled as they rolled their eyes and asked for more hints.

"That's all you're getting. The hunt is on, or the hunt is on in the morning. Diane, please get us there." Jess handed her the keys.

Jess slept so soundly that it took several minutes before she had awakened enough to realize where she was and to find the house phone as it rang.

"Hello." The sleep was thick in her voice.

"Jess."

"Arthur, why are you calling? Are the kids OK?" Now thoroughly awake, she stood up to ground herself, finding her cell phone in order to check the time: just after midnight.

"I assume the kids are fine. I'm not calling about the kids. I couldn't reach you on your cell." The anger in his voice was palpable.

"Arthur, why in the world are you calling me after mid—"

"What are you doing, demanding those airline miles? Why on earth do you think you should have them? Who put you up to this?" He raved on, until he finally paused to take a breath. "What exactly are you doing?"

Jess moved from a wine and relief–infused dead sleep to warrior mode in less than five seconds, then ratcheted back to enjoy his tirade.

"Seems only fair, since I was keeping the home fires burning while you were traveling the world for so many years, that I should get something in return."

"Ah, so this is about revenge? I thought you were above that."

"What's fair is fair, Arthur. And this seems fair to me."

"Well, it's not going to happen. So don't plan any trips yet. I will reopen the negotiations."

"At your own peril, I would say . . ."

She could faintly hear Arthur sputtering. He went quiet for a few seconds, then said, "Don't be so sure about that, Jess. By the way, have you found the pictures?" *Click.*

"Jess, is everything OK?" Diane peered into the master bedroom. "A late-night phone call always makes me nervous."

"I'm so sorry. Did the phone wake you?" Jess felt her heartbeat slowing at the sight of her friend.

"Well, yes, but it's fine."

"What about Claire?"

"Haven't heard a peep. The downstairs bedroom door is closed, so she may not have heard anything."

"Thank God. She needs her sleep." Jess exhaled slowly.

"So do you, my dear. What's up? Do you want to talk about it?" Diane started walking toward the great room. "Or at least come see the moon."

Jess followed her, and they both took in the breathtaking sight of an autumn full moon, in all its colorful splendor, splashing light on the lake in front of them, beyond the deck.

Diane broke the spell. "So beautiful and peaceful. Are you ready to go back to sleep?"

"Nope, don't think that'll happen for a while. How about you? Sleepy?"

"I don't expect to be sleepy until you tell me what happened just now."

Jess smiled. "I don't know what I've done to deserve a friend like you, but I'm grateful." They sat on the couch so that they could still see the moon.

"I'm becoming a cliché, Diane. I'm a middle-aged wife whose husband has left her for a younger woman—just as her children have left the nest. And now the divorce is almost finalized, all negotiations over, and I've acted emotionally and thrown something out there that I knew would be trouble."

"Hey, you're not a cliché. Far from it. You're an awesome, bright woman who is going through a tough time with incredible class. I didn't know the divorce was so close to being done. Good for you." Diane said.

"Yes, well, I want closure. I really do. So why did I throw a spear at Arthur?"

"Honey, you know there's not a straight path through these things. You two were married for a long time, had a wonderful life together, raised two beautiful children. There are a lot of memories to sort through before you can heal and file them away. You need to give your heart time to catch up with your head."

"But I can do that, Diane. That's why this is so frustrating. I lived through my parents' divorce. I know what it takes." She looked up at her friend through tear-filled eyes. "I'm resilient and strong—but so tired of needing to be."

"You may have survived your parents' divorce, but we both know what it cost you. Those were terrible times for you. You'll carry that with you always."

"And now so will Beth and Tom. I failed to protect them from that."

"You know this situation can't compare to what you went through with your parents. Polar opposites. You did whatever you could to avoid hurting your kids."

Jess eased her head back on the couch cushion. Diane walked the length of the great room and brought them each a glass of water.

"Diane, I hope my experience hasn't turned you off to marriage. I feel guilty sharing all of this with you, when you should be in thrall with your own sweet romance."

"Not to worry. Remember, I have my own parents' marriage as a goal. If indeed this romance . . ."

"Ah, gotcha." Jess laughed. "That's as close as you've come to admitting that things are serious between you and George."

Diane took a drink of water. "Hmm . . . we'll see."

"It was the last picture that made me lose it. When I realized that one was missing and I still had to find it, and Arthur was so cool and dismissive about it . . ." Jess knew she was rambling. "I directed my attorney to go after his rewards miles."

"His what?"

"He has millions of rewards miles from all of his travel. He gets very excited about how to grow those rewards. It's a game for him."

"And he's ticked about it?"

"He's beyond ticked. Enraged is more like it."

"*That's* why he called after midnight?"

"Well, Portland is two hours behind us, and he said he tried my cell first, but you know we don't have good reception here. Anyway, yes, that's why he called."

"Do you want these miles?"

"It's not the miles. It's the pain I was going for," Jess whispered.

"Sounds like you got it, girl!" Diane chuckled, and Jess joined her, until they were both laughing uncontrollably.

Finally gaining some semblance of poise, Diane said, "So, are we tired yet?"

"Getting there. I've gotta sleep on Arthur's last words before I can sort this out completely."

"Last words?"

"Well, he sort of implied that the missing picture would remain missing until I gave up the miles."

"What? You're kidding! Does that mean he has it and we're on a wild goose chase?"

"Could be that, or he's bluffing. I have no idea."

They sat silently, both contemplating the odds, for a few minutes. Jess knew that had she been alone, she would have searched all night after that phone call.

It was after two a.m. when they went back to bed, and more than an hour after that when Jess last checked the time. What was she missing? Finally, she let her mind go blank as she listened to the waves spill over the rocky shore.

Chapter 24

⋄⋄⋄⋄⋄⋄⋄⋄⋄⋄⋄⋄⋄⋄⋄⋄⋄⋄⋄⋄⋄⋄⋄

The moment Jess arrived at work on Monday, Cindy, an associate at the firm, flagged her down and followed her into her office. "Hey, girlfriend. How was the weekend?" Cindy opened Jess's door and grabbed her briefcase from her. As Jess walked in, Cindy turned to face her. "You get through it OK?"

"Could have been worse, I guess, but it was still hard. I'm glad I had friends with me. They kept me from getting too teary about it. Plus, they helped me cart out the stuff I brought back."

"Did you bring much?" Cindy's voice relaxed.

"Nah, just some books, clothes, and personal mementos: the lake house guest book, which Arthur never wanted, and a couple of homemade kid ornaments that I couldn't part with. It made it easier to leave knowing that my children will find it familiar when they visit."

"So, Arthur doesn't plan to sell?"

"I don't really know. But for now, we've agreed that we won't upset either household. I'm not privy to his living situation in Portland, but I assume he's not in a tent." She looked up at Cindy and laughed. "I'm OK, really. But thanks for checking in on me. The divorce should be final this month." Jess headed for her desk.

"Oh. Glad to hear that, Jess."

"Yes, it's time to close this chapter and move on. Drama can be exhausting." She laughed again, hoping to put her friend at ease. "So, did I miss anything here on Friday?" She glanced at her inbox.

"Actually, I do want to bring you up to date on something. But I was just running to the corner to get a fancy coffee. Can I bring you one?"

"That sounds wonderful, Cindy. I'll do a quick e-mail check and be ready when you get back." Jess was just about to sit, then added, "Surprise me with something new and different, please."

She could use the caffeine. After Arthur's wild call had interrupted her night, she and Diane and Claire had turned the place inside out on Saturday, looking for the pictures. Finally, Jess had hit a wall and called a halt to spending any more time or emotion on a photo of her that might or might not still exist. She vowed not to fall into Arthur's trap, and Diane and Claire cheered her decision. But it was a decision she had to live with, and it was only day two.

She had dealt with a dozen e-mails by the time Cindy returned with a double-mocha, double-shot latte. "A treat with some punch." She passed it over to Jess.

"I look a little tired, huh?" She took the cover off the whipped cream–topped concoction and smiled at her friend's concerned expression. "It looks delicious. Thanks."

"You were going to catch me up on something from Friday," Jess prompted, taking a first sip with her eyes closed in appreciation.

"Yes, something new and different happened here on Friday—something that may open a new chapter for us."

"Good segue, Cindy. Do tell." She smiled between sips.

"Well, it happens that Dick Morrison called Dan over for an impromptu meeting, and Dan asked me along."

"What's up with Midwest Health? Merger business still?" Jess asked.

"No, that's all tidied up. He actually seemed very pleased with the work the firm did for him, which is why he's asked for our help with a new initiative."

"That's good. I bet Dan was pleased. New legal work for you, then?"

"Not exactly, so I'm giving you a heads-up about what happened at the meeting."

"Sounds mysterious. Go on."

"Evidently, Dick is thinking that Midwest Health, now that the university acquisition is all set, is ready to make a play to add some community clinics. Seems like they're ready to take advantage of their new capacity to bring in more patients by buying clinics. And, that brought him to—"

"Wow, that's fast. That merger must have been pretty smooth if they're ready to take on more complexity. It's only been a few months. I'm impressed."

"Well, here's the new-and-different part. Maybe your ears were burning Friday afternoon, because your name came up at the meeting."

"Really? Why is that?" Jess studied her closely. Cindy had no idea how Jess and Dick had faced off the previous spring, as she had been out on maternity leave at the time.

"Well, Dick apparently checked with his network for the best local talent on practice acquisitions and came up with your name. He wants to retain us to help with this new strategy, if you'll agree to be lead."

Jess felt her cheeks flush. "What, me?" She got up from her chair, headed for her coffee supplies, and made a full-blown mission of locating a spoon for her drink.

"Well, Jess, what do you say to that? Quite a compliment, right?"

"Yes, wow, that's very nice to hear." Jess regained her composure and took her seat, concentrating now on stirring the drink and taking a long swallow. "And what did Dan say to that?"

"That's the interesting part. Dan didn't jump on it at all. I was amazed. He sounded almost uninterested. Anyway, they excused me at the end and met for maybe ten more minutes. Dan was pretty closed-mouthed about it as we left, but he did tell me he plans to talk to you about it early this week."

◇◇◇◇◇◇◇◇◇◇◇◇◇◇◇◇◇◇◇◇

After work, Jess met Claire, whose nesting instinct had arrived. Time to prepare the nursery.

"OK, so this is the one." Claire caught Jess's attention as they entered the kids' furniture showroom and pointed to the cherrywood crib.

"Oh, I love that, and you'll need a rocker . . ."

After they had made their choices and arranged for delivery, Claire insisted on dinner. "I'm famished. Among the most surprising experiences of pregnancy is the never-ending desire for food—all kinds of food, any time of day, and in copious quantities."

"Oh, I remember the cravings I had, for salty, then sweet. My big thing was potato chips and ice cream in the middle of the night!" Jess laughed. Then she took a long look at her friend, still stylish in her ninth month, her jade jersey drape jacket lengthening her petite frame and accentuating her brilliant green eyes, and added, "Anyway, whatever you're eating is obviously working for you. You look great—glowing, as they say. And Kenneth is working wonders for you." She thought of all the shopping she had done with Claire until they'd found Kenneth, who had become their personal shopper and emergency go-to guy for a must-have outfit on little more than a moment's notice.

"Yes, he was a bit surprised by my situation but never skipped a beat in making me look good. Even the footwear!" Claire had switched out her Kate Spade four-inch heels for sensible but still stylish shoes with straps for the duration of her pregnancy.

They walked two storefronts over to a local bistro. The hostess led them to a table, rather than a booth, after taking a full-length look at Claire.

"Thanks for your help with the furniture shopping. I'm feeling better now that all that is set. I can't believe it's so close now."

"And you're doing beautifully. At this stage, your excitement starts to overcome your increasing discomfort."

Once their food was served, Claire tackled a new topic between bites.

"Jess, I know these past months have been hard for you. But I feel like this weekend was a milestone in getting some emotional distance from Arthur. And, of course, you'll continue with your recovery. But I think it's time for you to consider dating. I think it would help you to move forward."

Jess put her fork down. "You must be joking. That's absolutely not something I'm considering and am not sure when or if I ever will." Jess had resolved not to allow herself to be vulnerable again. The pain of any potential betrayal was more than she could risk.

"But you need to get out there and see," Claire insisted. "You're an extremely attractive woman who deserves a great man to appreciate you. And you're not going to find one by hanging around with a pregnant woman." She laughed then and paused to land her point while appraising Jess. "We should put Kenneth on alert to dress you for dating!"

Jess raised her eyebrows, then looked at what she was wearing: a conservative navy-blue wool crepe suit, and answered, "Too soon." But Claire's advice hit a nerve. Her social world had clearly narrowed in the past months. Funny how the married friends she and Arthur had socialized with had more or less disappeared. Perhaps they thought marital woes were infectious. She hadn't sought them out in her heartache, so maybe they really didn't know how to approach her. Now that Arthur was out of the picture, she wasn't sure what they had heard through the grapevine and didn't make it her business to find out.

Eager to change the subject, she said, "So, you'll never guess who wants me to do some work for him."

With her mouth full, Claire didn't try for a response, so Jess continued, "Dick, Midwest Health Dick, who expected me to keep Arthur here to keep his merger safe. He wants me to lead a new initiative for him. Can you believe it?"

"Yes, I can easily believe that. I know it was hurtful to you when he did what he did last spring. But he's a businessman who isn't taking any of this personally."

"So, you think I should agree to do it?"

"I think you should do it if it's something you want to do," Claire responded. After taking the last dinner roll from the basket, she added, "Actually, it may be just the thing to put that chapter behind you."

As Jess drove home, she marveled at how Claire could pose the question so clearly. Now she just had to figure out the answer. What *did* she want to do?

Chapter 25

⟡⟡⟡⟡⟡⟡⟡⟡⟡⟡⟡⟡⟡⟡⟡⟡⟡⟡⟡⟡⟡

The next day, Jess treated herself to a French-vanilla double latte from the corner coffee shop and met Dan as she entered her building's elevator. "Good morning. I was going to track you down later. How was the Chicago trip?"

"You know how these advisory conferences can be—one mind-numbing day to fill your head with trends, while the real learning goes on when you bump into colleagues who are also trying to stay awake." They shared a laugh. "So, what's up?"

"I understand Dick is interested in getting our help with a new acquisition strategy."

Dan looked surprised. "How . . . Cindy?"

"Yup." She smiled.

They reached their floor and got off. "Do you have time to talk now, Jess?"

"Sure. Let me drop my stuff, and then I'll come to your office." Dan seemed tense. Jess hoped he hadn't told Cindy to keep this hush-hush.

"C'mon in. Let's sit over here," he said when she entered his office. As she sat, she took in the view of downtown lights brightening the darkness of an early November morning.

"Dan, I didn't mean to corner you on this, and, gosh, I hope it wasn't a secret . . ."

"No, of course not. I'm glad you brought it up. We need to talk about it." He looked up at her sheepishly. "I guess I was trying to figure out how to approach you."

"You mean you were a bit worried about how to approach me after Dick kicked me off the last project?"

Dan looked at her quizzically. "That would be a yes."

Jess laughed softly, and Dan joined in. "Well, the man has nerve—we can agree on that. What is it he wants us to do?"

"That's the thing, Jess. It's not us he wants—it's you. You just happen to be in this firm now. He did his homework and got your name as the top choice for clinic acquisition work. Not even a close second." Dan shifted in his seat and took his glasses off.

"But, given your history, he wasn't sure you'd hear him out, so he called me. I brought Cindy along, thinking it was about legal work. But that's not the focus, at least not on the front end. He wants you to take the lead on deciding which practices Midwest Health goes after, and then to help them sort out the how."

"Cindy doesn't know about Dick's role in my decision to transition out of the merger work." Actually, nobody at work did, except for Dan.

"No, and she didn't find out about it at the meeting. Once I saw where this was going, I excused her. Then Dick asked me point blank if I thought you'd agree to work with Midwest Health again."

"And?" Jess felt for the clasp on her necklace and shifted it to the back of her neck.

"I told him I didn't know." He eased back in his chair. "I also told him you had every reason never to give him the time of day again. I must say, I enjoyed that part." He smiled.

"Wow. I wish I'd been there." Jess returned the smile. "So, where did you leave it? And what would you like to have happen here, Dan?"

"I told him I'd talk to you and that you could take it from there. If you want to explore it, fine, but if not, Jess, that's OK with me. It's not like we don't have work to do here. We're not begging for clients right now."

"No, that's true." Jess gazed out the window, her thoughts mixed. Dick had had no way of knowing the status of her marriage when he'd presented his ultimatum to her, but it had still been a sexist move on his part. "Do you think he learned anything from this? Did he give you any sense that he's gained some insight into how to treat women in the workplace?"

"Hard to know. I do think he realized that he'd miscalculated his leverage point with Arthur." Dan stopped abruptly and looked quickly at Jess. "Oh, God, that sounded awful."

"Go on. What do you mean?"

"Well, he's very intelligent. But the man must be missing an empathy gene when it comes to people. And he seems to think that's OK if he has a larger purpose in mind." He shook his head. "I wouldn't describe him as an evolved leader."

"Nope, I wouldn't either, Dan." They laughed.

Dan looked at his watch. Jess saw his assistant, Amy, peek through the glass. Time to start the business day. They both stood. He walked over to put his coffee cup on his desk. "Anyway, think about it. If you're willing to hear him out, he'd like to take you to lunch and talk about it. Your call."

"Oh, I'll hear him out, for sure. But on my turf. I'll ask him to lunch at the Saint Louis Club." She threw Dan a brilliant smile and left him chuckling.

◇◇◇◇◇◇◇◇◇◇◇◇◇◇◇◇

A few days later, Jess drove to the Pierre Laclede Center, where the Saint Louis Club was located. She parked a block or two away, close to the old county courthouse. It was a blustery autumn day that sent flying leaves collecting at the base of the few trees in front of the building. It was a relief to get out of the wind and into the foyer. She headed up to the fourteenth-floor Back Door dining room.

"Ms. Lawson, I've seated your guest," the host announced.

Jess checked her watch. Two minutes past noon—perfect. As she made her way to the dining room, the CEO of the Jenny Project, a nonprofit she had worked with pro bono awhile back, flagged her down. She greeted him, then looked around. She saw Dick Morrison studying his menu and facing the wall.

"Hello, Dick. Thanks for meeting me downtown." He rose when she reached the table and gave her a formal handshake. Three degrees shy of firm—decidedly weak for a so-called power player.

"Of course. Thanks for taking the meeting." Jess detected a touch of humility in his voice.

"Well, Dan tells me you have quite the proposal for me, so I wanted to hear you out for myself." She paused. "I see you've already studied the menu. Are you set to order?"

He nodded, and she caught the eye of the headwaiter, who approached and asked, "Are you and your guest ready, Ms. Lawson?"

Dick gestured for Jess to go first, but she waved him off, flipping his script. "You go first, Dick—you're my guest." She closed her menu and after Dick ordered, said, "Paul, would you have them poach a couple of eggs and top the spinach salad?"

"Just as you like it, Ms. Lawson." Paul wound his way among the small tables to the kitchen. The lunch crowd was beginning to show up.

Dick scanned the room for a bit, then focused on Jess and said, "Dan may have told you that I did a lot of research to find the right person to lead this project. I hope you're proud of your reputation in the community." Jess tried not to show her surprise at his flattery and smiled politely.

"I'm curious: Why did you take your business to Dan's firm?" Dick relaxed into his chair, his charisma oozing from every pore.

"Dan and I have a shared value system. We take on projects we believe serve a greater good. I was at the point where I was turning clients away, so I wanted the extra capacity that a larger firm could give me, without having to spend time growing it myself. I wasn't looking to build an empire; I just wanted to do meaningful work."

"Well, I think you'd find this meaningful, Jess. I need someone who knows the community practices here to direct us to those that are the right fit. We're ready to grow and need to bring the clinical work to our larger system. Did you get the position paper I had couriered to you?"

Lunch was served. "Thank you, Paul. It looks perfect." Jess smiled at the waiter. She couldn't care less what Dick ate.

"Yes, I did receive the paper, and read it. Dick, what's your ultimate goal with all of this?"

He smiled as he met her gaze. "To get you to agree to develop and implement our strategy for clinic acquisition."

"I know what this lunch is about. I'm asking what your ultimate goal for Midwest Health is."

"For Midwest Health to be the model of a public-private partnership able to preserve the academic mission of a university through excellent clinical care and responsive community service." Dick sounded rehearsed, parroting a line his marketing department must have supplied.

"And is that your ultimate career goal, Dick, or do you see this as a stepping-stone to a bigger job?"

He had started on his sandwich and took a drink of his iced tea before responding. "If you're worried that I won't see this strategy through, you needn't, Jess. This is important to me personally. I'll let the career path take care of itself." She noted a bit of arrogance seeping out.

"Well, you certainly have achieved success with the merger. I'm pleasantly surprised to hear from Dan how well it seems to be going—and happy for everyone involved." She smiled, then glanced down at her left hand, noting the birthstone where her wedding ring should be. *"Happy for everyone" might be an overstatement.* She now knew the merger strain hadn't been what had ruined her marriage, but it would always remind her of its choppy end.

"Thank you, Jess. We still have some loose ends, but by and large it's been smoother than I expected." He started on his soup.

"So, no mass exodus by the faculty, then." Jess glanced up from her salad and looked him in the eye.

Dick was taking a sip of soup. It went down the wrong way. He choked, sputtering and coughing loudly as people turned to look. Paul came over with another napkin and refilled Dick's water glass. He took two swallows of iced tea, then pulled out his handkerchief to blow his nose and wipe his eyes. Finally, he took a deep breath and swallowed hard before he was back in control.

"No." He spoke softly, handkerchief put away, his red nose the only evidence of his coughing fit. "I need to apologize for my behavior toward you last winter. I misjudged the situation, and I know I put you in an untenable position. I'm sorry for that."

"My policy then and now is not to discuss my personal life with a client, but, since you brought it up, I will tell you that it not only was unprofessional but also showed a total lack of sensitivity on your part."

"I know that, and I'm truly sorry." He cleared his throat again. "And I can see that it's too much for me to expect you to put that aside and work with me on anything again. This was a mistake."

Jess let him wait, his sandwich half eaten, his soup put aside, no utensils in hand.

She placed her fork across her empty plate and drank the last of her water. "You know, Dick, you and I have something in common. We'll both give our all to see something through, to reach a goal. I respect that in you and recognize that trait as one that can be hard to control at times." Jess stopped herself from delivering a full-blown lecture. She could see that Dick was already listening.

She leaned forward, her arms folded on the table.

"Here's my position. I've always recognized the value of academic medicine for this state. That means that Midwest Health, now that it owns the university hospital, needs to thrive. If I agree to work with you on this strategy, it's because I want to make Midwest Health stronger—not because of you, but in spite of you." She paused and locked eyes with him. "If I were to work on any new project with you, I'd have to have total control—within certain financial parameters, of course."

Dick did not respond but kept eye contact.

"So if you feel that these terms could work, you know where to find me." She broke eye contact, glanced down at the table to find the bill, signed it, and rose. "Enjoy the rest of your afternoon."

With that, Jess left him at the table and made her way to the elevator.

If she hadn't been wearing her killer heels, Jess would have skipped back to her car. She felt like she could now conquer the rest of the world. But the winds had whipped up even more during her meeting with Dick, and she barely made it into the driver's seat before the rain started.

She got to her office and turned her cell phone back on. Another phone message from Arthur. Ten days since the lake. Every day, at least two voice mails or texts. *All right—enough already!*

She shook her hair back into place, slipped off her heels, and e-mailed him: "Turn over the picture, and you can keep half the miles. Offer expires in 24 hours."

She turned on her office sound system to soft jazz and dealt with e-mail and paperwork until four p.m. Then she was off to a massage appointment amid the November evening's gale.

Chapter 26

◇◇◇◇◇◇◇◇◇◇◇◇◇◇◇◇◇◇◇◇◇

Sideways rain and wind made the drive to the massage studio challenging: cars crawled along, and a traffic light was out at the busiest intersection on the route. But Jess, still feeling the rush from her meeting with Dick, arrived with a smile on her face.

The low light and soft music of the studio enveloped her. She hadn't realized her body was tense until she was on the table and warm, oiled hands were working the knots out of her upper back.

Her mind drifted to Arthur. She conjured up an image of him reading her e-mail. He would be furious. It made her smile but then sad. Memories floated in: happy family moments at the lake; she and Arthur attending school activities as proud parents; teaching their kids to drive. Why couldn't those good times have lasted?

Anyway, what does it matter now? she asked herself. *There he is in Portland, with a whole new life.* She remembered helping him set up his office in St. Louis, his favorite art on the walls, a piece of sculpture they had found on one of their escapades in Italy. Had he boxed all that up and put it in his new office?

What about family photos? She knew he had a favorite one of her and the kids: Tom still a toddler, Beth barely older, smothering their mother in their no-holds-barred embrace.

Maybe the new love had helped him set up. She felt her body tighten at the thought. The new love would mean different pictures on his desk, for sure. She forced herself to block any further thoughts of Rebecca.

The masseuse helped her flip over onto her back. Her leg muscles, tight from running, protested at the targeted touch, but she knew this pain was therapeutic. She stayed with the touch and forced her mind to go blank.

Jess was always a bit dazed after a massage. She dressed slowly and sipped the tea the masseuse had left for her. She turned her cell back on and noticed that she had received a response from Arthur: "Tickets for the kids to Portland for Thanksgiving. The rest of the miles are yours."

She fell hard back into her chair, gut-punched, and dropped her teacup in the process. It broke, loudly, on the tile floor. Her teeth clenched as she squeezed her eyes tightly against oncoming tears.

Memories of Thanksgivings past floated into her consciousness, until she grabbed one: Beth and Tom proudly helping to decorate the table with their preschool construction-paper place cards; Arthur making his special stuffing.

A soft knock on the door pulled her out of her past. "Is everything OK in there?"

"Uh, yes, thanks. I just spilled my tea. Sorry. I'll be out in a minute."

But it took ten minutes to right herself and navigate out of the room, carrying teacup shards and apologies with her.

The rain was coming down in sheets outside, and the wind pulled her every which way as she made her way to her car.

Chapter 27

◇◇◇◇◇◇◇◇◇◇◇◇◇◇◇◇◇◇◇◇◇◇

Jess was halfway home before she conquered her emotions and recognized the win for the miles. She should have been prepared for Arthur to twist the knife as he lost this skirmish, and for the reality of holiday traditions that would go by the wayside now. Her body stilled. Arthur had revealed himself once more. Never again would she allow herself to hurt this much at his hand.

She had just pulled into her garage and was still sitting in her car when her cell phone rang.

"Oh, thank God I got you, Jess. It's time. My water broke." Claire spoke clearly but excitedly.

"Wonderful! Now, breathe—it'll be fine. I'm on my way. Are you at home?" Jess quickly shifted into gear and looked at her watch. She entered the house, grabbed her hospital bag, and changed her shirt while putting Claire through an essential Q-and-A session. The answers did not challenge her equanimity one iota. Claire had called her doula and the midwife and had been directed to go to the hospital, as planned. Her contractions were still a few minutes apart and not incapacitating.

Jess was out the door in five minutes, at Claire's house in fifteen, and at the hospital inside of thirty. Not bad. It was still blustery, but the rain had subsided.

Claire was holding up beautifully even amid the contractions, which were coming ever faster and stronger. She didn't protest when they helped her into a wheelchair for the ride to the midwife unit.

Jess could barely suppress her excitement. "OK, let's go in and have a baby!" she exclaimed as they arrived at the door of the unit.

Claire responded with a hard-to-find smile. Her eyes glistened, and she took Jess's hand. "Thank you for doing this. I may swear at you soon, so I want you to know I do appreciate that you're here!"

The doula, Sofia, greeted them warmly, then checked Claire into a bed. Sofia declared promptly how much progress Claire had already made and then set about procuring all sorts of comfort—except, of course, the most important part: whisking that baby right out of Claire's body and into her welcoming arms.

Claire asked, "How much longer?"

Sofia, who must have known the drill backward and forward, answered tactfully, "First labors are always hard to predict. Let's see what Alison says. She'll be here in just a couple of minutes. But I can tell you that everything is proceeding very well."

Alison came and went and came and went. Sofia did the same. Jess brought ice, popsicles, distracted the mother-to-be as much as possible, and stayed calm and positive throughout. Jess watched their every move, experiencing labor from a different, and much more comfortable, angle, literally and figuratively.

Claire didn't swear at her but did show some impatience when Jess attempted to get her to conjugate verbs in French to distract her between contractions.

"Really? You can't be serious. Is that the best you can do?" Claire whined. "How about movie categories or something creative?" So they took turns thinking of movies in which they would have liked to be cast as leading women, until they realized they would mostly have preferred the male roles.

Claire had been adamant that a midwife attend her delivery. Jess had agreed but insisted on a hospital birth with coverage by attending staff available to the midwifery service. At the advanced age of forty-three, Claire was technically a high-risk mom. Jess also wanted a neonatal unit on-site. When Claire had asked Jess to be her support through the pregnancy, birth, and child rearing, she might not have bargained for such strong opinions. But when it came to the safety of those she loved, Jess was uncompromising.

Jess had done the homework on Alison, a bright Seattle University grad with an impressive CV and excellent clinical outcomes. She was experienced with mothers over forty and nonjudgmental about Claire's decision to go it alone.

Claire approved immediately after meeting her and loved her exuberant yet professional style. She was part twentysomething, red curls bouncing around her head, and part wonder woman who had seen her share of the miracles and tragedies that make up the life of a midwife.

Jess left the room to make a few calls, when Sofia beckoned her back. "Would you like to be here for the main event?"

"Are you kidding? I wouldn't miss it for the world." She sashayed back in with a bright smile and met Claire's eyes. "Let's meet this baby. Are you ready?"

"More than ready. Let's do it!" Claire responded, huffing and pushing as directed. Moments later, a beautiful baby boy came into the world, screaming his head off. "Peter in honor of my brother, James for my father, PJ for short."

"Oh my God, he's so beautiful. Claire, you were wonderful. Thank you for letting me share this with you!" Jess gushed.

Exhausted and teary-eyed, Claire hugged her doula and her midwife, thanking them in turn. After they left and Peter James was positioned on her chest, she said, "Jess, I'm not sure I could've done this without you. Thank you for taking such good care of me throughout this . . . well, *journey* covers it, right?" Her voice broke.

Jess gathered them both into a giant hug and said, "Are you kidding? It was the least I could do after you saw me through my own challenges this year. We're now family, of the best kind. We've chosen to be." And with that, PJ squealed.

Later, Jess left Claire to get some sleep. She let her mind drift to the birth stories of her own children. Happy events both, Arthur, the proud father, showing them off. But then she reminded herself that he had been nowhere near the labor room for either child. He had popped up so often to leave, to chat with the doctors he saw coming and going at the care station, that she had finally sent him away so she could get the job done. *Amazing how you forget the pain of childbirth*, she thought.

She hoped someday soon she would forget the pain of her separation and divorce. But, starting now, she vowed to forget that damn missing picture and close the silly chapter about airline rewards miles. Arthur would always be the father of her children, and she would not do anything to break that tie. She knew better. Time to move on.

◇◇◇◇◇◇◇◇◇◇◇◇◇◇◇◇

"George, you're a gem!" Jess praised Diane's boyfriend after checking his work on the baby car seats he had installed in both her car and Claire's.

George closed the door on Claire's new SUV and said, "I'm glad you talked Claire into getting a more sensible car. I wouldn't have been too excited about putting a baby seat in a Jaguar."

"Yes, and it helps that she has garage space to keep the Jag. I'm not sure I would've been able to convince her to make a full switch!" Jess laughed. "Thank you for doing this. I might have been able to figure it out, but it would have taken me more time than I have at the moment." She remembered how many times Arthur had laid claim to a fix-it or setup job around the house, only to put it off for so long that she had usually ended up furtively enlisting a handyman.

"No problem. Piece of cake. Diane is at Claire's house, laying in supplies, so it was no big deal for me to do this now. Let me know if anything else comes up. I'm happy to help." George walked to Jess's car and opened the hatch. "Do you want me to take this box into the house for you, as long as I'm here?"

Jess peered in to see what he was looking at. "Oh. I almost forgot about that." She saw the storage box she had brought back from the lake house, filled with her stuff. She knew she had to go through it, but this wasn't the day. "Nah, leave it there. Maybe I'll have some downtime at Claire's to look through it." Jess gave him a warm smile. "Diane is so lucky to have found you, and she deserves you—actually, you deserve each other. Thank you again, George."

He beamed, his crinkly blue eyes showing his appreciation, and Jess almost cried. She seemed to be on the verge of tears almost as much as Claire was, but it felt different from a few months earlier, her weeping then the result of a domestic order changing irrevocably. Fortunately, that was over now.

Jess planned to take a few days off to get Claire settled in, so she had used Claire's three-day hospital stay to get her work in order. Dan was a great guy and very supportive, but even so, she always covered her back at work, overachievement a survival skill she had learned as a child.

Once the car seat was installed, Jess drove to the hospital, picked up Claire and PJ, and took them home. Diane met them at Claire's front door, which was decorated with a bright blue WELCOME, PETER JAMES sign and balloons just inside the threshold. Leave it to Diane to see to the extras that helped keep life worth living.

"Claire, you look amazing! Mothering must agree with you," Diane said. Claire was sporting glowing skin, shining eyes, and a never-ending smile.

"And this little bundle of a boy. He's very handsome. Hello, Peter James. Welcome home!" Diane took the baby from the car seat and, once Claire was steady on her feet, handed him back to her for the important first trip into the house.

Claire cooed, "Here we are, PJ. Home sweet home," as she carefully watched her footing up the steps. She stopped just inside the door and snuggled her son. "It's you and me, babe, and we're gonna be so happy here." She looked around and added, "Oh my God, it's so good to be home. I can't wait to sleep in my own bed!"

Once Jess had lugged in all of the paraphernalia and they had caught their breath, she sniffed and said, "Diane, what have you concocted here while you were waiting for us to arrive? I smell marzipan or almond. Could it be?"

Claire laid a sleeping PJ in the bassinet in the great room, started for the kitchen to put on the kettle, and then noticed the table was already laid for tea. She walked over to Diane. Tears spilling down her cheeks, she gave her a long hug and sobbed unabashedly. After crumpling into an armchair at the table, she managed, "I totally hit the jackpot this past year. A poor decision on my part to have unprotected sex led to a pregnancy that I never knew I wanted. Now, here I am, surrounded by incredible friends and a gift from the heavens that I will cherish forever. It's almost too much to take in. I'm overwhelmed."

"And exhausted and hormonal," Jess added. "You'll soon regain your equilibrium and be the brilliant and powerful executive you were born to be. And you'll do it with us supporting you." She rounded the table and gave Claire a hug before sitting down.

"And now, Diane, you haven't answered me yet. Is it almond tart or a marzipan kringle? Do we need to feed the young mother here something else first, or go straight to the . . ."

Diane didn't answer; she simply went into the kitchen and returned carrying a salad of farro, spinach, mangoes, and black beans, followed by a steaming cranberry-almond tart to serve as a centerpiece that would motivate her diners to eat their vegetables first.

Diane lifted her glass of sparkling apple juice. "To Claire and Peter James, a loving duo forever, through sleepless nights, dirty diapers, temper tantrums . . ." They all clinked glasses and laughed.

The first week with PJ was certainly a change of routine for both Jess and Claire. Peter James was a good baby, but even good babies need time to adjust to the world. However, Claire seemed a natural mother and was so enamored of him that she happily let Jess wait on her hand and foot.

When not busy fetching and carrying for Claire or oohing and aahing over PJ, Jess had time to reflect on helping her friend with the challenges that accompanied a surprise mid-life pregnancy. Jess met many comments fraught with guilt, regret, and fear on Claire's part with what she hoped was calm, rational, realistic input. Focusing on Claire and the new life she was preparing for also saved Jess from going over the edge into despair about Arthur. That, and needing to stay solid for Beth and Tom.

Claire knew well that the stigma of having a baby alone could harm her rise up the corporate ladder, which was still filled mostly with men, some more enlightened than others. Jess remembered Claire's humorous take on how a conversation might go in the anteroom of a corporate boardroom between a powerful CEO and a headhunter pitching Claire for a position. "So, what's the story on her personal life? She's raising a baby on her own?"

But even the potential negatives couldn't outweigh the irresistible value of creating her own family. Claire had been hungry for a child without being able to identify it. Seeing her with PJ now, Jess could tell how powerful that emotion was.

It helped that Claire had been proactive in sorting out her situation with PJ's father. After making her decision to keep the baby, she had done the right thing: she had flown to Belgium and discussed the situation with him. In recounting the story later for Jess, Claire said she wasn't sure who was more relieved: the Belgian, who was already engaged and didn't want his fiancée to know anything about his indiscretion, or Claire, who happily left the country with a good understanding of his family medical history and a signed document relinquishing his paternal rights.

◇◇◇◇◇◇◇◇◇◇◇◇◇◇◇◇◇◇

Jess looked hard at the storage box from the lake house, now tucked away in a corner of Claire's porch. She couldn't justify more delay. The nanny, Melody, would start tomorrow, and PJ and Claire were down for a nap. If she took time to go through it now, she could sort out the items she no longer wanted and drop them off at Goodwill. No sense bringing into her own house stuff that would remind her of things she should forget. She made a cup of tea and headed for the den, grabbed a few brown bags, and began to sort.

Pretty easy to decide she wouldn't be keeping the out-of-style shorts, faded shirts, and worn jackets. And the boots had seen better days. She steeled herself not to let her mind wander to the good times she and Arthur had enjoyed on the Katy Trail, along the banks of the Missouri River. Not so easy to decide if she should keep the commemorative poster of the Lake of the Ozarks Festival. But where would she put it?

The books. She had left the ones that she thought Tom or Beth might someday choose to read at the lake. She had been undecided about the volumes on wildflowers, so she had kept them. Now, looking at those she had hauled home, she wondered why. She had read them, so it was time to share. Maybe Claire or Diane? If they didn't want them, she would save them for the library book sale next summer.

She teared up when she spied the pottery vase that Beth had made for Mother's Day and the woven basket that Tom had crafted under the guidance of the local resort owner. "I'll keep these forever." She put an end to her tears with that declaration and gently moved them from the box. As she did so, she saw the lake house guest book. She thought now that it was almost like a time capsule; it memorialized that era for her. She was glad that Arthur didn't want it. Bearing an old-fashioned leather binding with ribbon ties, she knew the book chronicled entries from guests through the years, as well as jottings about the weather, wildlife sightings, and assorted gems. She took a sip of tea and argued with herself about whether she should tempt her emotions by opening it now.

No real decision made, she halfheartedly paged through it. She especially loved Tom's cryptic notes about the lake, which he entered devotedly every time he was there. "Gray on gray." "Silver with dark blue overtones." She smiled. She recognized the names of friends who had enjoyed the lake house with them over the years—grateful comments from city folk awed by the beauty of the setting.

This would be a great keepsake, if she didn't get too morose about it. She sighed. She was about to put it in the "keep" pile, when she noticed the scrawl of a name she couldn't read, following a lengthy comment: "So thankful we had the winning bid. A great spot! Deer came around morning and night to check on us, and the sunsets were gorgeous. Romantic evening on the deck. Thank you, Dr. Steele, for your generosity."

Winning bid? She looked at the date: two years ago, August. She looked at the scrawl again. She was stumped. She emptied the remaining books from the box and started putting the items from the "keep" pile back into it. She now had a pile of books to offer to her friends, two bags of clothing for Goodwill, a bag of books for the library sale, and a much lighter box to lug back out to her car.

As she hoisted the storage box up and headed to the door, she connected the dots and stopped in her tracks. Winning bid. The golf tournament sponsored by the university hospital medical staff. Arthur had donated a long weekend to the silent auction for the benefit of the hospital's cancer-research program. It all added up. Someone had made a generous donation and used the lake house for a weekend. She remembered it vaguely but not who had won. She put the box down by the door and walked back to the den to look more closely at the name. Doctors and their signatures. Never easy to read. Oh well.

She had just finished loading the big box and bags for Goodwill and the library in the back of her car, when a van turned into Claire's driveway. A young man got out of the driver's side, after checking his packages, and headed for the door. He removed his earphones and approached her. "Is there a Jessica Lawson at this address?"

"I'm Jessica Lawson, but this isn't my residence. Who is it you're looking for?"

"Then I'm looking for you. I was redirected from your office to this location. I was told I'd find you here, and that if I didn't, I should keep looking until I did." He handed her a large manila envelope and a clipboard to sign.

"Thanks for finding me, I guess." She smiled at his grin. Jeez, she'd been out of the office for only a few days. What now?

Chapter 28

◇◇◇◇◇◇◇◇◇◇◇◇◇◇◇◇◇◇◇◇◇◇

Jess closed the car hatch and headed back toward the house with the envelope as a VW Bug with floral decals on both side doors pulled alongside her car in the driveway. A young woman moved smoothly out of the car and extended an arm.

"Hi, I'm Melody Barnes. You must be Jess," she said in such a well-modulated, sweet voice that Jess wondered if her parents had waited until she could talk before they'd named her. Not only that, but Jess couldn't stop looking at her hair, and then, when she was over the shock of seeing a bright purple stripe of short hair cut on a diagonal on one side of Melody's head, she couldn't stop looking at Melody's clothes. She was dressed in a bright pink camisole nearly covered by a black silk blouse, and a rainbow-checkerboard short skirt with purple leggings and matching bright orange clown shoes.

Before Jess could respond, Melody quickly went on, "You probably think I'm kinda freaky. But I just got off work at the puppet theater, and this is how we were dressed for the finale. I wanted to keep this appointment and didn't have time to go home and change into other duds. Sorry to surprise you."

Jess realized she must have been standing there with her mouth open to have received such an explanation, so she quickly responded, "I'm happy to meet you, Melody. Claire is so excited that you'll be helping her out. Come on in."

Jess peeked into the nursery and found Claire awake and nursing PJ. She greeted Melody with a huge belly laugh, which threw poor little PJ off the breast, and then they all started to laugh, except for PJ, who whimpered a bit until he was repositioned.

"Melody's a playwright for a puppet theater, and she sometimes works as a puppeteer. I know we talked about her as an artsy type who was looking for steady work, but maybe we never really got into much detail about her. Given that I'm such a right-brain, focused person, I wanted PJ to have a presence from another sphere with him in his early developmental stages. And, as you can see, I believe Melody will add a lot of color to his life!"

"I've worked as a nanny off and on for four years," Melody said. "Babies are my specialty. He's adorable. Can I stay a bit and hold him when you're done nursing?" she asked.

◇◇◇◇◇◇◇◇◇◇◇◇◇◇◇

Claire walked Melody to the door and found Jess checking the giveaway stack in the porch. "I see you've been busy."

"I have. I went through that big storage box from the lake and sorted stuff. Do you have any interest in any of those books? No big deal if you don't."

Claire smiled. "If I ever have time to read again, you mean? What's that?" She pointed to the envelope. "Are you getting stir crazy?"

"I'm not sure what it is, but they tracked me down from the office. Guess they miss me." Jess raised her eyebrows, tore open the envelope, and scanned the contents. "Unbelievable." She sat down and read more closely.

"What?"

"It's a contract offer from Dick for that project he wants me to do. I more or less told him off when he asked me about it." Jess paused and looked up at Claire. "And not only does he want me to do it, but the terms are open. He wants me to name my price."

"Wonderful! Another reason to party. We're celebrating your last night sleeping over with takeout. I just ordered pizza; it should be here in fifteen minutes."

Just then, PJ's cry alerted them. Claire was halfway to the bedroom when the crying stopped. She returned, happy for a few extra minutes of freedom.

Diane arrived before the food. She carried a bottle of wine into the den and presented it to Jess with a flourish and a warm squeeze. "It's time to recognize another new beginning. For Jess, the divorce is final. Ready to move on to the next chapter?"

The doorbell rang, pulling Jess out of her momentary lapse. "Wow, it's hard to believe this one's really over."

Diane went to the kitchen for a corkscrew and glasses, and Claire answered the door for the delivery guy and then called out to Diane, "Hey, a glass for me, too! I'm more than ready to have my first wine after childbirth!"

Jess exhaled deeply and let her mind unwind. Between PJ's birth and getting him and Claire settled at home, she hadn't had much time to think about the true end of the marriage. How did anyone really celebrate the end of a marriage, anyway? The papers were finally signed, so the deed was done. At best, it was bittersweet.

The marriage had ended long ago for Arthur. She found it ironic that he could leave his family as easily as he had because he knew how strong she was. She had developed that strength early in life to help her survive the melodramatic failure of her parents' marriage and their inability to shield her.

"You didn't tell me it was final," Claire said. "When? And, more important, how are you feeling?" Claire carted the pizza box to the dining room table, and Diane reappeared with tableware.

"The news from my attorney came in while you were still in the hospital. Arthur finally let go of the air miles." Jess paused. "More easily than I expected, actually. And that was the last issue."

"OK, that's the 'when.' But how are you feeling?" The question stopped time, like suspended animation in a movie. Diane was poised to pop the cork from the wine bottle, and Claire was just about to sit. They waited.

"Relieved, but sad, too," Jess started slowly. "Not sure how I'll feel about it next week or next month. It's somewhat anticlimactic right now, yet still a bit raw," she finished with a trembling lip.

Claire and Diane both started toward her, but Jess headed them off. "But right now, I'm very excited about having my first taste of wine in a week." She picked up her glass and held it toward Diane. "Pop that cork, please!"

Over dinner, Jess told them that Tom and Beth were going to Portland for Thanksgiving. "I know it's what Arthur wants. The kids are hesitant to go, but they did agree. And I'm not going to make it hard for them, any of them." She looked up at her friends and found the support she needed.

"But they'll be here for three full weeks over winter break at Christmas. Yay!" Jess cheered. Claire and Diane joined in. "Claire, is there any chance you would consider having the christening when they're home?"

"What a brilliant idea! Yes, let's do that."

"They're both so excited to meet PJ!"

As Jess was drifting off to sleep during her last night in Claire's guest room, she was pleased that she had kept her cool when she had shared the news that the kids wouldn't be with her for Thanksgiving. Just as well that there had been so much activity. It kept her mind occupied. Her last thought was of the envelope sitting atop her suitcase.

Chapter 29

◇◇◇◇◇◇◇◇◇◇◇◇◇◇◇◇◇◇◇◇◇◇◇◇

"This is amazing." Dan whistled as he finished reading through the short contract from Dick and looked up at Jess, who was enjoying her breakfast while awaiting his reaction. They had agreed to meet at their local diner, Peter's, on Jess's first morning back, as she had no groceries in her house.

"Isn't it? Am I missing anything? I read it as a full engagement offer with terms to be defined at my pleasure. Right?"

"Yes, that's my read. And it's consistent with what he told me when he couldn't get to you last week. This guy is clearly intent on having you act as his agent in all things related to this new clinic-acquisition strategy. Pretty incredible."

Jess pushed her plate away and took a minute to register her first day back after a week of life-altering events: the birth of PJ, the official end of her marriage, and then this totally unexpected new opportunity with Midwest Health.

"By the way, I hope you didn't mind that we had it sent out to Claire's house. Dick was pretty insistent on getting it to you ASAP, and"—Dan grinned—"I guessed you might appreciate the special attention, especially coming from him."

Jess chuckled. "Life is crazy, isn't it? I had written this off, you know. No way I thought he'd be man enough to allow me to call him on his behavior and then turn around and make an offer like this."

"Well, are you going to do it? This is the man who required you to promise to keep your husband in town in return for staying in your job on the merger team."

"Same man, yes. But, as you remember, I didn't play his game then, and now I get to set the rules in a new game. Of course, *we* are going to do it! I'm not going to pass this up. This is a chance to take Midwest Health to a new level, to strengthen the combined system. Absolutely!"

Dan laughed. "Ms. Lawson, I daresay you sound quite excited about this. I wasn't sure you'd go for it."

Jess laughed with him, then got serious. "I'll be watching this very carefully. My terms will include an opt out at the slightest concern on my part. But the chance to make this system stronger is too tempting for me not to take the risk."

"Sounds like the right way to approach this, Jess. What would you like from me?"

"I'm going to take today to draft my proposal. I'd like to go over it with you tomorrow so we can consider what staffing and resources we need and get the right legal protection in line. Then we'll meet with Dick later this week and tie it down. I'd appreciate it if you could be at that meeting."

"An extra set of eyes and ears?"

"Yup, you got it."

∞∞∞∞∞∞∞∞∞∞∞∞∞

After their lunch, Jess anticipated that Dick would be a bit wary of how she would handle the meeting to formalize their agreement, so she changed things up. He had never seen her as her most charming self.

"Dick, I'm so excited about working on this project." She reached out a hand in greeting and smiled warmly. "Dan has graciously served as a second pair of eyes for me and reviewed my proposal, and I asked him to be here to make sure you know how seriously we take this opportunity." She read Dick's obvious surprise at Dan's presence as confirmation that he was aware Dan was there as a witness, not a coach.

Dick nodded at Dan, then zeroed in on Jess. "Jess, I'm thrilled we've been able to reach an understanding of how to approach taking Midwest to the next level." He led them to the furniture grouping at the end of his office suite.

After some gratuitous discussion about the artwork on the walls, Jess pulled a folder from her briefcase. "I know your attorney has reviewed and signed off on the papers, so here are the three sets of originals, with objectives and timelines, for your signature."

Dick took the papers and scanned them quickly. "Of course." He retrieved a pen from his suit pocket, then handed the signed papers to Jess, who looked him straight in the eye and said, "Thanks for the work, Dick. I look forward to a strong partnership." To herself, she said, *And if you blow it, you'll hear about it and I'll walk . . . But I hope you don't.*

"As do I, Jess." Dick grinned at her. "Strong personalities make the best partnerships. Glad we got there."

The meeting over and the papers signed, Dan and Jess agreed on the team from the firm, and she chose Cindy to be her lead legal advisor.

The following week, Jess took Cindy with her to the first meeting with Midwest Health's outreach staff to get the ball rolling.

"It's good to see you again." Jess offered her hand to Sam Hirsch, the medical director, as she and Cindy entered the conference room at Midwest Health's medical staff executive offices. Sam was an old hand in academic circles at the U. He had played the role of kindly uncle to many fast-trackers over the years. Jess remembered Arthur confiding in her that Sam had taken him aside and counseled him to control his temper a time or two. She wondered now if he had ever counseled Arthur on managing his personal life.

"And you, Jess. Great to have you back, helping us out with this new venture." Sam winked at her and shook her hand. She noted the portraits of previous deans hanging in a row on the conference room walls. How little had changed here in the many months since her last meeting at the medical school—and how much had changed in her own life.

Roy and Matthew, the outreach staff members whom Midwest Health had provided to support Jess, stood and shook hands with her and Cindy and introduced themselves. Roy was a tall, wiry lad wearing a brown suit and a purple tie. Matthew had somewhat shaggy blond hair and wore rumpled chinos and a blue blazer. Their backpacks were stowed on a chair in the corner. They appeared to have a combined age of fifty. Jess wondered whether these two pups, who looked to be fresh from business school, knew what this business was about. It was up to her to decide whether to use them or bring resources from her own firm for this phase of analysis.

Sam left the room to ask Gloria, his assistant, to send in coffee while they all took seats around the conference table.

"Ms. Lawson, Ms. Newton, I'm going to show you a map of the medical practices that currently refer patients to Midwest Health, and then Matt will walk you through our prospect list, also mapped." Roy pointed to their individual packets and the PowerPoint presentation he was starting. Jess noticed that his hands were a little shaky as he began, but he spoke with growing confidence as they moved through the material.

"Roy, I see you've graphed the number of patients referred over the past three years from each of these medical practices. But have you accounted for demographic changes in each of these geographic areas as well?"

"Yes, ma'am. If you take a look at Table Five in your materials, you can see how we controlled for the population shifts." Roy spoke quickly and glanced at Matthew to comment.

"A very good question, Ms. Lawson. We know that these areas are shifting quite a bit. If we move to the prospective maps, you'll see how we anticipate marketing opportunities for the new, combined Midwest Health." Matthew shot out of his chair and used his laser pointer to indicate the data Jess had asked about. "If we're able to successfully market to the first of the practices noted here, we project a worst-case scenario of two hundred new patients."

They spent the next hour discussing the data; both the quality and the presentation of the analysis were spot-on. After a quick break and private conversation with Cindy, Jess said, "Let's see what you have on the university side. Are the data as specific?"

Roy and Matthew seemed to deflate. They looked at each other, then at Sam, who turned to Jess.

"Nothing?" Jess thought this must a joke, but the blank stares told her otherwise. "Really?"

"Really," Sam finally said. "There's nothing, and we've looked. Each department of the medical school has its own way of keeping track of referrals, but there's no central repository. No data set has ever been attempted."

"Hmm . . . interesting," Jess said. "But not the end of the world. That's where we need to start. Roy and Matthew, your first task will be to come up with a plan to get this information from each department and put it in some usable form. Sam, I know I can count on you for this."

"Yes, whatever you need." Sam seemed pleased. Jess knew that he had Dick's direction to support her with all the resources at his disposal, including political influence with the medical-school departments.

"Great. We can't prioritize until we have that information. Roy and Matthew, I'd like to hear how you intend to proceed, and how long it will take, by Friday. That gives you two days. Does that work?"

At this request, Roy and Matthew puffed up considerably and smiled broadly as they replied jointly, "Yes, Friday works."

"And, guys, you can call us Jess and Cindy, not Ms. or ma'am, OK?" Now that the boys knew they were still in the running to support her project, Jess was certain she would get what she needed by Friday.

When Sam walked them out of the conference room and into the anteroom, his administrative assistant, Gloria, was in a heated telephone conversation with someone.

"No, that will not do," she said. "This arrangement has been in place for the last five years, and you can't just cancel our reservation. We have a deposit down."

"Oh, poor Gloria. She's having problems with the golf course venue for the annual medical staff tournament," Sam explained. "Event management is no fun, let me tell you. Doctors are fussy about their events and not easy to please." He shrugged.

Jess listened as Gloria was pushing her argument, and something clicked into place. "So, your office handles these events?"

"Yes, we do."

Jess made a mental note to ask Gloria who had won the silent auction bid on her lake house two Augusts ago.

◇◇◇◇◇◇◇◇◇◇◇◇◇◇◇◇

November was nearly over. Thanksgiving came. Diane's parents invited Claire and PJ, along with Jess, to join them for the holiday, which turned out to be the best possible distraction. This was the first holiday she wouldn't spend with her children. If she hadn't had the trip to Goodrich on the docket, or the opportunity to spend Claire and PJ's first family Thanksgiving with them, she knew she would have spent the day going through photo albums of her own family holidays past, imagining what they would be doing if this were a normal holiday, before the divorce. She missed her kids and her past. She wasn't sure what a new normal was yet.

Fortunately, there was one child in the mix today. It was PJ's first big trip, and he cooperated beautifully, taking some of the pressure off George, who was still getting to know Diane's parents. On the car ride back, Claire shyly asked Jess, "Can I adopt them as honorary grandparents?"

"They're wonderful people, aren't they?" Jess thought back to the many hours she had spent in refuge at Diane's house while growing up. "I suspect they would love that. Diane and George may not have children, and it's obvious that her parents were delighted with PJ. Maybe you should feel it out with Diane, and then invite them to the christening next month."

"That's a really good idea. I suppose I should get that planning started. So far, I have my church date set."

"Oh, and the christening gown. Beth and Tom agree with me that we would like you to use the same gown that they each wore. It's a family treasure, and beautifully hand-embroidered. And we'd like PJ to be an honorary family member." Jess had been watching Claire from the driver's seat and saw her dab at the tears trickling down her face.

"Oh, Jess, that's so generous of you. Honestly, I'm not sure how I deserve all of this. But it feels wonderful. I feel like I have a family." She wiped away her tears and then added, "Are you sure it will fit PJ? He's growing like crazy."

"Not to worry. Both of my babies were robust." Jess laughed. "PJ will look divine in it."

"So, how's Thanksgiving going in Portland? I saw you take a call just before dinner. Going OK?"

"Well, it's the first time Beth and Tom have ever eaten Thanksgiving dinner in a restaurant. And Arthur has them staying in a hotel, which was a surprise for them. Evidently, the lady of the moment is out of sorts about something, so they're not meeting her this trip."

"That sounds weird."

"To them as well. But they love their dad and are happy to see him. That leaves lots of time to see Portland, I guess."

"You sound pretty calm about the whole thing."

"My kids are incredible, and they'll get through this. Only a few weeks until they'll be home. I can hardly wait. I'm already planning parties for the holidays so that we can keep things bright and happy—a neighborhood open house, a party for Tom and Beth's friends who'll also be home from school—and we're very excited about the christening. Let me help you plan the after-party?"

"Sure. But, Jess, are you sure about all this activity?"

"You know, I love to have parties, but I've given it up for the last few years. It's fun for me. But yes, I need to keep busy right now. I'm still buying time for my broken heart."

◇◇◇◇◇◇◇◇◇◇◇◇◇◇◇◇◇

When Diane joined forces with Claire on the issue, Jess knew she couldn't fight them. They had signed her up for a dating service that did some matchmaking for professionals who were too busy to devote the time themselves. This one catered to those who didn't go in for the bar scene and could afford something beyond an online service.

Jess couldn't really trust her feelings about dating yet. On the one hand, she realized Arthur was way ahead of her in his recovery and that she should catch up already; on the other, she didn't think she could cope with casual dating. Her feelings were still too raw. Still, she had reluctantly agreed, mostly for her friends' sake.

The day of her first date, she parked a couple of blocks away from the restaurant in order to walk undetected for a bit. Taking a few deep breaths and telling herself she had survived worse, she propelled herself through the door.

Fortunately, she was not the first to arrive. She was shown to a table where Kevin, her date, was already seated. He half rose to greet her, smiled, and took her hand. "It's nice to meet you."

She tried to get a good look at him while they talked about the restaurant. How did one judge the looks of middle-aged men? She tried to imagine him as a twenty-two-year-old but couldn't. Gray, thinning hair, bifocals, clear eyes with deep circles underneath, a thin physique, maybe six feet tall. No instant jolt of electricity signaled love at first sight.

"I'm a banker and always have been. I graduated from college in business and have worked for only two local banks since then."

Well, if he was trying to sell her on consistency and reliability, that was the ticket. Did that matter to her? She didn't really know.

"I work in the health care field," Jess said. "I'm divorced"—she cringed as she realized this was the first time she had said that aloud—"and I have two college-age children."

Jess didn't see a ring mark on his finger, then remembered that his profile mentioned two divorces, the most recent only a year earlier. *Can't blame a guy who keeps trying.*

They ordered. He was not a conversationalist. Jess decided to play this like a business lunch and made small talk about the food, the weather, hobbies. He didn't ask much about her at all. He did like to talk about golf. A lot.

"Do you golf?" he asked. When she shook her head no, he gave her a subtle shoulder shrug in response. Evidently, "no golf" was a nonstarter. She wondered if that was a deal-breaker, and whether she cared.

"I love to travel, mostly adventure travel," Jess said. "My favorite trip was to a rain forest in Costa Rica. I really liked the hiking and whitewater rafting there."

"Wow, that's too far for me, and way too hot," Kevin responded. "I couldn't stand to sweat that much." Then his eyebrows shot up and he looked at her with what Jess imagined were his bedroom eyes. "At least not while upright."

Jess swallowed and held his gaze out of curiosity, then looked down quickly at her plate. *Nope. Don't ever want to get sweaty with this guy.* When the check arrived, they each proffered a credit card to split the bill. It was pretty evident that this would be their only lunch.

As she walked back to her car, Jess wondered if she cared. She breathed deeply and said aloud, "Absolutely not." She laughed, lightened her step, and congratulated herself on having jumped the first hurdle. She realized there was a lot to think about if she wanted to date. Although she surprised herself with the realization that she did have preferences after all; she knew Kevin didn't make the cut.

On her way home that night, she stopped by Diane's, and from there they called Claire. Both friends expected a report, so she didn't disappoint them. As they peppered her with questions, she laughed lightly and teased them that Kevin would be a better match with Claire, since his golf game was so important to him.

"Jess, remember, we signed you up for six months of dating opportunities," Diane said. "So don't get disenchanted after the first one. It's good for you to get out and meet new people."

"And don't say you'll be too busy with your fancy new project, either," Claire added. "We're watching you."

Diane walked Jess out to her car after the phone conversation with Claire. "I see a new glint in your eye, my friend, one that I haven't seen in a while. You've come a long way."

If it hadn't been so dark, Jess would have looked in her car mirror for evidence. She was pleased that her friends had pushed her to take this next step on the road to recovery. She never would have done it on her own.

She drove home slowly. What exactly *did* she want, now that she was single again? She found herself whistling for the first time in years. She looked out both windows to see if anyone was watching. What kind of amazing life could she conjure up? And did she dare?

◇◇◇◇◇◇◇◇◇◇◇◇◇◇◇◇

The holidays came. The neighborhood open house was a hit. Longtime relationships bridged the changes in her family life more easily than Jess had expected. Someone suggested that the party become an annual tradition. When Mariel told Tom and Beth about Trixie and how Jess had taken her in for several days, they insisted on meeting her, and after they reappeared from a visit to Mariel's house, Beth said, "Mom, Trixie's really sweet. Why didn't we ever have a cat?"

"Well, your dad's allergic to them, and we didn't want to cope with the schedule a dog requires." Jess remembered the one summer when Beth's lobbying for a pet had been in full swing, but it hadn't lasted and they hadn't succumbed to the pressure. Parental unity, at least that time.

Beth and Tom were delighted with PJ, and the christening was a high point for everyone. Jess had searched out the baby pictures of each of her kids wearing the christening gown, and Claire had the photographer take similar shots of PJ with the kids so that they would all have a keepsake of the day and their new relationship.

On Boxing Day, Arthur surprised Jess with a late request. "I know this isn't planned, but I'm hoping it's OK with you if the kids spend New Year's with me at the lake." His voice was almost timid on the phone.

"Where are you now?" Jess asked.

"Still in Portland. I didn't want to pressure you by showing up. But I'd like to fly in on Wednesday and pick them up. I haven't spoken to them about this yet."

Jess processed this information. Arthur wasn't rushing her. Ushering in the new year at the lake was a family tradition. He was politely asking if he could keep that going. Memories of cross-country skiing, hot chocolate, and candle luminaries on the path to the house crowded her mind. She felt a pain in the palm of her hand and saw her nails pressing into her skin.

She breathed and relaxed her wrist. "Well, I don't know what their plans are, but we have nothing firmed up together, so, yes, go ahead and talk to them."

With that, Jess spent New Year's Eve watching old movies with Claire and toasting at ten p.m.

"Is this a hard night for you?" Claire asked while pouring champagne into their glasses.

"I thought it might be, but I'm all right. It's been some kind of year. Thank God it's over. I'm ready to move on."

"Yeah, a year ago, who would have figured a divorce for you and a new baby for me? Amazing. It makes you wonder what will happen next year, right?"

∞∞∞∞∞∞∞∞∞∞∞∞∞

The kids returned from the lake with just a few days before they needed to go back to school. Both were subdued, and Jess knew not to pry. They huddled together in Tom's room for a while, then raided the refrigerator for leftovers, claiming they were starving.

The next day, she took them out clothes shopping for the next semester's essentials, and they stopped for dinner at a new restaurant that had just opened in the neighborhood. No memories here. After they shared a dessert, they finally gave Jess a glimpse into their new world.

"Mom, did you know Dad is thinking about selling the lake place?" Beth was near tears.

"No, I didn't."

"He didn't say that exactly, Beth," Tom said. "She hinted about it, but he didn't say that."

"She?"

"Rebecca. They're together. Living together, in Portland." Beth looked worried. "You knew that, right?"

"Yes, Beth. I knew."

"And she's not crazy about the lake house, I guess." Tom shrugged. "She doesn't even cross-country ski."

Jess's heart ached for her children. They obviously felt conflicted about how much to share about their father's new life, and she wondered how to comfort them without making false assurances. "Well, I would guess the decision isn't made yet. Did you get a chance to talk to your dad about your feelings about it?"

"No, not really," Tom said.

"It wasn't easy to talk—*really* talk—about anything. It was weird," Beth said with finality.

"And anyway, if Dad truly cared about our feelings, he'd still be here," Tom blurted, then looked away, then at his sister, whose eyes were welling up.

"Hey, you two. Look at me." Jess waited for them to oblige, then said, "It's a weird time for all of us, I know. And it's hard. But we'll find our way through it. Please know that we can talk about whatever you want to talk about at any time, and that I'll give you my best shot at a sensible answer. Right now, when the opportunity presents itself, if you feel you want your dad to know about your feelings about the lake house, you should tell him."

That seemed to be the end of the conversation, for now. Jess hoped she had at least opened a couple of doors for them—a door they could open to talk to their dad, and one that they could always open to talk to her.

When they left the next day, she knew they were flying to their separate coasts and their increasingly independent lives. If only she could protect them.

Chapter 30

◇◇◇◇◇◇◇◇◇◇◇◇◇◇◇◇◇◇◇◇◇◇◇

The holiday hiatus behind them, work started heating up again. Cindy and Jess sat at the worktable in Jess's office with files of background information on Goodmoor Family Medicine scattered about. "What's in this for Midwest Health?" Cindy asked. "With so many changes in the industry, I can understand why Goodmoor wants to take shelter in the loving arms of a large health system." She paused and pointed at the group's financials. "However, it doesn't look like the group has any financial problems to speak of."

"That's a good question." Jess took a quick study of the financial statement Cindy indicated. "I'd say the Midwest Health folks want to make sure they look inviting to the old, established practices now that they have the U in their family. They need the referrals to fill the beds, and those academic doctors don't immediately change just because of a merger. Midwest Health needs to break down any existing "town and gown" barriers to referrals. I like your question, but turn it around: What does Goodmoor need? I want to make sure we get to all the questions so we can bring any issues to the surface."

Jess pushed her chair back from the worktable and closed the file. Roy and Matthew were still working to get the overall data analysis completed so they could set priorities for their clinic-acquisition strategy, but Jess was restless and eager to start. Fortunately, Sam Hirsch had called the previous day with this promising opportunity. Since Goodmoor was interested in a relationship with Midwest Health, why not start here?

"I know it isn't much notice," Jess said to Cindy, "but can you join me for a meeting with Goodmoor later? I just found out that today is their monthly business meeting. I'd like to get this assessment going as quickly as we can. We could get started with introductions tonight."

"Yes, of course," Cindy answered. They made arrangements to meet at the clinic at six p.m., and then Cindy gathered her papers and left.

They arrived at Goodmoor a few minutes early and walked down the hall to the meeting room. A tall man with a lean build caught up to them. "Cindy, is that you?"

"Hey, Ian. How fun to bump into you. Is this where you work?"

"Yes, I'm an internist here." He pointed to the embroidered name on the pocket of his white coat. "Are you our guests from the law firm?"

"Yes. Ian Brewster, meet Jess Lawson. We're here for the meeting. I had no idea this is where you practice. Jess, Ian is a marathon runner I see all the time at meets. Are you running the half marathon for Habitat next month?"

"I am. Even if it's miserable." He grimaced.

"Jess, this reminds me, I was going to pitch you to join me, since you're a runner too." Cindy's voice grew excited.

"The course should be beautiful by the parks," Ian added. "Let's hope it's not too cold and icy."

"That doesn't sound very tempting, but I'll think about it." Jess laughed. Cindy seemed to come up with activities for her every week. "It's to get you out and about," Cindy always said. But Jess guessed it was really about encouraging her to meet a new man.

As they neared the meeting room, an older doctor, bald, with wire-rimmed glasses and a natural scowl, approached them. "Ms. Lawson?"

"Yes. Are you Dr. Personne?" She stretched out her hand for a handshake, but he didn't take it. *Maybe he didn't see it*, she thought. "Please call me Jess. Thanks for making room on the agenda tonight on such short notice. This is my legal associate Cindy Newton." Jess tried to meet his eyes, but he kept shifting the angle of his body, making that difficult. She offered her hand again, and he took it this time. "As I mentioned on the phone, our purpose in being here tonight is just a meet-and-greet so that physicians in the practice know who we are and why we'll be meeting with them. Does that still work?"

"Yes, yes, of course. Whatever gets this rolling," Dr. Personne responded quickly, still not looking at her. "I'll introduce you when everyone gets here, and then you can do what you need to do."

Dr. Personne left them, and Adam Bright, a young internist, approached Jess and whispered, "So, have you met the charming Larry Personne before tonight?" When Jess shook her head, he raised his eyebrows and said, with a sarcastic grin, "Well, wasn't that a treat?"

She was glad she had turned down Dr. Personne's invitation to join them for dinner. Much better to stay near the door and chat with the latecomers than risk having spinach in her teeth when it was time to present.

The room filled up. Jess and Cindy pulled up a couple of chairs as Dr. Personne finished his dinner and stood to open the meeting. Before he could introduce the guests, Dr. Bright remarked, "Well, Larry, looks like you've finally succeeded in getting women into the room without having to recruit them to the practice!" Several physicians snickered. Others looked ill at ease.

Dr. Personne's eyes cast daggers at Bright, but he made no response. "Gentlemen, let me introduce our guests. Jess Lawson and Cindy Newton are from the law firm that's going to consider options for us with Midwest Health. They're here tonight to describe how this will work. Jess?" He gestured for her to speak and quickly sat down. Jess wondered if the purpose of his very brief intro was to be expeditious or to distance himself from the project. He didn't look like a warm-and-fuzzy leader.

Jess smiled. "Thanks for letting us come tonight. We know you have other business on the agenda, so I'll just take a few minutes to describe what will be happening over the next several weeks. I'll also answer any questions you may have." She spoke slowly and looked at their faces to get a read.

She had their attention and continued, "At this time, Midwest Health and Goodmoor Family Medicine have each expressed interest in forming a closer business relationship. Our firm has been retained to determine the merits of an arrangement to both parties. We have deep experience in this work, and our process is tested. We're here tonight just to be introduced, but we'll interview each of you over the next few weeks. Another team, under our direction, will be conducting the business analysis and assessment of the practice as it now operates." She saw a few physicians exchange sideways glances but didn't hear any snide comments. "Are there any questions at this point?"

"How long will all of this take?" asked Ian, the runner.

"It should take six to eight weeks, depending on how quickly we can get on your calendars and complete our analysis."

There was a pause. Then a doctor who had arrived late and was still in the buffet line asked, in a loud voice, "What happens to the interview findings?" The soft clinking of silverware on china stopped abruptly, and all eyes turned to the questioner, then to Jess.

"Glad you asked. The individual findings are blinded and aggregated. With Dr. Personne's permission, we'll share them with you as a group." All eyes zoomed to Dr. Personne, who looked as if he had just awakened from a nap. He snuffled a bit but didn't answer. That put an end to the questions. Jess noted that the unidentified doctor who had asked the million-dollar question was making his way to the table with his full plate, and that Dr. Bright was staring straight at him.

Next, Cindy spent five minutes describing possible relationships that their firm knew of with other groups and hospital systems. Jess then concluded with her most important point. "Due diligence is as important at this stage as being honest about the reasons the group might be seeking a new arrangement. For instance, I would guess from Dr. Bright's statement earlier that you may be having difficulty recruiting women to the practice. There are clearly ways to respond to that challenge without a full-on merger with a hospital system. So we'll look at all of that with you."

Jess noticed a couple of raised eyebrows and glances across the table. The possible upset of any practice always caused some nervousness. She gauged this group's anxiety level to be about average. It was time to leave. The tires had been kicked and found solid, she hoped.

"We'll be moving ahead, then. Thank you so much for your time. We look forward to meeting with you one-on-one in the near future."

On their way out of the room, Jess stopped and whispered to Larry Personne, "Do you want a quick debriefing in the hallway?"

"Not necessary." *Ouch.*

As they left the room, Jess saw that the doctor who had stopped the group cold with his question was watching her closely. She had a feeling this project was going to be complicated.

Chapter 31

◇◇◇◇◇◇◇◇◇◇◇◇◇◇◇◇◇◇◇◇◇◇◇

Just as Jess was about to open the exit door, a man coming in opened it for her and Cindy. When she walked by him, he pivoted abruptly and asked, "Jess, is that you?"

She turned toward the voice. It was Jim Nathan, a colleague in Arthur's department at the U. She hadn't seen him since before his wife had died of cancer, right around the time when her difficulties with Arthur had come to a head. "Jim. Hey. Hello. Nice to see you. It's been awhile." He had aged, certainly, was more crinkled around the eyes, but he was still handsome.

"Uh, what are you doing here?" She focused and walked a few steps back to the entry where Jim waited. She thought about all the changes each had been through in the past year. There had been such reverberations in the department after Arthur's departure that Jim doubtless knew of their marital breakdown. Everybody there did.

"I'm on the Goodmoor meeting agenda. The U surgery group, now Midwest Health, does some of their surgeries, and I'm here to discuss doing more. How about you?"

"We just met with the group on a project." Jess turned to look at Cindy, who was waiting patiently. "Oh, forgive me. This is my colleague Cindy Newton."

They shook hands, and Cindy made noises about the practice, but Jim just stood looking at Jess. Neither spoke. Jess's face flushed. Finally, Jim said, "Well, I should let you two get home. It would be nice to catch up. May I call you?"

"Sure," she said, entirely too quickly. She recognized in Jim someone whose world had also been rocked and instantly felt a common bond.

"Great. I assume you still live in St. Louis Hills?"

"Yes, but I have a new phone number." She fumbled with her briefcase and finally fished out her card and handed it to him.

"OK, then." He smiled. "I'll call you. Have a nice evening. Great seeing you again, Jess." Jim seemed stuck in place. Jess stood there too, until Cindy started walking toward the parking area.

Cindy stopped at Jess's car. "Well, that was unbelievable. What just happened? He seems quite interested in you."

"You're imagining things. Jim's just an old friend." Jess took a deep breath. She needed to calm down and think. She headed toward her car door, but Cindy blocked her, folding her arms in front of her.

"Not so fast. Is he available? Those brown eyes are something. Oh my God, this is exciting!"

"Don't be silly. As I said, he's just an old friend. He lost his wife awhile back, and he knows about my divorce, so he probably sees me as someone to commiserate with."

"Well, I don't buy that 'just an old friend' bit for a second." Cindy grinned.

Jess searched her pockets and briefcase for her keys, avoiding Cindy's intense gaze.

◇◇◇◇◇◇◇◇◇◇◇◇◇◇◇◇◇◇

The next night, Jim Nathan called to set up a coffee date for that Saturday afternoon. Jess found herself looking forward to the opportunity to talk with someone who was also just recently single, then chided herself for considering their circumstances similar. Jim had lost his wife to cancer; Jess had lost her husband to another woman.

But it wasn't hard to find common ground. They met at a popular coffee shop midway between them. Casually dressed in jeans and a flannel shirt, Jim seemed years younger to Jess. Conversation came easily. They talked about rattling around in a big house alone, sorting through business matters to become single after more than twenty years of marriage, parenting college kids through disruption—all shared challenges. They laughed about how their longtime couple friends weren't sure how to deal with them now, as if they had grown horns or something. "We just no longer fit the mold, I guess," Jim said.

Then Jess changed the mood. "Jim, I'm sorry I didn't reach out to Sally when she was sick. I didn't know."

"She was very private about it, and it went fast. A blessing, really." He looked away briefly. "The end was rough. It's been tough for all of us, but the kids are amazing. We'll make it."

"I'm sure you will, but still, I'm very sorry for your loss." As she reached out and squeezed his arm, she thought about how difficult this would be for his kids, Marty, a college junior, and Joanna, the same age as Tom.

"And, Jess, I'm sorry about what happened with you and Arthur."

"What do you know about what happened?" Jess couldn't stop herself from asking the question.

"Jess, a third party never knows what goes on in a marriage, but after Arthur announced he was leaving, I heard the stories about him and the graduate fellow he was evidently involved with." He held her gaze. "I'm sorry it happened."

"Thanks. Me too." Relief swept over her like a wave. Hearing him state the situation so clearly and without hesitation seemed to make it less extraordinary, cut it down to size. "But things do happen sometimes." She smiled at him.

Before they parted, they laughingly agreed to stay in touch regarding matters of complexity in newly single circumstances. As she walked to her car, she said to herself, *He was really easy to talk to—wow. That was actually pleasant. I could definitely do that again sometime.*

◇◇◇◇◇◇◇◇◇◇◇◇◇

That Monday, Jess launched the project team for the due diligence of the business side of the Goodmoor practice. There was a lot to organize, and it was a busy, productive week.

By the weekend, she was happy to spend some downtime with Claire and Diane and to cuddle little PJ. It wasn't too chilly, and the pavement was clear, so Diane and Jess decided to get a run in before breakfast at Claire's.

"Do you think she'll have the coffee on, or should we give her a quick call?" Diane asked while keeping to her stride on their closing turn around the Soulard Farmers Market.

Jess laughed heartily. "Diane, my dear, it's nearly nine a.m. on a Saturday, and Baby PJ has been up for hours. He may even be down for a nap. Believe me, his mother has definitely made coffee. And I brought some eggs and goodies from the bakery for us. They're stowed in the car, so we should be set."

Not only did Claire have the coffee ready, but she had also poured water and juice and was dressed and looking alert when she met them at the door. "Thank God. I really need some adult conversation. I fear baby talk is my default now, and I have to get fit for the office soon. Oh my God, did you bring cinnamon rolls?" The aroma was heavenly even before Jess put them in the oven for a quick warm-up. "How am I supposed to regain my figure with these temptations?"

Jess smiled. "Not to worry, Claire. I'm going to scramble some eggs and tomatoes, and we'll share the rolls. But life is sweeter with a treat now and then, and you deserve it. Besides, I know you missed these."

"You do know me well, Jess. Thank you. I love being taken care of." They walked to the kitchen, and Claire got out the tools to make eggs and chop tomatoes.

PJ woke up with a sweet whimper, and Diane got to cuddle him for a while before he insisted on eating.

"So, what's going on in the adult world? Anything new?" Claire asked innocently.

Jess felt herself flush. "I think I've been asked out on a date," she blurted out. "And I'm not sure I like it."

Simultaneous shrieks from both Claire and Diane resulted in a blushing Jess's having to dish the details. She told them how she had bumped into Jim, a former colleague of Arthur's, who was now a widower. They had met for coffee to catch up, and it had gone OK. They had caught up on kids and their lives and offered each other condolences of a sort. And—

"OK, OK, let's get to the date part," Diane interrupted. "What did you say?"

"Well, I haven't really said anything. There's a message on my phone that I haven't responded to yet, and—"

"What was the message? What did he say?" Claire asked in eager but muted tones as she began to nurse PJ.

"Dinner. He wants to take me to dinner. Doesn't that sound like a date? You know, I'm out of practice, so I'm not sure. But it feels like it. A date inquiry. And it makes me uneasy. It's different than just catching up over coffee." Jess could scarcely admit her nervousness even to her best friends.

"Hallelujah and praise the Lord! Yes, my dear, it sounds like a date!" Diane was giggling like a schoolgirl. "The fact that it makes you nervous makes it the best kind of date! And you're definitely going!"

Jess concentrated on chopping tomatoes and whipping eggs.

Claire joined in the giggling, and she and Diane dug out the details about Jim's past and present, marital history, professional life, and, of course, physical appearance.

Jess answered all their questions formally, as if she were being deposed in court, but then hesitated before describing his looks. "He's handsome and friendly, even chatty." A softness came into her voice, and her friends both caught it.

"Honey." Diane took her hand and looked her in the eyes. "Of course you're nervous, but he seems like a nice guy, and it's only dinner. He sure sounds like a better dinner date than the golfer would have been."

"Ugh, don't remind me. I would never have had dinner with the golfer. The fact that I *want* to have dinner with Jim is what makes me nervous." And with that, they all laughed, and kept it up while Diane told them a few horror stories about dates she'd had over her many single years before she'd found George.

Jess promised to respond, to accept. But she knew she would put it off awhile. She needed to get comfortable with the notion of a "date." What did that even mean nowadays?

◇◇◇◇◇◇◇◇◇◇◇◇◇◇◇

Putting it off was easy. Jim was booked the following weekend, and that gave Jess time to think about it. Although she'd first felt drawn to Jim as a fellow victim of midlife single status and enjoyed the comfortable conversation they'd shared over coffee, something about how this evening was planned changed it from a continuation of the coffee date into something else. When she said she would meet him at the restaurant, he insisted on picking her up, even though it was a long drive for him. And his choice to go out on a Saturday night at eight made it sound like a date for grown-ups.

By the night of, she had decided to enjoy herself—*I'm a grown-up, after all.*

"So, tell me about this restaurant; I don't know it," Jess said during the drive.

"I don't either, and I was hoping it would be new to both of us. It just opened three months ago, and I've been wanting to try it but didn't want to go alone." He turned to smile at her.

Jess chuckled to herself when she realized she was his dinner date in order to avoid one of the complexities of being single: solo dining.

The northern Italian food was excellent, but the service needed work. It made for an excellent backdrop to keep the meal slow and mellow as Jess and Jim shared news of their lives before they'd become acquainted as spouses thrown together occasionally at the university.

"I had a great childhood. My parents are still living and are super. Dad is a sports fanatic and follows all of the Florida teams. Mom's health is a bit compromised by arthritis, but she's still a ball of fire." Jim laughed. "They were great about helping with the kids during Sally's illness. Joanna adores her grandma."

"So, you met Sally in high school?"

"Yes. She was my one and only girlfriend, and then my fiancée at the end of college at Duke, and my wife by the end of med school at Penn."

"Wow, that doesn't happen very often."

"No, it doesn't. We were lucky. Sally became an elementary school teacher and worked until we had kids, then stayed home to raise them."

Jim motioned to a passing waiter for the promised basket of bread, then added, "Hey, I've been doing all the talking. What about you, Jess?"

Jess took a sip of wine and contemplated how different Jim's childhood and marriage were from her own, and how much she was willing to share.

"Well, I'm afraid mine was not a storybook childhood. My parents were not well matched—abusive, actually. They were volatile to the extreme, and their divorce was excruciating for everyone. I left home during my senior year and haven't been back since." Realizing how tragic it sounded, she hastened to add, "But circumstances sometimes cause bold action. When I left with a full scholarship to Harvard, I excelled at school, got some counseling, and poured myself into my professional life."

Jim took it all in without batting an eye. "That's a lot to overcome. It takes incredible strength of character to get through that." He poured her another glass of wine. "How does Arthur enter that picture?"

"Professionally, of course." She laughed. "We were partnered to lead a medical team in the jungle and found we were compatible."

"Hmm . . . So, this was much later, then?"

"Yes—clearly, after I thought I was over my childhood trauma and well on my way career-wise. I certainly didn't expect to marry him. But we came to recognize the benefits."

She looked up and found Jim listening with such care that she felt safe, and continued, "In many ways, it was a very successful partnership, but in other ways, it was not a successful marriage." She paused. "I'm not sure I knew what a good marriage was, actually. And I think I stayed in mine longer than I should have, trying to avoid the pain of divorce and family dysfunction that I experienced."

Jim reached over and took both of her hands in his. "Jess, you did nothing wrong. And it's over now."

She felt a sudden jolt in her body and then allowed herself to be enveloped in the warmth of his touch and the empathy in those sincere brown eyes.

When the waiter came by to tempt them with dessert, they ordered tiramisu to share, and coffee. Jess had a moment to reflect on how much she had just revealed to Jim, and how easy it had been. She couldn't remember ever having talked to Arthur with such honesty. But somehow she didn't feel exposed.

Over dessert, Jim lightened things up with funny stories of his trip to a Gators game with his son and father over the past weekend. It was after eleven when they left the restaurant.

On the drive home, Jess's mind leaped to what it would be like to be driving home to one house, as a married couple, after a Saturday night out with Jim. She shut down that thought quickly, but not before she realized that Jim and Arthur were total opposites.

Back at Midwest Health, Roy and Matthew had made such strides in data analysis that they were now working with a preliminary prospect list. Jess spent some time with the duo over a couple of beers to conquer the generational divide. They were now speaking the same language and gelling as a team. She had given Dick Morrison a thumbs-up on the pair weeks before, and they were ready to move ahead.

She wished things were going as well with Goodmoor. The project was moving, but slowly. Larry Personne couldn't get his people to stick to the original schedule, and Jess had talked to him about it more than once. Finally, he had dialed back clinical time to get the last few physician interviews scheduled. That was not a popular move with the group, but it didn't take long for Jess to realize he was not a popular guy. Meanwhile, her team at the firm was working on the audit.

"Thanks, all of you. Sorry it got so late. Thanks for staying on task," Jess said as the due-diligence meeting concluded.

She stood to stretch and start picking up, when she noticed that Cindy was still in the room. "This is always the most interesting part of a project like this: figuring out how the group ticks. I'm still not sure about this one. What about you?"

"Well, I'm not sure we're getting the straight scoop from the doctors, and I'm still not sure what's motivating them to want to cozy up to Midwest Health. That's the same question I had when we started this. But listen, I didn't hang around to talk about that. What about your date with Jim?"

Jess looked up quickly and slowly started for the door.

"C'mon. I need to know how it went! I hope you finally had this date that's been on the horizon forever. Tell me you didn't cancel." Cindy was up now and heading to the doorway.

"Oh, that. It was fine."

"Fine?"

"Well, it probably helped that we delayed it for a while, since he and his son were traveling over a long weekend and I was busy with stuff, too. By the time it actually happened, I wasn't really nervous at all. We had a nice dinner and may do it again some time. We'll see."

Just then, Cindy got a phone call and they both left. Jess was glad for the interruption. Her spine tingled to her toes. She wondered how much casual speculation she would have to deal with while she sorted out her own feelings about the date—both dating in general and dating Jim in particular.

Chapter 32

⟨⟩⟨⟩⟨⟩⟨⟩⟨⟩⟨⟩⟨⟩⟨⟩⟨⟩⟨⟩⟨⟩⟨⟩⟨⟩⟨⟩⟨⟩

Jess was enmeshed in paperwork at the office when she took a call from Diane, who, along with George, was babysitting for PJ until Claire got home. "George is having such fun with the baby that I'm on kitchen duty."

Jess felt a wave of nostalgia as she pictured Diane and George preparing dinner and fussing over PJ. She had always loved that cozy feeling in her family's house when dusk brought house lights on, furnaces kicking in, and everybody talking at once to share the day's events. How she missed those moments!

Diane spoke quickly, baby noises in the background. "Jess, you sound a little down. Are you still at the office?"

"Slow down, girl. I'm fine and just finishing a few things here. Almost out the door."

"Are you sure? Why don't you join us?"

"No, no, no, I'm totally fine. You guys enjoy. And, Diane, I appreciate the concern, but maybe it's time for you to stop worrying about me."

"But it's such a habit now." They laughed.

Jess was transported back to Diane's porch swing, where the background notes of her mother's organ wafted outside as she practiced for Sunday church in the next room. Safe, nurtured, loved. Jess had depended on Diane's emotional support then and still did. But she wondered if it was fair to Diane now.

"You need to immerse yourself in your lovely romance right now—not worry about me."

"Promise you won't cross-country on me again?"

Silence, then a quick recovery, but only after Jess received the message. She knew Diane felt responsible for not having vetted Arthur when Jess had eloped after dating him for only a few months.

"Diane, I'm a big girl," she said, a slight edge in her voice. "I release you from responsibility for me. I promise I won't do anything foolish."

For a long minute, she reconsidered her plan to stay in the office for another hour or two and thought she might instead just go home, turn on the fireplace, cook a real meal, and listen to jazz while sipping a glass of wine. It struck her that maybe that sense of leisure was why she was enjoying her dinners with Jim—three now in the past three weeks. *Of course, the companionship is a good thing,* she thought. Then she wondered, would Diane approve of Jim? Diane knew her better than anyone, and when Diane had met Arthur for the first time, after he and Jess were already married, Diane had clearly not approved of him.

She stayed in the office for another hour, trying to decipher the information from the Goodmoor business office review. Floyd Ramsey, the group's practice manager, had tragically been killed in a car accident several months earlier. He had been at the helm for the past fifteen years. The interviews she'd conducted thus far indicated that he'd had a tight grip on the business side of things, and the group was confident that all was in order. But they were having a difficult time tracking the receivables, and even more trouble with insurance billing.

Floyd may have been a taskmaster, but he didn't seem to have been able to keep staff very long. She saw a handwritten note from him, chewing someone out—presumably, one of his office employees. Who signed nasty notes with such a flourish? It did seem to explain one of the reasons the group wanted to join Midwest Health. Because Floyd had been the go-to guy, the practice leaders had no clue how to do things without him. There was no real attempt to replace him, so they were relying on temporary help. She needed to sit down with Dr. Personne and try to get a better understanding of their current situation, if he knew it.

But first she needed to follow up on that internal Medicare audit. Joyce should have preliminary results this week, and that would help decipher the weaknesses they were seeing with their own friendly eyes, rather than having Medicare come in. Something didn't feel right, but she wasn't sure what it was.

She left the office to drive home and realized it was still quite warm. Spring in St. Louis was hard to beat. It could be a bit brisk, but it was always a wonderful surprise to see the start of green in the yard and the crocuses peeking out.

As she unlocked the door and dropped her briefcase, the phone rang. "Hello."

"Hi, Jess. How are you?" Jim asked.

At the sound of his voice, her heart rate quickened, yet she also felt relaxed as she responded warmly, "Oh, hi, Jim. How are you?"

"Good, good. I'm good. Actually, I just wanted to touch base. It's nice to hear your voice."

"It's nice to hear yours too. How was your day?"

◇◇◇◇◇◇◇◇◇◇◇◇◇◇◇◇

Early the next afternoon, Jess took a call from Sam Hirsch about Midwest Health's prep. "That sounds like good progress, Sam. If they could have that diagram and sensitivity analysis ready by our meeting Wednesday, that would be great. Tell Matt and Roy I'm excited to see what they've got."

She was about to hang up, when she remembered: "Oh, Sam, is Gloria there? Great. Can you transfer me to her for a minute? Thanks. See you Wednesday."

"Hi, Gloria. Jess Lawson here. I hope this isn't too much to ask, but I'm wondering if you keep records from the medical staff's golf outings over the years."

"Oh, yes. We have to keep all the records for the family history, you know." Gloria laughed lightly. "What were you interested in, Ms. Lawson?"

"Well, this is a little awkward, but you might know that Dr. Steele, my ex-husband and I, offered a weekend at our lake place for the silent auction a couple of years back. I never really knew who won and enjoyed the time there. Do you have that information in your history?"

"Should have, yes. Let me take a peek and call you back. Is that OK?"

"Of course. I appreciate your looking it up for me."

Jess walked down to Cindy's office to relay the good news and settle her nerves. She had almost forgotten that damn picture, and now that she had found an easy way to determine who had been at the same house where the picture might have gone missing, it made her jumpy.

"At our Midwest Health meeting Wednesday, we should have all the data we need to start prioritizing target clinics for them," she said when she arrived.

"Wow, that's quicker than I expected. Those outreach guys moved pretty fast." Cindy smiled.

"Yes, they did. It'll be interesting to see where Goodmoor comes in on the list."

Cindy nodded. "You're right. Come to think of it, Good-moor came to us. We didn't have to put that practice through a screen at all. Should be a good test of our matrix." Cindy got up and put on her coat. "Gotta go. Meeting in Brentwood. See you tomorrow."

Jess fought back her anxiety and returned to her office. There was a voice mail. She tensed up before she accessed it.

"Ms. Lawson, this is Gloria from Dr. Hirsch's office. I found the information you asked about. The silent-auction winner of your lake place that year was Floyd Ramsey. He's not a physician. Looks like he signed in as the office manager for Goodmoor Family Medicine. Community physician groups often fill in with office people. Hope this is what you wanted. It's really all I have in the records. Bye, now."

Jess gasped. How could that be? What were the chances that the winner of the weekend was the office manager she was learning so much about? She stood up and took a turn around her office. Suddenly, the other shoe dropped. *My God, he's dead. The winner is dead. The winner of the weekend at the lake place, who could have found my picture, is dead.* Her heart beat faster as a combination of relief, followed quickly by guilt, confounded her. *How can I feel relieved about someone's death?* She needed to get some air.

Jess checked her calendar to see whether she could leave the office. She decided to take a drop-in yoga class in her neighborhood, starting in thirty minutes—just the thing to calm her. She drove to the class, still trying to process this revelation. There was something just beyond reach in her mind, something still unsettled.

She got to the yoga studio, changed, and laid out her mat in the classroom by four p.m. The class started with some easy poses. Jess concentrated on her breathing and tried to clear her mind. Her muscles started to respond to the gentle stretches, but her brain was still working overtime. Forty-five minutes in, she finally started to relax.

Just as the instructor called for corpse pose, Jess's subconscious mind locked onto its target. It was the signature! Now she remembered why it had caught her eye. She had been going through Goodmoor office files, looking for anything that might help clarify their situation, when she had come across the scribble of a signature. It had seemed so odd that Floyd Ramsey, the Goodmoor manager, had signed the nasty note to an employee with such a flourish. And she had a similar-looking signature in her guest book from the lake house. If they matched, she would know for sure that Floyd had been there.

She fought the impulse to run from the studio as the other students near her continued lying as if dead. But the minute class ended, she would take the steps she needed to check the signatures and get the closure she needed so desperately.

She forced herself to walk calmly from the class and got into her car. She reached Joyce by phone at 4:55 and asked her to put the box of Goodmoor files in her office before she left for the day.

Jess's heart raced as she drove the five blocks to her house, dashed in, and made a beeline to the guest book. One minute later, she quickly found the page, glanced at it, and hurried back out to the car.

She made it to her office by five thirty. Almost nobody around. The box of files sat on her table. She closed the door, stood over the box, and rifled through its contents. She found it. The nasty note. Floyd's scrawl at the bottom. She took the guest book out of her coat pocket, pulled the note out of the box, and placed it next to the entry in the guest book on her conference table. She compared the writing. Could it be?

Her body trembled. She exhaled loudly. A match. *Thank God!* The man had a terrible signature, but it was terrible in both places. She sat down and concentrated on breathing normally and talked herself down. "The man who may have found the picture died in a car accident months ago—end of story. You were scared, but it's over now."

With that, she closed the box and felt her body go limp with relief that this ridiculous situation had finally been resolved.

Chapter 33

◇◇◇◇◇◇◇◇◇◇◇◇◇◇◇◇◇◇◇◇◇◇◇◇◇◇◇◇

"Is there a piece missing? Something that we might not be seeing that could explain this?" Jess asked Joyce. The billing-audit specialist had just briefed her on possible overbilling at the Goodmoor practice. Joyce and Cindy had been poring over the audit results and were not happy; their empty coffee cups and papers were strewn across the conference table after several hours of frustrating effort.

"Well, nothing in life is certain," Joyce responded. "But this is the data from their own office and covers the past seven years. Between the business manager's death and the lack of long-term employees to decipher this, it's hard to know for sure."

"Cindy, what do you think?" Jess asked, frowning. "Does it look like it could be the result of sloppy work by poorly trained staff, or does it look deliberate?"

"We need to spend more time on this, right?" Cindy glanced at Joyce, who stood up to stretch and nodded in agreement. "Maybe the next step is to see if we can tie individual staff to the incidents of overbilling. Of course, that could still be just larger-scale negligence. It's too early to point to a cause."

"OK, and in the meantime, let's keep this information among us. I'd hate to get a rumor going that could foil a deal or stop people from cooperating with this process." As medicine became more of a business, Jess knew, MDs who had spent countless years learning the science and art of practicing medicine were tempted to allow those interested in, and supposedly expert at, managing the business to do so.

"How about if I order some lunch for you two?" Jess offered, and got hearty thanks from both women. When she left the room, she called Dr. Personne to let him know she would be dropping by to see him at the end of the day. She needed to get a read from him about whether he knew of any irregularities. She would give Dan an update based on Dr. Personne's response. Dan didn't like surprises any more than she did.

Later that day, as Jess drove onto the Goodmoor lot, Larry Personne crossed in front of her on his way to his Lexus. She stopped and called to him from her car. His fingers released their grip on the door handle. He responded like a schoolkid sneaking out early. "I wasn't sure you were going to make it."

"Sorry. I didn't expect you to be finished yet. I got held up at the office." She gave him a moment to recover. She had clearly told him she wouldn't be there until five forty-five, and it was barely five thirty. "Are you available to chat for a few minutes now?"

Jess could see the conflict on his face. He responded with a weak smile, "Of course." He looked up and down the street for a moment, then said, "Let's walk down the block to Gabe's. I'll buy you a drink."

He walked slowly and without a word, but by the time they reached the bar, he seemed to recover his composure and became quite chatty.

They talked about the weather and the state of road construction nearby. He was still nursing his vodka tonic after twenty minutes, when he started in on the forthcoming St. Louis Cardinals season. At this rate, he might go on forever.

Jess looked at his ringless left hand—probably no wife at home, making his dinner. Larry didn't seem to be friendly enough to socialize with his staff, so Jess knew he was stalling. She held up her hand to refuse a second glass of wine from the attentive waiter. Time to move this along.

"We need to talk about some confusing findings on your audit. My team has spent considerable time on it now, and there are some inconsistencies in the Medicare billing that we need to understand."

He downed the last of his drink and eyed everyone in the quiet bar. Finally, he shrugged and spoke in a pronounced whisper, as if sharing a secret. "You know, Jess, I don't really know anything about any of that."

"Larry, Floyd was an experienced manager, at the peak of his career. I can see why you delegated so many of the practice's business dealings to him. But as head of the group, you were ultimately responsible for what he did. How did you two interact?" Jess wasn't about to let him off the hook easily.

Larry jiggled his keys in his coat pocket. "Floyd handled everything. His death was such a blow to all of us, although of course I realize now that we should have been . . ." He hesitated and looked away. "I should have been more involved in the business aspects of things."

Jess kept at him. "So, did the two of you have regular meetings and review the financials?"

Larry looked away.

"Often, a head physician pulls the manager and the lead billing person together to review the past month. Were you doing that or anything like that on a routine basis?" She wasn't sure how much further she could push him.

"All right, all right. I wasn't involved. I wasn't interested, OK?"

Continuing to look him in the eye, Jess waited for the payoff.

"So, what do you want me to say? That it was my responsibility and I let everyone down?" His voice rose. A guy at a nearby table looked their way. Larry fought to regain control. He slumped. It took him some time to gather his words.

"You know, when I was a kid, I realized I wanted to help people stay well and make them better if they were sick. I never once wanted to run a business. Managing people, keeping everyone happy in the group, keeping track of the business side of medicine—none of that is my interest or my forte. I can't believe I've been doing it this long, and now that Floyd is gone . . . well, I realize how little I've actually done. And how much I've let my group down." His face drooped.

"Is that why you initiated a potential arrangement with Midwest Health?" Jess asked softly.

"Yes. Once Floyd was dead, I was clueless. I could see I had no understanding of our finances, much less of how to move forward to replace him. I panicked."

"It's very difficult to lead a group in this day and age," Jess said. "Many have succession plans in order to avoid burnout for any one group president, or they rotate roles so that everyone understands the business and is basically forced to evaluate decisions that affect their livelihood." She slowed down to let that idea sink in before asking, "Did you ever think about stepping down and allowing new leadership to emerge?"

"Yes, yes, I did." Larry made eye contact again. "But nobody wanted the position. I failed to groom a successor, and I failed to learn and perform my job as president. And now the group has pinned its hopes on Midwest Health."

He paused and took a deep breath, exhaling slowly. "I'm so grateful that Jim Nathan mentioned a purchase by Midwest Health as a possibility. We've got to make this work." His voice stronger again, he slapped the table with the heel of his hand. "It has to work."

"Oh, so Jim Nathan suggested this to you?" Jess asked carefully, covering her surprise at this new information, a shiver tickling her spine.

"Yes. Jim's been our senior surgical consultant for years and knew how we had depended on Floyd. He gave me the idea and set up the first meeting with the outreach guy at Midwest Health. And now here you are to do the assessment. There's been no forward movement by the practice in the several months since Floyd was killed in that car accident. I'm really just treading water until this deal gets done." He looked spent.

Jess responded with a lukewarm smile. "Larry, I appreciate your sharing this with me. I can understand what a great burden this is for you. But knowing this will help us sort things out."

She noticed he was following her every word, and she needed more. "It would help if you could tell me if there's anyone on the billing side who you think has a better handle on the history of the group's financial practices."

His posture straightened as he thought for a moment or two, then, in a stronger voice, said, "Alice Lang may be able to give you a better understanding of the business than anyone there now. If I call her, she might agree to meet with you. She retired early, and we were all sorry to see her go, except for Floyd. She was one of the few people he didn't appreciate. I could never understand that."

They left Gabe's at nearly seven p.m. and walked in the growing darkness back to their cars. Larry said little but seemed more at ease. Jess made soothing conversation but wasn't sure he deserved it at this point.

She drove home slowly, thinking about Larry's demeanor during their meeting and how humbled he had seemed while admitting his failings to her. If he believed he had nothing to offer, that could explain how distant he had been during the assessment process. But something still didn't feel right. She made a mental note to find Dan immediately in the morning. And what exactly was Jim's role in all of this?

Chapter 34

◇◇◇◇◇◇◇◇◇◇◇◇◇◇◇◇◇◇◇◇◇◇◇◇◇

Jess didn't sleep well that night. She was up later than usual, thinking about her strange meeting with Larry Personne and about what they might find out next about the practice. Now that she had a big project for Midwest Health that she could get excited about, she hoped it wouldn't be derailed before it even got started. She cringed to think about the possible havoc it would wreak on the physicians in the group if, indeed, the financial irregularities were found to go beyond simple negligence.

She was just out of the shower when the phone rang. *Too early for anything good*, she thought, but then her mood shifted 180 degrees when she realized who the caller was. "Beth! What a wonderful morning surprise. How are you?"

"Pretty good, Mom, but crazy busy. I miss you, though, and so does Tom. We have a proposal for you. Remember how my theater group is going on tour? We'll be in Chicago next weekend, and Tom would like to fly in for the performance, but only if you come too!"

They both whooped and then laughed at sounding so much alike. Jess remembered that at one point Beth hadn't been sure she liked being similar to her mom in looks and manner, but now they both found it amusing.

"You're kidding. How and when did you two come up with this scheme? And when's the performance?" Jess thought back to the trip she and Arthur had taken to Stanford a year earlier, when Beth had mentioned this theater tour and Arthur had dodged the question. She again felt the fool as she remembered his duplicity during that time. She wondered if he knew about this trip. If he did, would he feel left out?

"Our group's at the University of Chicago on Saturday night. Tom can get into Chicago easily Saturday morning. This was really his idea. Is it OK with you?"

"Is it *OK* with me? Are you kidding? I'm thrilled! I'd love to spend time with you two!"

"Good." Beth's voice dropped, but the pace quickened. "Mom, I've got to get to class, so I'll e-mail you later. And of course Tom's using the miles you gave us for Christmas, so you should go ahead and make your own flight plans, OK?"

"What? It's unbelievable that you kids planned this on your own. I'll book my flights this morning. Can't wait to see you!" Jess smiled as she congratulated herself for going after the air miles. What better use than this? Arthur might not feel that way, but she no longer cared.

"OK, Mom. Gotta go. Love you." And, in a rush, Beth was gone.

The buzz from the phone conversation kept Jess smiling all the way to work.

When she arrived at the office, she found Cindy chatting with another attorney in the hallway. She greeted Jess with a sly smile and followed her toward Jess's office, where the door was unlocked and the lights were already on. *That's funny,* Jess thought, hanging up her coat and heading toward her desk with her second cup of coffee. A floral scent led her to a huge bouquet of flowers on her conference table.

Cindy joined her, still with her sly smile. "What have we here?"

"It's not my birthday, and Beth just called to arrange a weekend trip, so I don't know why she'd also be sending flowers. But hey, let's take a look." Jess unwrapped a beautiful bouquet of tulips, forsythia, and red buds to oohs and aahs from Cindy.

She located the card: "Looking forward to Saturday night. Jim." Jess got tingly from her scalp to her toes and knew she must be blushing.

Cindy looked over her shoulder to read the card and uttered, "Ah—the romance is on. I knew it. Excellent!"

Just then, Dan entered the room. "Good morning, ladies. Jess, you wanted to see me right away. Is this OK? Wow, beautiful flowers!"

"Aren't they?" Cindy quickly took the card from Jess and placed it under the vase. "Morning, Dan. I was just leaving. I'll check back with you later, Jess." She turned to give her friend one last glimpse of that same sly smile.

Jess kept the warm glow to herself and recovered quickly. "Dan, hey, thanks for making time. I wanted to give you a heads-up about the Goodmoor practice assessment. Do you need more coffee?" Dan shook his head.

They settled at her desk. "You know we aren't very far along with this," she said, "but I'm getting a bad feeling about the audit findings. I could be off base, but I don't think we want any surprises here, so let me tell you what we're finding and what it may mean. You remember Joyce, our billing expert?" Jess swiveled her chair so she could get a glimpse of her flowers.

"You mean Joyce, the human miracle who knows how to sniff out inconsistencies?"

"That's the Joyce I mean, yes. Her team has completed their internal audit, and while they worked on individual pieces, she pulled it together and reported on it to Cindy and me yesterday. Lots of issues. I'll stop short of calling it overbilling right now, but I can tell you that all three of us were concerned enough to keep it close. We'll have just Cindy and Joyce do the next review, testing for patterns, staff involved, et cetera."

"OK, good." Dan's body language remained relaxed, but his brow had tightened a bit as he slowly considered this information. "What about the docs? What do they know?"

"Well, I had an odd meeting with Larry Personne last night. He says he doesn't have a clue about anything on the business side. Floyd, the business manager, took care of all that. Unfortunately, that manager was killed in a car accident several months ago, and Larry admitted that he's been, in his own words, 'treading water until this deal gets done.'"

"Hmm," Dan mused. "You and I have certainly seen our share of overtaxed doctors wanting to dump the business to go to a staff job somewhere. Is it more than that, do you think?"

"It could be. He seems desperate, and I want to find out more about why." Jess thought of the physicians in that practice who were victims of this incompetence. Was Larry Personne really just a pawn himself? Her cell phone rang. She took it from her bag, silenced it, and put it on the desk within easy reach.

"So, anyway, we're going to go deeper to see what we can find. I did at least get Larry to give me the name of someone who's now retired but who may have some history on the billing side. There's just no bench strength in that practice with this Floyd fellow gone. It's a shame."

"OK, sounds like a plan." Dan stood up and exhaled. "Well, I guess this is why we do these exhaustive assessments. We clearly want to know what's going on before we represent anything to either client about any potential arrangement." He stood. "Where did this Goodmoor referral come from again?"

Jess's heart stopped, but she didn't miss a beat. "From their consulting surgeon at the university hospital, now Midwest Health." She registered a quick nod from Dan, and no questions, thank God.

Opening the door to leave, he said, "I assume Cindy's in this loop so she can advise on the legal aspects if we get in deeper, right? Is she doing well?"

Jess smiled warmly and nodded. "She's on top of it, and totally up for doing it right. Cindy's a talented woman. Up for partner soon, I hope?" she teased lightly.

She walked him out and slipped over to her conference table. She had intended to play with the angle of the vase of flowers so she could see them from her desk, but somehow that didn't seem right now.

◇◇◇◇◇◇◇◇◇◇◇◇◇◇◇

It was Jess's regular night for a massage and a pedicure. Her friends had talked her into this indulgence during the months leading up to the divorce, and she had kept the monthly routine as a treat for herself. On the drive to the spa, she reflected on how her troubled night had given way to a surprisingly good day: a wonderful trip conjured up by her children, and flowers from Jim. That was very sweet, but now she had to let him know she couldn't have dinner on Saturday night.

During her massage, she briefly considered the Goodmoor business and Jim. She wished she could rule him out of any involvement there. Then she let her mind wander a bit to what he had in mind for Saturday night. A little longer wait would make it all the more interesting. She smiled. They had time.

Her body was sore, and she felt as limp as a ragdoll when she got home after the massage and poured a glass of wine.

Just as she gave herself over to a growing sleepiness, the doorbell rang. *Odd*, she thought. It was after seven p.m. She turned on the porch light and opened the door to a smiling Jim.

"I hope I didn't startle you," he said, standing there with his hands in his pockets. One look at a slightly flustered Jess, and he added, "I guess I should have called first."

Dressed in leggings and a hoodie, her bright red toenails shining, Jess realized her hair must still be a mess after the massage. She regained her poise and smiled slightly. "Hey, you just surprised me. I'm not used to unexpected company after dark. Come in."

"I'm sorry. I wanted to talk to you in person, not on the phone, so I took a chance on just dropping by."

She gestured toward the living room. "Would you like a glass of wine, or any other kind of drink?"

"No, thanks. I can't stay." He stepped into the entry, looking boyishly sheepish, his hands still in his pockets.

"The flowers are beautiful. That was sweet of you. How did you know that I love that combination of spring blooms?"

"Wonderful. I didn't know, but I do now, and I'll remember."

Jess smiled. "You know, I'm feeling really appreciated right now. I had a good day, and I realize how many good things and people I have in my life right now."

"Well, I hope you won't take me off your list of admirers when I tell you that I have a complication concerning Saturday night."

"Oh," she said. "Really? So do I. What's your complication?"

"My daughter, Joanna, called and said she was feeling a little low, thinking of her mom's first birthday since her death, and wondered if I could fly out to her and spend the weekend. She and Sally were so close. I wish I'd thought of it myself. I need to go." His brown eyes searched hers for a response.

Jess could feel her heart open for this parent helping his child through a heartbreaking loss. "Oh, Jim, of course you do. Grieving her mother's death will take some time, probably a very long time. And you're a good father to help her with that. It's absolutely the right thing to do."

"I knew you'd understand, but I do feel bad that I won't see you." He gently took a loose strand of her hair, put it behind her ear, and reached for her hand. Jess felt her long-lost libido kick in as the soft touch of his fingers sent flutters all the way to her toes.

"Now, what's *your* complication?" Jim asked.

"This is an odd coincidence. I just heard from Beth this morning that she and Tom will both be in Chicago this weekend for Beth's theater troupe's performance, and she asked me to join them. So I was just going to call you to tell you I can't see you Saturday night."

Jess saw such warmth in Jim's brown eyes that it made her think about how nice it would be to curl up with him right then.

They laughed, and then, after a pause, he cleared his throat. "Jess, do you think maybe we could schedule a weekend away as a rain check?"

"I think that sounds lovely."

Jim took her other hand and drew her to him, and she melted into his arms.

◇◇◇◇◇◇◇◇◇◇◇◇◇◇◇◇

Jess hummed softly as she sat in the coffee shop, awaiting her four thirty p.m. meeting with Adam Bright. She used the time to reschedule a few things on her calendar so that she could have a weekend away with Jim. Claire and Diane were merciless in their teasing, and Cindy was trying to pry details out of her every day. The only downside of having these glorious friends was the transparency of her life. *Well*, she thought, smiling to herself, *some things will definitely remain private.* Her mind drifted to the romantic weekend Jim was planning for them. Was it too early to sleep with him? She wondered how well Adam knew Jim. She wondered how well *she* knew Jim.

When Dr. Bright arrived, she flagged him down. He greeted her with a businesslike handshake as they headed for the line to order. She was curious about him. Medium height, with Harry Potter glasses and a sincere, somewhat boyish demeanor, he looked harmless enough. She wondered what had prompted him to challenge Larry Personne the first night she'd met the group.

"Thanks for coming to my neighborhood. I have parent duty at five thirty and have to pick up my son at his friend's house. This works better for me than driving across town during rush hour."

"Not a problem. It's fun to get out of my everyday routine now and again. I take it you live here in Maplewood?" Jess asked.

"Yes, we've been here for five years now. We chose it for the house, the good schools, and all the wonderful bike paths and parks."

Jess nodded, and they retrieved their drinks and returned to the quiet corner where she had been sitting. She started off with a reminder that whatever he told her would remain confidential. His first questions surprised her.

"How far along are you in the interviews? What have you learned so far? Any early conclusions?"

"Well, actually, we've had some trouble getting many of the doctors scheduled. Of the fifteen we plan to interview, you're only the fourth, so I don't have any results or conclusions yet. Do you have any idea why the doctors might be reluctant to talk to us?"

"Hmm, I'm not surprised," he said slowly, seeming to weigh his words carefully. He looked her in the eye. "You've been around the Missouri health care scene a long time. I did a little research on you."

Jess smiled. "I would expect nothing less from you, Dr. Bright. Is there something you'd like to know about my background specifically?" It was so easy to search someone's profile these days. She was sure he hadn't had any difficulty finding out about her. Larry Personne had certainly reviewed her résumé. Maybe he had shared it? She took a sip of her drink and let Adam consider his questions.

"No, you checked out. You've got a very impressive track record. I'm glad you're the one working on this." He met her eyes again and leaned in a little, as if to share a secret. "So, do you *promise* I can take you at your word?"

Jess put her pen down by her notebook. "I promise."

He folded his napkin and placed it under his drink, then said, "OK, here goes: I don't think anyone believes what they say will matter. It hasn't yet. Personne is totally clueless, and Floyd was an autocratic jerk. We don't even know how the practice is being managed now. The doctors think that the Midwest

Health acquisition is inevitable. Those who are talking to me think of it as an unknown but probably a good thing. But a lot of them are waiting to see what happens before they make any personal decisions."

Jess noticed that Adam's face had flushed. She slowed him down by asking a couple of questions. "Tell me about your own experience with the practice. Did you try to get involved, learn about the business aspects?"

"Yes, I was a very eager young doctor when I arrived five years ago. I had a dream of making a start as a clinician in a well-respected practice and then eventually helping to shape a new health care system. There's no way physicians starting out today can ignore the changing health care environment. We'll either shape it or inherit whatever others shape." He took a sip of his coffee and checked his watch before continuing.

"I had the audacity to want to learn from Floyd: how things worked"—he counted off on his fingers as he continued—"how the revenue came in, how the insurance contracts were negotiated, how we hired staff, how we determined where our patients should be hospitalized." His voice now had an edge. She noticed his shoulders tighten as he added, "I was hungry to learn every aspect." He rolled his eyes. "What a joke! I was totally shut down."

"How exactly were you shut down?"

"Floyd cut me off at every turn, saying, 'Your value to the practice is clinical, not administrative.' He used flattery to tell me that any old guy could manage a practice but that only the best and brightest could take care of patients. He conspired to keep information from me. He ran things so tightly that all of his staff were forewarned not to give me the time of day." Adam put his hand on his left leg to stop it from jumping.

"When I appealed to Personne, he backed Floyd up, then got me involved in peer review as a way of using my keen clinical talents in an administrative capacity." He sneered.

"How did that go?" Jess could tell that this interview was therapeutic for Adam, and she was all ears.

"Surprisingly, I enjoyed it." He loosened up and smiled for the first time. "And I've learned a lot about dealing with my fellow clinicians that way. I think I'm pretty good at it. But about two years ago, I was ready to try something new. Personne tried to appeal to my experience in this area to keep me busy and committed to it. And, of course, my colleagues had become reliant on me to do the job. So I more or less gave up on forcing the issue." He sighed.

A blast of cold air came in with a loud bunch of kids who were slow to close the door. Jess pulled her sweater tightly around her. "Adam, why do you think Larry Personne and Floyd Ramsey didn't want you to get more involved?"

"I don't know. At best, it may have been a matter of 'if it's not broke, don't fix it,' though that's surely shortsighted. And at worst"—Adam swallowed hard, his eyes darting around the coffee shop—"maybe they didn't want anyone else to know what they were doing."

Jess registered his hesitancy, then used the momentum by asking, "Was anyone else wondering what was going on, trying to get involved?"

"Not really. You know, most doctors don't really care much about the practice details if they're making decent money and the patients keep coming—much to our discredit, I think, but it's true. Nobody really came to my rescue when I made a stink about recruiting more MDs, especially women. It would mean fewer dollars for everyone for a while. But c'mon—that's so necessary for growing a business, or at least for having a good airing of views about the future of the practice." He paused. "I guess I just got tired of being the squeaky wheel." He glanced across the room. "And I didn't want to be the next Sloane."

"The next Sloane, as in Dr. Sloane?" Jess now knew the name of the doctor at the board meeting who had inadvertently cut off any further questions when he'd asked about what would happen with the interview findings.

"Yes, but you didn't get that from me. I'm not going to talk about that." He put his hands out to signal a stop. "Ask Sloane about his experience trying to shake things up. Let me just say, it was a cautionary tale."

"OK, I will." Jess wanted to be sure. "So, Larry Personne never solicited help from any of you, after Floyd Ramsey died, to help sort things out?" She flashed back to her meeting with Larry when he had presented himself as the vulnerable leader with no willing help from his group.

"No, he didn't." Adam exhaled as he spoke, appearing relieved to have this off his chest. "And, as you might expect, that wasn't because I didn't offer."

Jess returned a weak smile and sat silently for a moment, letting Adam's words sink in. His story certainly conflicted with what Larry had told her.

Who was telling the truth? She remembered her own recent experience with duplicity, wondering what was true and whom could be trusted and how the churn of that time still echoed in her. She could empathize with this young doctor, trying to get involved, yet never gaining any traction. "Wow," she finally said. "What do you want to see happen here, Adam?"

"Frankly, I'm glad it's coming to a head. I'm intrigued with whatever might come from a Midwest Health connection. But if that doesn't work, I've already made some overtures. Even if I have to leave this area, I'll go where I can actually do what I've wanted to do from the first—get involved in helping shape the future of health care." He looked at his watch again and started to gather his things to leave.

"I'm so grateful for your candor," Jess said. "Let me assure you that your eagerness to get involved in practice issues and the future of health care is admirable. I'm just sorry that you were 'shut down,' as you describe it—such a waste for you and for the practice. Too few young doctors have the desire and drive to get involved, and here you are!" She smiled at him.

When he stood to leave, he asked her to keep him in the loop if there was anything else he could do. "I will, Adam. And one last thing. Do you remember a woman named Alice Lang who worked in the business office?"

"Yes, I remember her. She was actually very nice and tried to explain a few things to me, but Floyd came down hard on her and stopped that. I think she retired shortly afterward. He was really annoyed if anyone crossed him. What a jerk. Terrible how he died, but he was the epitome of a control freak."

After Adam left, Jess thought about how many practices would praise the Lord for a young guy like him. Then she checked her calendar and noted that she was scheduled to interview Dr. Sloane in a couple of weeks. None too soon.

Chapter 35

◇◇◇◇◇◇◇◇◇◇◇◇◇◇◇◇◇◇◇◇◇◇◇◇◇◇◇

The much-anticipated getaway got off to a bumpy start. Jim was called in on a complicated case, and they were late leaving town on Saturday.

"Sorry about this. I really wanted to get an earlier start," Jim said when he picked her up. He smiled as he held the door for her and watched as she settled into his car.

The wait hadn't helped her nerves. But once she saw Jim, her mind released thoughts of *Should I be doing this?* and relaxed into a pleasurable, tingling sensation as his eyes focused only on her. "No problem. Augusta is just a couple hours' drive; we have plenty of time." She had to think hard to remember the last time she had been in the passenger side of a car, and she truly could not recall the last time someone had opened a door for her.

She saw Jim's stash of CDs and sorted through them. "Wow, you're a jazz man for sure. These are amazing. Should we listen?" Jess found some of her favorite musicians' names among his collection: Scott Joplin, Duke Ellington, Charlie Parker, Ella Fitzgerald.

She put on a John Coltrane CD. "I didn't know this about you. Keep driving. I'm in heaven." She chose several to play, Jim nodding at each. She pulled the last CD from the box, felt a tremor, and dropped it. Miles Davis. Years were erased in seconds as she remembered her early days with Arthur and their nights with Miles.

She shook it off. Nope. No memories of Arthur allowed this weekend. And no shop talk, either. She didn't want the Goodmoor difficulties to loom large, so she resisted the temptation to bring up the practice just to hear what might be top of mind for Jim.

It started to rain. The windshield wipers held up for a while, acting almost as a metronome for the music. The swooshing gained momentum as Jim changed the wiper speed to keep up with the rain, which fell harder and then turned icy.

"Mixed precipitation: my favorite driving challenge. At least we made it out of the city traffic first." Jim squeezed her knee before putting both hands firmly on the wheel.

Just as they were making headway through the late-winter sleet, chatting and singing along with Jim's sizable music collection, traffic stalled on the two-lane highway. Jim turned the wipers off, and they were cocooned in a crystalline world filled with the sound of ice pellets stinging car metal. The Missouri River bluffs were barely visible.

"Romantic, huh?" Jim grinned and leaned in for a soft kiss. The high pitch of sirens caused them both to jump back into position and added to the soundtrack of Wynton Marsalis. Jess got the giggles. No way this man could be involved in something sinister at Goodmoor. Or was that wishful thinking? She needed to find out for sure. But how?

Jim got out of the car to see what was happening and returned with a report. "Well, fortunately, it's a police siren, not an ambulance. A car hit a deer, and there's a four-car pileup ahead, but no injuries."

After waiting thirty more minutes for highway patrol to arrive and direct traffic, they were both getting punchy.

"Not the best luck for our getaway." Jim stopped drumming his hands on the wheel and glanced over at Jess. "I hope you aren't taking this as a sign."

She laughed, and he joined her. "Are you worrying I'm getting cold feet?" She couldn't help but think of the temper tantrum Arthur would have thrown by now. He didn't like it when things didn't go his way. She marveled at how Jim had kept his cool throughout. "You do keep a girl guessing—that's for sure."

Finally, the disabled cars were removed and traffic began moving in the open lane. They dropped their bags with the owner of their bed-and-breakfast at seven thirty and made it to the restaurant in time for their eight o'clock dinner reservation.

Jim took her hand and followed the hostess to a candlelit corner table. "Wasn't exactly how I planned it, but here we are!" He pulled her chair out for her.

"And what an adventure we had!" Jess smiled broadly, setting aside any misgivings. She had decided on a plan to get to the truth, but not tonight.

The server came with a bottle of wine from Mt. Pleasant, one of the local wineries, that Jim had called ahead to reserve. His brown eyes twinkled in the candlelight as he toasted their evening. "To our love of jazz and our getaway."

The mixed precipitation had stopped by dinner's end, leaving a glossy sheen on the boulevard trees and benches on the downtown Augusta walkway.

They held on to each other on the icy sidewalk and made their way to the only bar still open for a nightcap, before heading back to the B and B.

By then they were better friends, soon to become lovers.

◇◇◇◇◇◇◇◇◇◇◇◇◇◇◇◇◇

"So, *New York Times* in the breakfast room now, or save it for later, after our hike?" Jim asked when he came in with two mugs of steaming coffee on a dainty little tray, looking for a spot to put something down in the overdecorated, overstuffed room. Bric-a-brac was everywhere. Desperate but chuckling, he put the tray on the bed, where Jess still lay sleepily, wrapped in a sheet.

"Hey, it's Sunday morning," she said suggestively, feeling quite lovable and hopeful. "Our first Sunday morning together, I might add. Maybe we can just snuggle in here with our coffee and the paper. What's the hurry?"

Jim did not miss the invitation. In a series of exaggerated comic moves, he threw the heavy sham and quilt from the arm-chair and table, primly situated the tray on the side table, and threw himself at her, pulling her to him, preparing to ravage her. "Next time I make arrangements for a romantic getaway, please remind me not to book a fussy B and B, and to closely review things like Sunday checkout time."

"You're kidding." She pushed him away. "Really? We have to check out now? What time is it, anyway?" She squirmed out of his arms and toward the bedside table to find her watch.

"Eleven ten. Checkout was at eleven. They've held break-fast for us until eleven thirty, and they're holding a *New York Times* for us, too."

"Oh my God, I can't believe it. Did you know it was this late?" She jumped out of bed and grabbed her glasses. Fully dressed, Jim stood by without moving a muscle, enjoying the show as she cast about for her clothes and pulled herself together.

◇◇◇◇◇◇◇◇◇◇◇◇◇◇◇◇◇◇

Not until she tried to go to sleep that night in her own bed did doubts about Jim resurface. She should have waited until morning to check her e-mail and let the afterglow of her getaway lull her to sleep. Instead, a message from Joyce about their lack of progress on Goodmoor's billing problems reminded her of the unknowns she had yet to investigate. She hoped Jim wasn't involved, but she couldn't be sure of anything just yet. Had the practice made fraudulent financial gains? If so, had he played a part? Her mind spun with questions, until, finally, she drifted off.

Chapter 36

"We know you're busy getting ready to fly to Italy for Liliana's wedding, but could you handle a girls' dinner at Claire's Wednesday night? Or we could bring dinner and PJ to your house and help you pack? We miss you."

Jess smiled as she listened to Diane's phone message. *Yeah, right*, she thought. *They miss me, but they really want to know how my weekend went.* Well, they deserved a bit of fun, having carried her through some very rough spots. But she would have to respond later. She had a more pressing matter on her mind. She walked down to Cindy's office to see if she was free earlier than they had scheduled to meet that morning.

Cindy was just finishing a meeting. Jess saw Dan's office door open, so she ducked in for a quick greeting.

"How goes it?" he asked. "Getting Goodmoor sorted out?" He turned from his desk as she entered. "Can't be too horrible. You look very cheery."

"Well, still sorting, I'm afraid. But I should be able to brief you later this week before I leave town. And"—she smiled proudly—"I *am* cheery. My kids and I are taking a trip to Italy for a wedding."

"Wow! That sounds like fun. Someone close, then?"

"Liliana's the daughter of a dear friend, Vincente. She came to nanny for us when the kids were young, and we've stayed close. This trip will work pretty well with school breaks. We've been looking forward to it for the past year."

"Time flies, doesn't it? I can't believe Tom is almost through his freshman year in college. I remember his high school graduation party—seems like yesterday."

"Yes, they grow up so fast, and this year has been a challenge. But they're doing well." She paused, thinking about her own growing-up years and the central drama of her parents' divorce. "You know, Dan, my kids really have it made, compared with how I had to make my way, as did you." She squeezed his arm. "But I feel like they get that and are good people, caring and loving, and both will be OK. I'm very proud of both of them."

"No small credit to you, Jess. You've raised great kids." As if encouraged by her mood, he braved the next question. "I assume Arthur will be there—what's up with him these days?"

"Oh, yes, he should be there. He's pretty settled into the Portland community now, and he says his research is going well. So I guess he's fine." She felt her smile fade a tad, and she didn't meet his eyes as she spoke. She didn't want to discuss Arthur anymore.

She stood and took a quick look down the hall. "Looks like Cindy is free now. I'll give you an update before I leave. It hasn't been easy to untangle. Too early to be definitive."

Cindy met her in her office doorway. "Let's take a walk and get some coffee. I need a change of scenery, and"—she smiled—"I want to hear about your weekend."

"God! Can nobody have a private life around here?" Jess faked outrage as they started toward the elevator.

"You have to remember, I was there the night you two met! I have certain rights. Seeing that chemistry firsthand was so exciting. So, enough stalling," Cindy said. "How was the romantic getaway? And do not use the word 'fine.'"

They both laughed, and then Jess, feeling herself blush, offered, "It was lovely. Far enough away to feel removed from the familiar, yet not so far that we drove forever. Romantic without being sophomoric. We had some fun. I'd like to do it again."

"Is that all I get?" Cindy challenged.

"Yup," Jess answered, and they laughed again.

On their walk back to the office, Cindy told Jess about her meeting with Alice Lang. "She's retired now and was somewhat reluctant to meet. But when I told her what was at stake, she agreed to speak to me off the record. Alice really liked the doctors in the group."

"What did she say about the billing?"

"Enough that we can assume there were some overbilling issues, and that's why she had trouble with Floyd. She challenged their practices, and he tried to discredit her. When that didn't work, he made life miserable for her. She finally left without raising a ruckus, because that's not who she is."

Jess pulled a face at that, then asked, "Did she say anything else about Floyd?"

"She described him as an autocratic, mean man who was very short with the staff. But he had his favorites among the doctor group. She did point me to something we should check on beyond the billing. She said that Floyd took some of his favorite doctors on fancy trips to California and Mexico, sponsored by pharmaceutical companies."

"Who were his favorite doctors? Was Personne among them?"

"Oh, yes. He and Floyd were evidently very tight. And an internist no longer with the group—a Dr. Boyd. Alice also said that she challenged Floyd on a payment from Memorial Hospital for the ongoing consultative directorship of a doctor who had actually left the practice years earlier."

When they finished their walk, they popped back into Cindy's office to finish up.

"Well, I'm sure it wasn't easy to get Alice to open up, but, thanks to her, the picture is coming into focus. Good job, Cindy."

Jess shared the Adam Bright interview findings, and they both drew the same conclusion: it wasn't good.

"I'm going to call on an old friend at Memorial to check out this doctor arrangement. Can you or Joyce follow up on the sponsored trips? Under the circumstances, I don't want to ask Dr. Personne about either of those things."

They agreed on a plan, though Jess knew Cindy was as worried as she herself was about what they might find.

◊◊◊◊◊◊◊◊◊◊◊◊◊◊◊◊

The cooling breeze of a springtime dusk shook the fresh green buds off the trees as Jess rounded the final corner of her running route back to Claire's. She slowed down to a walk for the last block, controlling her breathing and smiling at the anticipation of seeing her friends and PJ.

Jess had always been able to compartmentalize, and the Goodmoor quandary couldn't keep her from enjoying this fun evening. But the possibilities of what this puzzle meant intrigued her. Larry Personne had kept his distance from her since their meeting. Was he embarrassed about having shown his weakness? Or did he know that she was still digging? Adam Bright had seemed to shine a light on what was going on, and Alice had certainly solidified her earlier suspicions. Once Jess had done a few more interviews and Joyce and Cindy had crunched more data on any discernible billing inconsistencies, she would have what she needed. And, fortunately, she had booked a breakfast meeting the next day with her old hospital administrator friend at Methodist to inquire about the medical directorship.

"Oh, you look so energized." Diane walked to meet her, having just parked in front of Claire's. "I wish I could have run with you."

"Is that code for 'you look sweaty and should take a quick shower before hugs'?" They laughed as they walked up to Claire's front door.

Out of the shower, Jess went to the kitchen, where Diane handed her both a bottle of water and a glass of wine.

"Ah, I could get used to this. Will you marry me?" She now hugged Diane. "Such loving affection and service. I hope we're ordering in. I've come empty-handed and assume nobody is cooking, right?"

Just as she finished that thought, Claire swooped in and said, "Oh my God, yes. I ordered Thai food. It should be here in about forty-five minutes. That's just enough time to get us situated on the porch and PJ into his prebedtime nursing routine. But"—she pivoted to look at Jess—"ah, yes, you look . . ." She hesitated and grinned widely. "You look like you've had some lovin'!" Claire whooped and grabbed Jess for a jig step.

A sudden squealing from the nursery caused Claire to release Jess and lead them to her son, but not before Jess grinned and pronounced the weekend "very enjoyable" while silently thanking PJ for having let her off the hook for saying any more.

PJ was delighted to see his mom. Melody departed for her puppet theater, and the three friends headed to the porch.

"It's so nice to be able to enjoy spring out here, but we'll appreciate a wrap soon. There's still a bit of a nip in the air in the evenings." Diane grabbed a shawl from the pile in the basket by the door and threw one at Jess.

They made goo-goo eyes at PJ and took turns holding him, sipping their wine, and catching up on Claire's transition back to work. "If you're exhausted, Claire, you don't look it. Motherhood becomes you. How are you feeling?" Jess asked.

"Pretty good, actually. Physically, I'm fine. One of the best decisions I made was to hire Melody and keep her happy keeping PJ happy. That, and scheduling my own gym time. If I didn't stay in shape, I'm not sure I could do all this. It also helps to have money to be able to pay for all this cushioning for myself. How moms do this alone otherwise, I don't know." She shook her head.

"And how about work? Have you been able to keep that contained a bit?" Diane asked.

"Well . . ." Claire paused. "That's the hardest part. Ratcheting down is hard for me. I've always been on the fast track, so all I can see is what I'm *not* doing. It's weird—it's like I'm outside myself, looking at me not doing what I used to do. But so far, I can handle it. We'll see how it goes." She shrugged.

"Ah, balance—the elusive goal for women now and forever. I wonder, will it always be so?" Jess raised her glass to toast the question just as the doorbell rang.

Diane brought the food in on a tray and prepared a plate for Claire. "Here, you eat, and then I'll eat when you're nursing him. Too hard to enjoy the food otherwise." She took PJ from Claire.

"OK, your turn, Diane. What's going on with you? Is the building progressing?" Jess asked as she grabbed a plate for herself.

Diane beamed. "It's so exciting to finally be building! Can you believe after three years we're in the second phase of construction? Fortunately, my work on it is mostly done. The pledges are still coming, and we're so fortunate that we remain a healthy nonprofit with a wonderful board to see this through."

"You should be so proud of yourself, Diane—to have navigated through all of the local and state jurisdictions on this and to have successfully raised the money. They're lucky to have you running the show. And, knowing you, I bet you have something new on the horizon. What's next?" Jess said before she took a big bite of pad Thai. She looked beyond PJ on her lap to Diane, who was blushing and hiding her eyes.

Diane repositioned PJ so he could see his mom, and squirmed a bit. "Well, I do have some news," she said very slowly. "George and I are getting married."

Both Claire and Jess jumped up at the same time, screaming and high-fiving each other and Diane and hugging PJ, who by now was seriously fussing.

"You sly old thing. Tell us everything," Jess said as Claire took PJ and a shawl and got comfy in the wicker rocker to nurse. "George is such a wonderful guy. I'm so happy for you both. You belong together. I wasn't sure you were going to marry, but

I'm so happy for you." Jess thought about how skillfully Diane had deflected questions about her relationship during these past months, so that finally her friends had all just put them together as a couple and accepted that as a final deal. Now Jess wondered if Diane's reticence had been designed to save Jess's feelings.

She put on her bravest face, knowing that Diane could read her like a book and had been doing so since they were five, but she saw Diane register the pain behind her facade. Diane took a long look at her and said, "Jess, I'm sorry this is so soon after your divorce . . ."

"Hey, life happens, right? Please don't let my situation deter you in any way. I'm fine and couldn't be happier for you." Jess lifted her glass and toasted her friend and was thankful that Diane didn't press the issue.

Claire and Jess played twenty questions until they were satisfied that they had the scoop.

"We're having a short ceremony in Goodrich, at the family church. My parents will be so delighted. They've waited so long." Diane smiled. "I want to do that for them. But then we'll have a reception here in St. Louis for our friends—hopefully on-site at the new building. We may be wearing hard hats, but the foyer area and outdoor patio should be finished by late summer, so we're thinking fall. George is so excited about that part, not only because it's such a special site but also because we met over the design table."

"Diane, I've never seen you happier. I couldn't be more thrilled." Jess reached over to take her hand. "Please put me to work in any way you wish. It would be a joy to help you with this. Anything you need."

Jess looked up at Claire, who was rocking her cherub and smiling like a Madonna. "How lucky we are to have such good things to look forward to!"

At least, I hope we do, she couldn't help adding to herself.

Chapter 37

◇◇◇◇◇◇◇◇◇◇◇◇◇◇◇◇◇◇◇◇◇◇◇◇◇

"So, how long has it been?" Steve asked as he slid into the booth opposite Jess at the Louisiana Grill in the Central West End. "Was the office building for Henderson the last project we worked on together?" The Louisiana was a favorite meeting place for up-and-comers, and she saw Steve take a moment to search the room for anyone he should greet while there.

"I think so, Steve, and that was almost three years ago. I've been reading about you in the 'People Under Forty to Watch' mentions in the *Biz News*. Memorial must appreciate you. What are you now, chief administrative officer?"

"Yes, have been for a little over a year." He smiled with understated confidence. He straightened his tie, smoothed his perfect hair, and looked at her full-on.

Jess knew the type: man on the move. She could almost hear the hard drive in his head calculating how much value a continued link with her might be. Right now, she knew he was considering her reputation in health care in greater St. Louis and the fact that she probably knew all the local power players.

No doubt he was also aware that she and Arthur were no longer together. He would buy into the least charitable version of the stories about her failed marriage: that her star researcher of a husband turned out to be an opportunist, ditched the university just as merger papers were being signed, took his research money to Portland, and shacked up with his sweetheart out there. Health care in this city was a small world.

"How's life been treating you?" he asked, just before the waiter approached to take their order.

He had been on a steep learning curve on the Henderson project, and she was counting on his remembering that he'd learned a thing or two from her during that intense month of negotiations.

They ordered, and the waiter left. "I'm great, actually." She smiled brightly, wanting to allay any worries he had that she might want to share chapter and verse of her marital woes. "I'm leaving town for a trip with my kids later this week, and I still find good work to do with Dan at his firm. So all is going well."

That seemed to satisfy his quota for polite conversation. "So, why did you want to meet, Jess? You said something about clearing up an issue for a practice group you're assessing. What can I do for you?"

"That's right. It's just a loose end I'm trying to tie up and thought you might know something about it. You know the Goodmoor Family Medicine group?"

"Is that the group whose manager died in a car accident awhile back?" Steve waved to someone across the room and checked his watch again.

"Yes, Floyd Ramsey. Very sad. Unfortunately, there isn't much bench strength there, so we're trying to get a picture of the health of the practice, which is hard."

Steve leaned back as their food arrived, and carefully placed his refilled coffee cup back on the saucer.

"Anyway, something we found leads us to a contractual relationship that Memorial had with a Dr. Deitz. Do you remember him or anything about that?"

Steve stopped chewing, shifted uncomfortably in his seat, and looked warily around the restaurant. "I'm not sure how much I can tell you, or should tell you. But, since you work for a law firm, you should check with them on the particulars."

Jess was afraid he was going to clam up; she had assumed he would enjoy dishing the dirt. She took a bite of her scrambled eggs and waited.

"There was a very messy situation, very awkward to dismantle. Floyd was a real operator—I can tell you that much. Sometime before I came to Memorial, he negotiated an arrangement for this doctor to be the medical director of a program that never got off the ground. But the payments continued for years, until we caught it in a routine audit."

"Wow, that must have been ugly," Jess encouraged. "What did Memorial do?"

"We discontinued the payments, but not before a very sticky situation developed with Floyd. He threatened to stop all referrals to Memorial from the group and to badmouth us around town. It got to the point where we were close to making a call we didn't want to make. Regulators get ahold of that . . ." Steve raised his eyebrows. "It was a tough time."

Jess was reminded how crazy it was that one man could wield so much power over a hospital. But the real threat of revenues lost from cutting admissions to a hospital and spreading the word that a practice had been treated badly could wreak havoc with other referrals. Hospitals didn't admit patients—physicians did. "I can imagine. How did you finally get him to back down?"

"Hmm, there was a lead physician at Goodmoor. What was his name? Kinda funny name. Peoples, um, something like that." Steve was enjoying his egg-white omelet and spread a heaping spoonful of raspberry jam on a piece of unbuttered toast.

"Dr. Personne?"

"Yes, that's it. Anyway, we had Dr. Ogilve, our chief medical officer, have a chat with Personne, and that seemed to end it. Evidently, Personne was pretty hot about it as well; he backed Floyd up initially, until Ogilve gave him a lecture or two about the legality of the situation. It scared him, I think."

"So, Personne was aware of the arrangement and that there was no work being done on that contract?" Jess needed this information.

"Oh, yes. What a shady piece of business. Boy, I haven't had to think about that for a while." Steve finished his breakfast and pushed his plate to the side, then asked, "Why is this relevant for you, again?"

"The group is trying to sort out its future, and it's hard to advise them unless we know whether there are any skeletons in the closet. I'm just looking for them."

Steve chuckled. "Well, I think you've found one!"

Chapter 38

◇◇◇◇◇◇◇◇◇◇◇◇◇◇◇◇◇◇◇◇◇◇◇

"I know you're busy getting ready, but I wanted to get a couple of things on your calendar. Can I pick you up at the airport Sunday night? I want you to meet my friends and come to the Symphony Ball with me and visit the lake the weekend after your trip. I'm so excited to share summer—"

"Jim. Jim!" She had to raise her voice to interrupt him on the phone. "Hold on, please. I can't process all of this right now—not yet."

In the ensuing silence, they both took a breath. Then Jess continued, "You're a wonderful guy, and we did have a great weekend—a really great weekend. But I can't think as far ahead as you on all of this yet." She continued to pack her bag.

"What does that mean?" He sounded hurt.

"It means exactly that. I have to process this a bit and not move too fast. And right now it means I have to get off the phone, pack, and get ready for my flight in the morning. And enjoy my trip to Italy. And, yes, I'd love for you to pick me up at the airport Sunday night. That would be delightful. Please?"

Jim exhaled loudly. "I'm sorry, Jess. I'm acting foolish," he said. "Of course you need to enjoy this trip and take some time. I'm embarrassed to be acting like a lovesick teenager. It's just that it's so good to feel alive again." His voice dropped. "I was overeager, and I apologize. Forgive me?"

"Nothing to forgive, Jim. Thanks for understanding. I look forward to seeing you Sunday. I'll text you my flight info. Good night."

Nothing to forgive, she thought as she finished packing, called to stop newspaper deliveries, and set up the automatic light. But something to note.

◇◇◇◇◇◇◇◇◇◇◇◇◇◇◇◇◇

"Yes, Dan. Cindy will be rolling up the financial analysis. And now that I've found out what happened at Memorial, the last thing we've got to do is research the out-of-town trips sponsored by pharmaceutical companies, and then . . ."

Jess was rolling her bag through the airport as Dan finished her thought on the phone with her: "Finish the research, and then sit with Dr. Personne to hear him out. This deal may be derailed before any work is done on the Midwest Health side, but better to find that out now than to bring both sides to the table."

They were in agreement. She was just signing off when she spied her beautiful daughter waiting curbside at the American Airlines door of the Newark airport.

"We made it. It worked!" Jess managed between hugs. "You look wonderful. Let me see you. Love those earrings!" Regardless of how long they might be apart, it always took only three seconds to regain their easy intimacy. Jess hoped that would never go away.

They took the shuttle to the international terminal and met Tom at the gate. They chattered about their impending adventure, seeing Vincente and Liliana, and the chance to see a beautiful part of Italy. The Three Musketeers, heading out.

"How is my philosopher chemist?" Jess grabbed Tom for a big hug and check-in as they waited for their flight to be called.

"You look very pleased with yourself. Are you still happy with your coursework?" She beamed.

"Oh, Mom, you know me. I'm pretty happy most of the time. This should be a fun week. I'm most looking forward to the food. Vincente promised he would have some information about a culinary course he knows about."

"And when exactly will you have time to do that?" Jess was curious.

"Well, I was going to wait and talk to you about this when it was more fleshed out. But maybe this summer? Vincente says there's a course offered near his house. It's a restaurant, really, but they provide meals in return for work, and Vincente says I can stay with them." He stopped. "Mom, would it be OK with you? I know you expected me home for the summer." He looked up at her hopefully.

Jess's heart dropped at the idea of Tom being gone, but she was determined to support her kids through their life choices, as she always had, regardless of her own needs. "I think it sounds marvelous, Tom, as long as you promise to cook for me when you do get home." Jess gave him another hug. "You've been busy planning, haven't you? Beth knows?"

He nodded, then reached for his phone to read a text, and his expression took a dark turn. He looked away and inhaled deeply, then announced in a wobbly voice, "Dad has schedule issues. He's not coming."

Jess watched her daughter take a quick look at her crestfallen brother. Beth didn't miss a beat—"Well, we'll just have to send him pictures of us hiking those hills he told us about"—but the look she gave Tom was 90 percent bravado and 10 percent little girl on the brink of tears. "Mom, will you join us?" she asked as she grabbed her own beeping phone, no doubt containing the same message her brother had just gotten, from her backpack.

Jess silently cursed Arthur for disappointing his kids but put on a bright face of her own and said, "I'm sorry your dad isn't going to make it, but we can't let that ruin our trip." She drew them both close. "I did bring my new hiking boots, just in case. I'd love to join you. Gosh, we haven't hiked together in a while. I hope I can keep up with you two."

Jess saw clearly that her children were taking care of each other, and while it broke her heart that they had to, she realized that the resilience they were building was what she had needed as well. It was a legacy she had not planned for them, but she was proud of them.

They traveled to Perugia, a lovely hill town in central Italy, for the wedding. Jess enjoyed several days and many hikes with the kids. Liliana was radiant in her mother's lace bridal gown, and Tom took pictures of the wedding feast, eight courses of gastronomical delight, for his burgeoning culinary album.

On their last night, Jess and Vincente shared a drink in the hotel bar while Beth and Tom joined Liliana for a fun picnic. It was their first opportunity to chat alone.

"Liliana was so sweet to save some time just for the kids," Jess said. "They were over the moon to have this chance with her. You've raised a beautiful person, and the new son-in-law seems like a great addition to your family. I can only hope mine grow up to be so wonderful."

"Your Beth and Tom *are* wonderful *now*. And they think the world of you. You know that, right?" He smiled. "I know how hard this past year has been for you. To see you with Beth and Tom, and the loving relationship you three have, it is impressive. When I think of how tough it must have been for you to stay positive for them . . ."

Jess shifted in her seat to avoid the late-day sunlight and the attention. Vincente jumped out of his chair and asked her to trade places with him. She protested, but he insisted. "This way, I can see you better, and you are more beautiful than ever. Italy agrees with you."

"Vincente, you are such an Italian charmer. I'm not used to this." She blushed. "Truly, this trip has been an elixir I didn't know I needed. It's so good to spend time with the kids and realize that they'll be whole and that our family can move forward."

Vincente toyed with the small vase of yellow flowers on the table. "I'm not sure if it makes a difference to you now, but Arthur doesn't seem happy. He seems to have relationship issues." He peeked up at her.

She took a sip of her drink and rolled her eyes. "Why does this not surprise me?" She chuckled ruefully. "But for the sake of my children, I'd like him to be happy. They don't need him to add drama to their lives. And for my sake, I'd like him to be happy so I don't have to think about him anymore. Does that make sense to you?"

"Yes, Jess, it does. I think it would be a good thing for you to be able to go ahead with your own life." He moved the flowers to the edge of the table and leaned back in his chair. "So, may I ask if you are seeing anyone special?"

"Ah, that's an interesting question." She smiled. "I don't know. I'm not sure about what I'm doing right now, beyond having a great vacation with my kids and enjoying your hospitality." The server brought them a small plate of prosciutto and melon.

"Hey, this reminds me. What are you doing, inviting my Tom over for the summer to learn to cook?" She took a bite of the appetizer.

"He sought out my advice. How could I refuse?" He looked down quickly.

Jess squinted at him. "Is it more than that? Tell me."

"Well, I've actually had quite a few conversations with Tom over the past several months. He was devastated by his father's duplicity and couldn't bear to burden you, so he turned to me." He looked at Jess as her eyes welled up. "I hope you're not angry with me for not telling you. I tried to provide some comfort and guidance, and I thought you had enough to deal with." He took her hand. "I'm sorry if I took liberties . . ."

"Dear Vincente. Of course I'm not angry. I'm humbled by your generous spirit. What a friend you've been to me." Tears streamed down her face. "I can't thank you enough for being there for my son."

He handed her his handkerchief and waited as she dabbed her eyes.

"Did you know Arthur wasn't coming?"

"Yes. I saw him at the Barcelona meetings last month and knew it was unlikely. But he called me just before the wedding with his final no." He suddenly took an interest in the street scene beyond Jess.

"Vincente, what aren't you telling me?"

"I feel torn. Arthur is my friend. You are my friend. I feel terrible about what has happened. I believe he has made some poor decisions."

"I can see this is difficult for you," she said. "Don't betray your friendship with him for me. But if you could help me understand anything that might upset my children as they try to cope, I'd appreciate it."

He pulled the flowers toward him again. "In Barcelona, Arthur confided in me that his relationship with Rebecca is falling apart and that he is filled with regret for having left his family. When he called a week ago, he was desperate to come but in the midst of chaos."

"So, it was chaos in his personal life that caused him to bail on this trip, not conflicting work obligations?"

"I'm not sure they aren't connected. I think the chaos in his personal life has caused him to retreat into work more than he should. That, and . . ." He looked up at her, as if wondering how much to share. "I'm not sure he felt he could cope emotionally with this family event—seeing you all and realizing what he's lost."

Jess felt her eyes fill again. Despite herself, she empathized with Arthur's delayed pain and tried not to relapse into her own.

"Vincente, I know there have been other women for a long time, but I don't know much about his current relationship, other than that she's in Portland. Tell me about Rebecca."

"Yes. She was his research protégée and then his lover. Then that wasn't enough. He thinks she's been obsessed with convincing him to marry her since she visited the lake house. And now she wants a baby, and, well, he's done with that phase of his life. He realizes he misjudged the situation—"

Jess's mouth fell open, and she cut in, "Wait, what? A *baby*? Wow, that's a surprise."

"Evidently to Arthur as well. He didn't expect her to want that. And he's not prepared to parent another child."

"And what did you say a second before that? What do you mean, she's been obsessed with marrying him since she visited the lake house? Arthur took her to the lake house for New Year's—actually, the kids joined them. What happened then that provoked her obsession with getting married?" Her mind leaped to how rough that trip had been for the kids and what they may have seen or heard, beyond Rebecca's interest in having their father sell the lake house.

"Oh, no, evidently it was last year when she visited the lake house, before the Portland move."

Jess could only acknowledge this news with a shudder. Rebecca had visited the lake house before New Year's, before Jess and Arthur's marriage had imploded. She wondered how Arthur could have taken a woman there without Jess's knowledge. There was so much she had missed. She looked away, her empathy for Arthur gone. She willed herself not to allow her mind to revisit the ups and downs of the prior year and smiled wistfully at Vicente.

"Jess, this is too much for you. I don't know how Arthur could have treated you so badly."

"It was hurtful for the kids that he didn't come."

"And you, Jess?"

She gave him a bittersweet smile. "Arthur's the father of my children and always will be. But the kids are my priority. I want what's best for them, which is why I'll always welcome him whenever he wants to join us. That's his choice. If he's dealing with poor choices now, perhaps he'll be more thoughtful in the future."

It took her the rest of the evening, but she finally realized that she didn't care about Arthur's personal problems anymore. Perhaps she had graduated.

Chapter 39

◇◇◇◇◇◇◇◇◇◇◇◇◇◇◇◇◇◇◇◇◇◇◇◇◇◇◇◇◇

"So, are your parents absolutely delighted? I wish I could have been there when you told them. Tell me all about it." Jess spoke to Diane in bursts as she jumped over puddles, navigating their run in Forest Park after a hard rain. She was determined for Diane to shine over these next few months before her wedding.

"Oh, they were so cute. They admitted to hoping but not wanting to put pressure on me. They love George and are so happy for me. Dad is so excited about walking me down the aisle, and Mom is already planning to come down here to go wedding-dress shopping with me. They want the whole experience, and I'm going to oblige." Diane was breathless, both from the run and with excitement.

Jess prodded her. "Isn't it wonderful that they're still around for this? And you know that the 'whole experience' includes a shower. Can I do the honors? Maybe we can do one in Goodrich for your mom's friends and family. And then let's do another one, here in town, for city friends."

"Really?" Diane looked at Jess in mock horror. "Bridal *showers*, plural. Do I really have to do that?"

"Of course—the first one for your mom, the city one for fabulous you! It'll be fun! Just say yes!"

"OK, OK. But I'm not going to let you do too much work on this. We'll go simple. Promise?"

"Promise. No ice sculptures or male strippers, I swear!" Jess smiled slyly as they paused to drink from the water fountain near the St. Louis Zoo entrance.

"By the way, your wonderful son sent me a postcard from Italy. He must have been raised very well indeed!" Diane teased, then hesitated a beat before asking, "How was it seeing Arthur?"

"Oh, he didn't show. He claimed he had schedule issues, but Vincente tells me there's trouble in paradise with the new love. The kids were hurt, of course. But we made the best of it and still had a great time."

"Do you hear from Arthur much?"

"Not much, which is fine with me. Thank God for e-mail. That's how we've communicated since the divorce. I know it's impersonal, but that saves me." Jess looked away a minute, surprised she had teared up. "And I have very little to communicate about with him, now that both kids are away at college."

They had reached their cars and caught their breath in the cool evening breeze.

"Hey, Jessica," Diane said, reaching out to touch Jess's arm. "If this wedding stuff is hard on you, let's not have you do all this."

"No, Diane, I really want to. This is real life, the ups and downs, and if you don't mind that I still feel bad sometimes, I want to feel the good stuff with you, without your feeling bad. OK?"

Sweaty as they were, they locked arms and held on for a big, wet hug, adding tears to the mix.

◇◇◇◇◇◇◇◇◇◇◇◇◇◇◇◇◇◇

"Are you saying that Personne and Ramsey were the ones who went on these trips?"

"Yes. We couldn't find any other trips that any other doctors took, and it looks like this was a regular practice over a several-year period; it ended this past year, after Floyd's death."

Jess pushed her plate aside and sighed. "This is getting pretty obvious. First, overbilling looks to be a systemic, not a special, issue. Second, there's the medical directorship kept alive even when there's no doctor providing services. And now we find out about these drug company–funded junkets to warm climates, with no educational component even hinted at." Jess pushed her chair back from the table in her office and took a turn around the room. "What's left to complete on our assessment? Is the quality review done?"

"Yes." Cindy reached into her folder to hand it to Jess. "It just came in as a draft, but I did discuss it earlier this morning with Dr. Moody. He made it clear that there was nothing in it to make him anxious."

Jess scanned it briefly, continued her walk around, and then stood with her hands on the table and leaned toward Cindy. "OK, this is what I'm thinking: poke holes in it." She waited for a nod from Cindy and then folded her arms, walked the length of her office, and turned to face Cindy again.

"Floyd is the bad actor. Maybe he started things that nobody knew about, just to prime the pump as he came in to juice up the practice years ago. Maybe Personne didn't know about any of it for a long time. Then Personne finds out, maybe by accident, and Ramsey persuades him that any change to their billing practices at that point will bring unwanted attention from the feds and lead to a large-scale investigation implicating him, as well as Personne, for current and past abuses. I don't know how much persuading it took, but let's say Personne becomes complicit and totally reliant on Ramsey, who continues to flout the rules. He makes sure nobody in the office stays long enough to get suspicious. He intimidates Alice out of the practice . . ." Jess paused to check Cindy's reaction.

Cindy's brow was furrowed, but she nodded and took the theory further: "And then Ramsey up and dies, leaving Personne in a bad place, alone. The other physicians are clueless, and Personne is stuck in his role as enabler. What a mess he's in! And when Ramsey dies, what can he do?"

Jess's turn: "He looks to Midwest Health to bail them out." Just then, with an involuntary shudder, she remembered that Jim was the one who had recommended Midwest Health to Larry Personne.

Jess's phone alarm went off. "Oh, gotta go to my interview with Dr. Sloane. He's the last of them, right?" Cindy nodded, and Jess continued, "OK, let's both think about this more on our own. We don't want to push it out too far until we're sure. And you were supposed to poke holes, not continue my thoughts." She winked at Cindy as she grabbed her suit jacket and grabbed the last bite of their shared cinnamon roll.

"Then you shouldn't have been so right!" Cindy returned the wink. "And before you leave, you might want to wipe the remaining frosting from your top lip—doesn't go with the image!"

Jess checked her theory as she drove. Was she pointing the finger at Floyd Ramsey because he was a convenient scapegoat? Was she being too easy on Larry Personne? And Jim: What role had he played?

"Keep an open mind," she said aloud. But crowding her rational thoughts like a storm cloud on the horizon was the anticipation of the pain that would result if she was right.

◇◇◇◇◇◇◇◇◇◇◇◇◇◇◇◇◇◇

Jess was breathless as she ran into the coffee shop amid a late-afternoon thunderstorm. Shaking out her coat and hair, she saw Dr. Keith Sloane sitting in the back of the nearly empty shop, reading from a tablet and drinking coffee from a steaming mug.

"I'm sorry to be late. I miscalculated the time in this traffic, given the weather. Will you give me a quick minute to get something hot? I'll be right with you." He nodded and went back to his reading.

When she rejoined him, he put the tablet away, sat up straight, and smiled, giving her his full attention. "What can I do for you, Ms. Lawson? What do you wish to know?"

His warmth and friendliness caught her by surprise. He had seemed to freeze the group with his flat delivery at the initial meeting, but now he was anything but detached.

"Tell me a bit about yourself: How long have you been at Goodmoor, and how did you get there?" She looked at his tablet and added, "And what are you reading?"

He grinned at her. "Grew up in California, came to St. Louis for a girl and to Goodmoor for a job. Reading Oliver Sacks because I have an interest in neurology, even though I haven't studied it formally."

"Ah, a man who keeps on learning. So, tell me what I don't know yet about Goodmoor."

"Have you interviewed everyone?" he asked coyly. He took his glasses off and looked at her with penetrating blue eyes. She noted his coal-black, curly hair, slicked back but still unruly, his late-day stubble just the right amount of dangerous.

"Yes, you are our last interview." She smiled. This wasn't supposed to be so pleasant. She took a swallow of her latte and let him talk.

"My interview will be different from the others." He paused briefly. "I'll assume you've learned nothing of great interest. It's a high-quality medical group made up of good doctors." His voice darkened. "But there's something rotten there. And I got too close for comfort." His smile didn't lose its warmth, but his eyes lost their gleam.

"A year ago, I challenged Floyd's interpretation of the rules regarding Medicare billing. I approached him directly, thought we could have a dialogue about it. I'd picked up some information at a medical meeting in Chicago. I'm always picking up stray bits of information." Again, that warm smile. "Anyway, I'd just gotten back from the meeting and asked for a minute at the end of the workday to talk to him. Nobody else around. He listened attentively and calmly told me my interpretation was wrong, but not to worry about it—he knew his way around Medicare rules.

"Two days later, Floyd told Personne that I'd been stealing narcotics from the supply closet and that I would have to go. Personne was about to fire me and report me to the National Practitioner Data Bank, when the missing narcotics were discovered in a file drawer in the chart room."

He looked away for a full minute. Jess held her breath. Finally, he continued.

"I suppose you're wondering why I didn't protest, fight, pull in reinforcements, et cetera." He paused again, then spoke softly. "I had a problem with substance abuse in my youth. That background, of which both Personne and Floyd were aware from my personnel file, would have made my stealing the drugs plausible. And, as you know, once you've been reported, you lose your livelihood."

"So, what happened?" Jess helped him get there.

"Well"—he regained his focus, and his warm smile and direct eye contact returned—"Personne offered me a break, I took it, and it was never spoken of again. And I knew what it required. So I'm biding my time until the Midwest Health deal either happens or doesn't, and then I'll leave."

Jess gave him another minute, as he took a swallow of his drink and exhaled with relief.

"So, you're saying that you were told to remain silent about the Medicare billing in return for the 'break' of keeping your job and not being reported?"

"It was never laid out in so many words, but yes, that's what I'm saying. Those two were covering something up. I still don't know exactly what, but clearly I needed to back away. I'm not proud of it, but that's what I did."

"Did anyone else in the practice know about this?"

"No, Floyd and Personne were careful about that. They isolated me by insinuation. They put my past drug abuse out on the rumor mill with a lingering question about a possible current problem, so I got a lot of cold stares and stilted conversations from my partners. Actually, Adam Bright was the only one to approach me about that. He's a good guy. I never told anyone about the incident and didn't try to explain away the rumor about my past, since it was a fact. It did distance me from the rest of the group, though. So there you are. I'm playing a waiting game." He smiled again, sat back in his chair, and finished his coffee.

Then he leaned forward with a serious expression and almost whispered, "I'm hoping, Ms. Lawson, that your firm does what's right. At the appropriate time, I'll be willing to help, but for now, I'm keeping a low profile. The 'girl' I mentioned earlier is now my wife. We have a child and a life here that I need to protect. And"—he grinned and stood—"it's my night to cook dinner, so I've got to get going."

Jess stood, they shook hands, and Dr. Sloane left. Jess sat and stared at the door, sipping her drink absently for several minutes before she could rouse herself. One thing she knew for sure: she no longer felt bad for Larry Personne.

Chapter 40

◇◇◇◇◇◇◇◇◇◇◇◇◇◇◇◇◇◇◇◇◇◇◇◇◇

Twinkly lights in the trees surrounding Jim's patio were just coming on, replacing the intense pink and orange colors of the sunset. Jim took orders for grilling. Jess sat with his friends around the table.

"Jim was a jock in high school. He was a three-letter man and always bested me—always." Jay, Jim's longtime best friend, was telling tales. "I recall I skipped football practice once and Jim here covered for me. Remember that?"

Jim looked up from his grilling. "You were always getting into trouble, Jay. Hard to remember all the times I covered for you!"

"At least I could challenge him academically, but not for long. He surpassed my intelligence and ambition when he went to medical school, and then kept on going."

Clearly Jay was a Jim fan from way back, but what kept this friendship going? Jess wondered, reflecting on the few times she and Arthur had encountered Jim and Sally at social events. She could see Liz as a best friend of Sally, Jim's wife. "How about you, Liz? What do you do?" Jess continued.

"Well, I take care of this guy." Liz giggled. "Which can be a lot of work!" The tan skin of her tennis-toned arms glowing, she arranged her bangles noisily and leaned into Jay as they exchanged a loving look. "And I raised two children to adulthood, or at least college." She sighed and looked at her husband. "We're hoping for adulthood soon." She giggled again. "I've always felt busy and fulfilled at home. My volunteer work with Sally, may she rest in peace"—she stopped and put her hand to her heart—"always gave me joy, and I'm trying to find my way back to that." She teared up, and Jay gave her a comforting squeeze.

"Three minutes out on the steaks," Jim announced.

There is a God, Jess thought. She escaped to grab the rest of dinner from the kitchen.

As she carried the food out to the patio, Jim came to help her and whispered, "Thank you for doing this. Are you OK?"

"Of course. They're very nice people." She smiled back. "But let's talk about something current over dinner."

When they returned to the table, Jim started in: "Any travel in the works for you two?"

"Oh, gosh, it's hard to think about taking a vacation without the kids. How many family trips do you think we took together?" Liz responded.

"Hmm." Jay looked to Jim. "We probably started when your two kids and our two kids finally had spring break at the same time." He paused for a moment. "Maybe when Jay Jr. was in fifth grade? So at least six. Four to Hawaii, and maybe two or three to Florida, and then that one trip to Costa Rica. Probably the best golf, right?"

"Yes, the golf was awesome there." Liz beamed and got nods from both Jim and Jay. "Sally and I were always looking for family-friendly places near challenging golf courses. We needed kids' programming or supervision so that we could golf with the boys for at least nine holes every day. Kept everybody happy!"

Jim attempted a course correction: "Those trips were a lot of fun, but that's old history."

Jess threw an appreciative smile at him, but he wasn't looking at her. If they were to be a couple, they would have to work on their signals.

"Do you golf, Jess?" Liz asked.

"No, I don't." *And I'm not likely to start anytime soon.* Jess smiled and passed the rolls.

"Have you met Joanna and Andy yet?" Liz asked.

"No, I haven't." Jess felt her smile tighten. *And meeting kids hasn't even come up with Jim yet. Slow down, Liz.*

But then, as Jess filled her wineglass, she forced herself to check her thinking. *These people have been friends for years, and you're a new woman in their world, after a tragic loss. Get a grip. They're making an effort.*

Jim got up to get another bottle of wine and squeezed Jess's arm as he passed.

"And how old are your two kids? Is it Beth and Ted?"

"Beth just turned twenty, and Tom is eighteen."

"Wow, all of our kids are around the same age," Liz observed, sounding a bit wistful.

"Yes, they're all starting to get out in the world on their own, as they should." Jim raised a glass. "To our young adults. Let them find their own path."

Jay added, "But not lose their way home."

As they clinked glasses, Jess felt a whiff of solidarity with these fellow empty-nesters. Perhaps the fact that they were all starting a next phase was a common bond to build on. She felt the tension in her shoulders release.

Until, bless his heart, Jim tried again. "Well, back to travel: I've always wanted to go to Japan, so I'd like that to be my next trip. What do you say, Jess?" He nudged her playfully.

"Hmm . . . I've never really thought about it." *Too early, Jim, and this isn't the right time or place.* She smiled and asked Jay to pass the salad.

◇◇◇◇◇◇◇◇◇◇◇◇◇◇◇◇

Jess and Cindy were working in Jess's office when Claire called her cell. She always answered Claire's calls, even if she was deep into her business day.

"Jess, good. Glad I caught you. I'm just heading out the door, but this will be quick: Will you come to Melody's first show?"

"You mean the puppet show she wrote? Her directorial debut? Of course! I'd love to come. When is it?"

"Saturday afternoon. I was thinking we could all go to the premiere and then come back to my house and have some dinner. That way, I can take PJ and get him to bed at his usual time."

"That sounds lovely; let's think about an easy meal." Jess tucked a stray strand of hair behind her ear. "Is it OK if I invite Jim?"

"Wow. Of course. Great idea. I'd like to meet him; this would be a good time to do that. OK, gotta run. Details later."

Cindy, seated at Jess's office table, looked up from her computer and smiled. "So, you're going to introduce him to the friends. That's great."

Jess returned the smile. "He's a very nice guy, and I'd like my friends to meet him." Jess fiddled with her hair again. "Speaking of friends, as Jim is one of mine and I'm thinking we may need to talk to him to complete the assessment, would you be willing to interview him?"

Cindy closed her laptop and followed the bright sun to the window to maneuver the shades until the work surface was without glare but shimmered in a prism of light. "Of course. What are you thinking, that we should add all the specialist consultants from the practice to the interview list?"

"No, not that. It's just that Jim was the person who directed Larry Personne to Midwest Health. I'm almost positive it was because he saw the group floundering after Floyd Ramsey's death. He's now part of Midwest Health's leadership, so I think he was motivated to keep them in the fold. But I want to rule out any other reason."

"Ah. If this whole thing blows up around Personne, you want to see if there was anyone else in the know." Cindy remained standing.

"Exactly. I'm pretty confident that the doctors in the group are clean, and that at least one, Dr. Sloane, had suspicions about the billing. But I don't know . . ."

"Whether Jim was aware and maybe looking the other way? Or if Personne confided in him after Floyd died and sought his advice?"

"Thank you for saying it so that I didn't have to." Jess exhaled softly. "We just can't finalize this before we know that."

Cindy leaned down to put her arm around Jess. "Hey, girl-friend. I get it and I've got this. I'll interview Jim, and we'll see where that leads us."

Chapter 41

◇◇◇◇◇◇◇◇◇◇◇◇◇◇◇◇◇◇◇◇◇◇◇◇

Friday midday, Cindy poked her head into Jess's office. "Interview just completed. Time for a debriefing while it's still fresh in my mind?"

"Oh, wow, you got that finished faster than I expected. Yes, please. Do tell." Jess headed to the seating area, and Cindy followed her, pulling her notes from her bag. Jess exhaled slowly, pleased that she could start off the weekend with more insight into Jim's possible involvement with Goodmoor's problems.

"OK, here goes. I arranged to meet Dr. Nathan—Jim—at his office on the university campus, now part of the Midwest Health system. I arrived early, and his assistant directed me to wait in his office, as he was running ten minutes late in surgery. So I used the opportunity to study this man's world a bit before he arrived. Remember, all I really knew before today was that he was good-looking, a recent widower, and a skilled surgeon. And, of course, that both the university and now Midwest Health valued him for his ability to reach out and keep referrals from the community physicians.

"So I looked around. There were three walls devoted to bookshelves crammed with textbooks, mementos, and family pictures. A chess set stood in the middle of a round table with no dust collecting on it. A plant on a corner of his desk looked healthy. Photos of Jim and his wife were all over his desk and shelves. There were pictures of his children, too: a girl and a boy. Judging from the photos, the family has already celebrated two high school graduations and one college graduation. His credentials were framed and hanging on a wall above a university regents chair stacked with journals. It seemed like a comfortable, masculine retreat, until he opened the door and the beep and hum of the busy hospital corridor reminded me where I was. That, and the fact that he was still in his scrubs."

Cindy stopped to grin at Jess. "And the green of the scrubs really set off those mesmerizing brown eyes."

Jess wasn't ready to relax, but she smiled back at Cindy. "Go on."

"He was very straightforward. He told me he was happy to help in any way he could to get Goodmoor into the new Midwest Health family."

"With that opening, I said to him, 'I understand it was you who suggested Larry Personne seek out a relationship with Midwest Health. Is that correct?'"

"He said yes, he'd been working with Goodmoor for twenty years and hoped he was part of the reason they had stayed in Midwest Health's orbit. Goodmoor sent them a lot of cases, important teaching cases. It means a lot to all of the faculty to keep those referrals coming."

Cindy checked her notes. "I specifically asked him to tell me how his initial conversation with Dr. Personne came about. He told me that it happened awhile back. He thought it was just a matter of noticing that Larry Personne was anxious. Certainly, it came as a big shock when their business manager died, and it was a real blow to Larry. Jim got the impression that, over the years, Larry had basically let that business manager call the shots. So, once that guy was gone, Larry must have realized he had to make some major changes to ensure the future of the practice.

"Jim made a point of telling me that, while in retrospect it may seem overtly opportunistic of him, Midwest Health had a stated strategy of bringing practices into the fold, so he just mentioned it to Larry and asked him to think about it. A day later, Larry called Jim and asked him to set up a meeting, which Jim did happily.

"I also asked Jim if Larry Personne ever specified the problems he was hoping to solve or revealed why he was so anxious. Jim said Larry didn't get specific, although he also admitted he didn't press Larry. That wasn't long after his wife died. He said he was still pretty much into righting his own world and didn't ask too many questions about other people's lives at the time.

"When I asked Jim if he ever met Floyd Ramsey, he wasn't even aware of who that was until I added 'the business manager of the practice,' so he definitely didn't know Floyd. He had heard through the grapevine that the manager ran a tight ship. Jim feels fortunate that he can stay clear of all the business aspects of how a practice runs. Evidently, he has no interest in it at Midwest, either. Businesspeople do that. He does surgery and teaches surgery. He gets no remuneration from Goodmoor. His fees come from the patients they send him who end up getting surgery there.

"I also asked him about the other physicians at Goodmoor, whether they ever offered him any opinions about the health of the practice or raised any concerns. He answered that he hadn't heard anything from any of them, but he also noted that he interacted with them only in clinical cases."

Cindy looked up from her notes and smiled at Jess. "You'll love this part. He said he may have seen some of them at the annual golf event for community physicians that the university hospital, and now Midwest Health, sponsors, but he didn't develop any close relationships with them. Not even with Larry, who Jim described as a quiet, morose sort of guy. His relationship with Larry Personne was a business relationship only. And Larry doesn't golf.

"In summary, he was very forthcoming and not hiding anything, from my perspective. I really enjoyed talking with him."

"Is that it?" Jess asked.

"Well, that's all concerning Goodmoor. But he did ask about you . . ." Cindy shifted her weight and leaned toward Jess.

Jess perked up a bit. "And?"

"And he was pleased that I knew you two were dating. Thought it was a good sign." Cindy chuckled.

Jess joined in. "Thank you, Cindy, not only for doing the interview, but for sharing this with me so quickly. The peace of mind is a gift."

"Hey, I'm just relieved I didn't have to shoot him," Cindy said. They laughed again, and Jess walked her to the door.

∞∞∞∞∞∞∞∞∞∞∞∞

The Puppet Master Theater was filled to capacity with noisy young kids squealing in anticipation of the performance. Jess had expected a library-type auditorium, but this was a custom-made puppet theater with dramatic lighting and a sound system to match. The raised, carpeted bench seating was clearly designed for a lively and ambulatory group.

"Wow, this isn't something I see every day," Jim said.

Jess scanned the audience for her group. "There they are." She grabbed his arm, and they headed to the front of the theater, where Claire and Diane had held seats for them. George couldn't join them until dinner at Claire's. "Sorry—we aren't late, are we?" Jess hugged her friends and turned to introduce Jim.

"I already like you," Claire said with a smile. "It's not every man who would agree to meet his girl's friends at a puppet show. But then you already know that Jess is not just any girl, right?" Jess saw Claire wait for Jim's quick smile, but when none came, Claire continued, "And this is Peter James, my son and Jess's godson."

Just then, the music started. The curtain parted and Melody Barnes, the puppet master for the premiere of *Peter and the Adventure in the Lost Forest*, was introduced.

At the end of the show, as the cast took their bows, Claire threw a bouquet of flowers up onstage. PJ giggled in recognition when he finally saw his nanny, blowing kisses his way.

When the group arrived back at Claire's house after the show, George was waiting there with barbecue. Claire disappeared to put PJ to bed while Jess, Jim, Diane, and George poured themselves drinks. They were watching dusk fall from the somewhat chilly screened porch when Claire rejoined them and moved them to the living room and the fireplace.

"Now, wasn't that a magical performance? Melody is really talented. I'm so lucky to have found her. Thank you all for coming to that show. George, you really missed out."

"Sorry, Claire, but I had to take care of a builders' issue. Customer service is necessary even on a Saturday afternoon."

"Are you worried that Melody will take off for a bigger opportunity, Claire?" Diane asked.

"Well, not right yet. I mean, gosh, she's so good that I hope she takes her talent wherever it leads her, but, selfishly, I hope that doesn't happen in the next two or three years." Claire crossed her fingers and looked at Jess for reassurance.

"That would get our boy to preschool and new adventures. But let's not worry about it yet. Melody's here, and she's ours for the moment. She's a first-class nanny." Jess stifled a giggle. "Let me tell you about when I met Melody." She looked at Claire, and they both told the story of the young woman's colorful first appearance.

When she finished, she noted that Jim was studying Claire closely, his features frozen on his face. She remembered his curiosity when she had explained Claire's situation. Claire was not the sort of independent woman Jim knew much about. She could almost see his mind puzzling over her friend's situation.

"So, Jim, what did you think of the puppet show?" Claire asked.

"I thought it was great," he replied. "It made me wistful about what I missed back when I was too busy to participate much in my own children's outings. And seeing PJ reminds me how quickly they grow up—"

"Oh, oh!" Diane interjected. "George and I have first dibs on babysitting. You were just about to offer, weren't you?" She teased.

Jim's face contorted in a look of such surprise and worry that Jess stood and walked toward the screened-in porch to give him time to recover. "Claire, I think it's time to think about putting the twinkly lights on in there. Look at that sunset."

Chapter 42

◇◇◇◇◇◇◇◇◇◇◇◇◇◇◇◇◇◇◇◇◇

"So, one thing I forgot to mention about Jim's office . . ." Cindy was priming Jess while they walked toward Dan's office the following Monday morning. "There's a full human skeleton in there!"

Jess smiled and, seeing Dan motion them in, opened the door.

"So, ladies, are we ready to wind this up?" He moved from his standing desk to the conference table in his office and offered them coffee.

Jess and Claire presented the material to Dan. It didn't take more than an hour for him to gauge the full scope of the problems. He took a quick break to take a call and then said, "I've seen enough. How should we approach Personne with this mess? The two of you together, since you both worked on the project? Cindy alone, as an attorney who can speak to the legalities if he needs that detail? Or just you, Jess, to keep it more personal and perhaps not as threatening as two-on-one? Or should I be involved? What do you think?"

Jess straightened in her chair. "I've been thinking about that and would recommend that I meet with him on my own. He came across as a real victim when I met with him the first time. Almost broke down, in fact. Clearly, we need to confront him with our findings in a nonjudgmental way. I think that's our best chance of getting him to come clean about his involvement and confirm our hunches. Cindy, are you OK with that?"

"Gosh, yes. I only saw the guy at that first meeting. It's going to be hard for him—he doesn't need an audience. Actually, it might be better, if he wants to meet later about some of the legal aspects, that I hold back."

They agreed that Jess would meet with Personne as soon as possible and that all would be quiet until after that meeting.

◊◊◊◊◊◊◊◊◊◊◊◊◊◊◊◊◊

"Just paying bills," Jess responded to Jim, who always seemed to start a phone conversation wanting to know exactly what she was doing. "What about you?"

"Barely home and looking at what I have to eat. Wishing you were here."

"That's a sweet thought." Jess wondered if he missed her or whether he mainly missed having someone there to cook. "I'm sure your lovely housekeeper left something for you to put together. She seems like a gem—you should keep her happy." She laughed softly. "By the way, thanks for joining me for the puppet show the other night. I hope you weren't too bored."

"Actually, I enjoyed it and also liked meeting your friends. Interesting people. I think Claire has a tough road ahead. Raising a child alone is a big responsibility. You never really know how big it is until you get into it."

"Yes, but she's strong and resourceful, and she has me to help her. She went into it with a clear head."

"Well, anyway, they were all very nice." He paused, then continued, "Jess, you haven't committed to the Symphony Ball yet. Are you planning to attend with me? It's coming up pretty soon."

"I'm glad you reminded me. I had a thought about that, and I hope you don't mind my making a suggestion. I know this was an event that was very important to Sally, and to you, and that you've always gone with a particular set of friends. It occurred to me that since this is the first one you would be going to after Sally's death, perhaps your daughter would want to accompany you, in honor of her mother." Jess paused for a moment, then continued, her voice soft and kind, "Remember how Joanna felt on Sally's birthday and how you went to be with her?"

"She always helped her mom get ready. The two of them would barricade the bedroom and get Sally all gussied up. It was a real family event for those two. For us three, I should say." He paused. "Do you think she'd really want to go with her dad?"

"Fathers are so important to girls and young women. And this is still not long after her loss—after your loss. I think it would mean the world to her if you asked her to attend in honor of her mother. And what a nice memory you two could make for each other."

"Wow, I should have thought of this. It seems like a natural thing to do. What a great idea! I'm going to call her now." Then another pause. "Hey, you didn't suggest this because you don't want to go, did you?"

"Well, fancy balls aren't my thing, but I *do* stand by my suggestion." She chuckled. "And will you invite me to your lake place for Memorial Day weekend, please? I'm dying to spend some time relaxing with you somewhere you love."

◇◇◇◇◇◇◇◇◇◇◇◇◇◇◇◇◇◇

Jess was waiting for Larry Personne at Gabe's when he arrived. She remembered how he had needed to loosen up a bit before admitting his failings to her the last time, and had thought meeting for a drink might work again, although the stakes were clearly higher now.

He looked much cheerier this time as he walked to her, putting his hand out to shake hers warmly. "So, Jess, I'm hoping we're ready to wrap this up and move forward. Are we?" As he sat down, he asked the server to bring him a gin and tonic and a refill of coffee for her.

Jess swallowed hard. "We're finished with our preliminary work, and before we close it out, I wanted to meet with you to make sure we're not missing anything or misinterpreting any of our findings. It's a courtesy we routinely extend to the heads of groups before we finalize our reports, in order to keep them in the loop and make sure they want to proceed."

"Well"—he exhaled and loosened his tie—"if that's all you need, I can tell you right now that I certainly want to proceed. I can hardly wait to get this deal done."

Jess wasn't sure how she could prepare him, so she opted to go for the truth, to get it out on the table and deal with his reaction then and there. "Larry, I'm afraid we've found some irregularities in the billing. They're quite serious—they're material, beyond the threshold of normal errors, and reportable to the authorities. They have consequences for your group and may have consequences for you, or for anyone else who knew that these practices were in place. And, unfortunately, they will stop us from recommending a business relationship between your group and Midwest Health."

Larry Personne's face lost all expression; his body sagged in his chair. He looked at her, soundlessly mouthing, "What?"

She gave him time to regain his composure by repeating the message again, this time a bit more slowly.

He drained his drink. "What does this mean?"

"It means that you should prepare yourself to understand the legal aspects of the situation your group is in and go from there. My colleague Cindy Newton is ready to meet with you about the specifics of the various infractions and how to report them. She'll be happy to refer you to an attorney after you understand a bit more about the situation."

He seemed to take that in. Still, he sat silently.

"Larry, this is beyond my purview, and you don't have to answer me, as you will no doubt need your own counsel to help you with these decisions, but were you aware of the billing issues and what was happening? Did you know what Floyd was doing?"

At the mention of his name, Larry lifted his head up and smirked. "Ah, Floyd. Good old Floyd."

Jess said, "I'm so sorry about this. I know you'll need some time to process it and to determine your next steps. Shall I have Cindy give you a call to schedule a meeting?"

Larry just looked at her and started on his second drink.

"Is there anything I can help you with right now, anyone I can call for you?" She wasn't sure she should leave him.

"No, just go." He made no attempt to engage further and wouldn't meet her eyes.

As she prepared to depart, she realized meeting him in a bar probably hadn't been the best idea after all. She guessed his reaction would have been the same anywhere, but perhaps at least she could have kept him away from booze for a while. She beat herself up about it during her evening run and tried to forget about it while she ate dinner. Finally, three hours after she had left him at Gabe's, she called the bar and asked to talk to the manager. "Oh, yes, we remember that gentleman. He was quite belligerent. We asked him to keep his voice down while he made a few phone calls, and he was not happy. He did agree to let us put him in a cab awhile ago, after it was clear he was in poor shape."

She felt no remorse for having given Larry the message that he and his clinic were in real trouble, but she did feel relieved that he hadn't hurt himself or anyone else driving home. Now what would he do?

She saw she had missed a call from Jim while she was on the phone. Too late for that now.

Chapter 43

Jess woke with a general sense of dread. Once it was light enough, she headed to the garden. She needed to divide hostas before they got too big, so she graphed her plan but stopped short of any digging, wondering instead how Larry Personne was feeling this morning after his night at the bar. Had he had a chance to think in a constructive way about what she'd said?

Suddenly, she found herself remembering her parents' divorce hearing. *Where did that come from?* she wondered. She thought that had been long buried, just as her family relationships had been. Both had expected her to testify against the other parent. She would have been willing to tell the truth, but that hadn't been what either of them wanted.

Sometimes the truth was hard.

The sun was still gentle and warm when she left the garden. As she got inside, she took a call from a very excited Jim. "Jess, you're amazing. I can't thank you enough for suggesting that I take Joanna to the Symphony Ball. She's on cloud nine. Evidently, there's a dress of her mom's that she wants to wear; the two of them both loved it. Joanna thinks it may need a bit of altering, but she's totally into this. You're truly wonderful."

"I know I am. I'm glad my hunch was on point." Jess laughed. His enthusiasm was catchy.

Almost as quickly as he'd begun gushing, he signed off. "Gotta go into a case. Just wanted you to know you're a special woman and I appreciate your intuition. Thank you."

As she hung up, she saw that she had missed a couple of calls while she'd been in the garden, one from Dan and one from Cindy. Rather than taking the time to call back, she texted them that she would be in shortly, took a quick shower, and arrived at the office forty minutes later.

Cindy had a meeting in progress but left it briskly and followed Jess to her office, closed the door, and skipped any preliminaries. "Personne has gone wild. He left a raving voice mail on Dan's line that he'll be suing us, that we're all quacks and don't know what we're doing."

Jess sat down at her desk and frowned as she emptied her briefcase. "I'm not surprised." After a brief pause, she said, "You know, I really did screw up on this. I should've had a communication plan ready so that things didn't stop with him. I knew his world was about to cave in. I was so eager to unload the bad news that I didn't think past that."

Jess gazed out the window for a moment and then continued, "Anyway, if he goes into a corner somewhere, we have to be able to communicate with his group. They shouldn't be left in the lurch because of the actions of a crooked business manager and a complicit physician leader. As it is, he may go off on a bender, or worse."

Cindy put a hand on her shoulder. "This will get sorted out. You couldn't know how he'd take the news. Dan's been trying to reach him all morning, and he hasn't responded. Did he express any interest in meeting to learn more about the legal realities and his obligations?"

"No, truly, he shut down and shut me out." Her early-morning sense of dread was back in full force, and now it had a shape. The Midwest Health project was dead before it could really get started: fifteen physicians' careers derailed and a rogue doctor wreaking havoc on the firm.

Cindy moved to the sitting area and gestured for Jess to join her. "I'm afraid it gets worse. Larry has made this personal and blames you for all of it. And he didn't just call Dan; he also called Dick Morrison at Midwest Health." Cindy paused, then added, "We think he may have called, or intends to call, Jim as well."

Jess noticed the voice mail light blinking on her office line just then. She was about to pick up and retrieve the message, when Dan walked into the office.

"Jess, don't listen to that." He guided her to the sitting area, where Cindy was waiting, and they all sat down. "I know Personne called you." He grinned. "He said some very bad things about you and called you some names that I haven't heard in a while. He has quite the command of colorful language."

Jess couldn't bring herself to join in the light laughter that followed. "Sorry, Dan. I guess I screwed up."

"On the contrary. You and your team uncovered some crazy stuff that this guy either knew about or should have known about, and now he's striking back. It just so happens that you're his target. Someone was bound to be."

"Dan, I think Amy is trying to get your attention." Cindy was looking through the hallway glass at his administrative assistant, who was standing with her arms full, waiting for a sign of permission from her boss.

Dan went to the door and let her in.

"I'm sorry to interrupt, but these came for Jess. May I bring them in?" Amy asked as Dan peered into the box.

"Couldn't be a better time for flowers." Dan clapped his hands.

Jess unwrapped the lovely bouquet, and the card fell to the floor. Cindy quickly picked it up and read it aloud: "So grateful that you're my team leader! I continue to have the highest regard for your integrity. Thank you. Dick Morrison."

"He enjoyed the rant last night as well, but when he called me this morning, it was to thank us, not to second-guess us." Dan looked bemused. "Jess, he knows who you are. You have a voice message from him as well. Erase the one from Personne and savor the one from Dick."

"Looks like he's a true fan," Cindy said. "He even underlined 'continue.' He clearly remembers and is appreciative, for sure."

Jess took a moment to enjoy the sweet scent of irises and lilies and to catch her breath. "I'm glad we didn't have to do a lot of damage control on that end of things. But wow, what a mess otherwise. What have you two been thinking our next steps should be?"

"Well," Dan said, "now that we know he was drinking last night and probably made the calls in that state, we should give him today to sleep it off and come to his senses. I have a call in to him, so that's enough for today. If he doesn't call by morning, I think we—and that means Cindy—need to figure out how to get to him to explain the specifics."

"It'll be so much better for him and the group if he works with an attorney to sort out how to approach this situation. Who knows—maybe he'll surprise us and retain someone today and call us. Cindy, if he doesn't have someone in mind, I assume you're putting together a list of attorneys for him?"

Cindy opened the notebook she had carried in. "Yes, I'm on it. I'm already developing a problem list to pass on as well. I'm prepared to meet with him whenever he's willing."

"And what about the group?" Jess asked. "If this goes on for more than a day or so, they'll begin to ask questions, especially if Personne isn't around. We should have a good outsource firm ready to refer them to for an interim manager. Many are just hanging on until this assessment is completed before they jump ship if the Midwest Health deal doesn't come about."

Jess was fidgety and couldn't stay seated. She walked to the window and then turned to face Dan. "If the practice can't be saved, Dan, we should be thinking about how to steer those who leave to Midwest Health."

Dan sat taller in his chair and smiled broadly. "God, yes. We should. Good thinking. That still works for Midwest Health's strategy, and you've already learned that the clinical quality of that group is very high. That could be the best solution for those physicians, as well as for their patients. Could save a lot of heartache for everyone."

"As long as the legal issues don't bog them down individually," Cindy added. "Remember, we did an assessment that will now be turned over to . . ."

"Yes." Dan stood and nodded in agreement. "And that legal process will take months, if not years. At least we know we did the right thing and can make the handoff with a clear conscience." He checked his watch. "I love problem solving with you two. So let's continue thinking along these lines and see where we are in the morning."

Jess worked on other projects through the next several hours, trying to keep her mind occupied. But later, when she left the office and headed to the parking ramp, she searched for her car for ten minutes before she realized she was on the wrong level.

Chapter 44

Jess took a glass of wine out to the patio to try to unwind. She breathed in the earthy smell of freshly cut grass and felt the gentle touch of a light breeze on her bare arms. She was tempted to go fiddle more with her garden, when Jim texted and said he was going to stop by on his way home.

As soon as Jess got a look at his face, she knew something was wrong. "Hi there. How are you? Tough day?" She poured him a glass of wine as he joined her near the patio table. His rigid body language did not invite a touch, nor did he reach for the wineglass, so she sat and waited.

"Not so much for me." He seemed to search her face. "Must have been a rough one for you."

"Did you get a call?"

"Yes, and it wasn't pretty."

"I bet not, and you weren't the only one to get one."

"Are you OK?"

"Yes, I'm fine. This isn't the first time I've been subjected to someone's misplaced anger."

"I can't believe it. Of course, I don't believe any of what he said about you personally. But I also can't believe that they're in legal trouble." He was pacing the length of the patio, lost in his own world.

"You know I can't talk to you about this stuff, right?" she asked, but received no answer.

"You know this clinic was important to my practice, right?" His tone was soft, a bit condescending.

She paused, trying to decipher that comment. "Jim, this isn't a good conversation to start."

"You know these guys are MDs just trying to do their thing, and without a manager to do the business piece . . . they're not trained to know this billing stuff. *I'm* not trained to know this billing stuff." His voice was getting louder, and he now stood stock-still, facing her. "That they could be held accountable for billing irregularities and face legal consequences—it's crap!"

How dare he bait me? she thought. She wouldn't go there.

"I'm sorry that you got a phone call, and I'm sorry that this whole situation may be difficult for your own practice. But I'm not sorry to have been involved in assessing the practice and following the facts. That's my job."

She rose to walk the edge of the patio and give him a moment to settle down. When she returned, he was in full smolder.

"Do you realize that Personne has probably lost his livelihood? Here's a guy in his midfifties facing legal trouble when he should be winding down to retirement. This isn't fair!" He started to pace again.

She silently counted to ten, then sat and poured herself more wine. "Overbilling Medicare is not a victimless crime," she said coolly. "And physician leaders have a fiduciary responsibility for overseeing their management. If they want to be business owners, they cannot default on that."

He stopped an arm's length from her, his voice now steely and low. "How could you see it only that way? How can you throw him under the bus? How can you live with yourself, having done that?"

Jess stood and walked away, trying to keep her trembling under control. She could hear the crunch of the gravel as he left the patio and headed for the front of the house.

Dusk had fallen, and it was chilly. She finished her wine, headed into the house, drew a hot bath, and soaked in it until she stopped shivering.

Was it really just this morning that he called me to tell me how amazing I am? she wondered. *That certainly wasn't what he was thinking about me tonight. But how much do I care?*

Chapter 45

◇◇◇◇◇◇◇◇◇◇◇◇◇◇◇◇◇◇◇◇◇◇◇◇◇

*T*hank God it's Friday, Jess thought as soon as she opened her eyes. She did a bit of stretching and spent some time at her computer before she left for the office. She caught Claire by phone just after Melody had arrived at the house.

"Hey, friend," Jess greeted her. "Do you and my favorite baby boy have plans for Memorial Day weekend?"

"No. But I thought you were going to spend the holiday at Jim's lake place."

"That's not happening. I can fill you in later, but I was thinking that a holiday would be just the thing for us. You haven't had a getaway since Thanksgiving, and I would really like a break. What do you say?"

"Well . . ."

"I'm thinking we can book a cabin at a resort I know well on the Missouri River bluffs. Then we can have our own place, and—here's the hook—there's a spa right at the lodge, and child-care, too. I believe you need to be treated to some TLC. Anyway, they're holding the unit for me, so I wanted to get back to them before they have to let it go. Are you in?"

"Massage, hiking, pontoon boat . . ." Claire paused. "Really, I could get excited about this. Are you sure you want to skip Jim's? Are you doing this for me?"

"Believe me, this is for me as well."

"Hmm. OK. Sounds like there's something I'm missing, but I'm game. Book it!"

"Great! And remember, brunch at my house Sunday with Diane to plan the wedding stuff—eleven o'clock."

◇◇◇◇◇◇◇◇◇◇◇◇◇◇◇

When she arrived at work, the receptionist gave her a note. "This fellow Adam Bright called on the general line but wanted to talk to you directly, not to your voice mail."

As she headed to her office, the elevator door opened and Cindy walked out. "Guess what? This is a nice surprise for us: Larry Personne called me last night and is heading in here this morning, with his attorney, at eleven."

Together they walked down to Dan's office and shared the news. "Excellent," he said. "Who's the lawyer? Someone we know?"

"Yes, actually. A very good attorney, Jack Silverman. We've worked with him before. He knows his stuff and would never advise anyone to play fast and loose where compliance is concerned. So if Personne has him involved, it's a very good thing for all parties."

They all exhaled at once. "Whew. I'm feeling a lot better about this." Jess said. "One other thing: Adam Bright called in on the general line to talk to me. I don't know what he knows, but I feel like I should call him back. Cindy, what are the legal limits of what I can say to him at this point?"

Cindy instructed Jess to stay away from legal specifics during any conversation with Bright, and they agreed to reconvene after Cindy's meeting with Personne.

Back in her office, Jess picked up her lake rock and rubbed it as she thought about Larry Personne coming in. Had he really come around, or would this be a meeting in which he'd fight their findings?

◇◇◇◇◇◇◇◇◇◇◇◇◇◇◇

Dr. Bright asked if Jess could meet him for a quick lunch near the clinic, and they settled on a little diner a few doors away. After a quick handshake, he offered a suggestion. "It's Friday, and the cook always has a great soup-and-sandwich special. Are you willing to split a sandwich with me?"

"Sounds like you know this place well. Of course." Jess smiled.

"I appreciate your willingness to meet with me. I'm sure there are some limits on what you can tell me about your findings, and I won't put you in an awkward position about that."

"Thanks, Adam. I can tell you that I met with Dr. Personne and gave him our preliminary findings Wednesday. He's conferring with Cindy, my legal colleague, about the details right about now."

"Yes, I know. Larry sought me out last night and bared his soul. He's in bad shape. He begged me to take over the practice and do what I can to save the group." He paused, cleared his throat, and then began again. "You know, I should have felt a certain satisfaction when he admitted his incompetence and utter lack of leadership. But I could only feel sorry for the guy."

The server appeared with two steaming bowls of homemade tomato soup and a grilled cheese sandwich divided between two plates. "Ah, comfort food. Perfect. Please tell Pete he's saving me today. Thanks," Adam said.

He looked up at her shyly and grinned. "Sometimes it doesn't feel good to be right."

"I can certainly agree with you on that, Adam." Then she asked, "Now, what would you like from me?"

"I was the one who found the attorney who Personne has in your office right now. He's a former law school classmate of a friend of mine. I know he's solid and will handle things right, but I haven't decided how much I want to be involved in this mess. I'm going to wait to see what the situation is and whether it can be salvaged, or if it's better for the practice to fold. And, truly, I don't know which it will be."

"OK, I'm with you so far," Jess encouraged.

"Good. I wanted to ask you to think about something. If it happens that we're all better off walking away from the practice, I want you to think about what it would take to start up a new practice with the same physicians, at least those who want to stay together. It's a good group; we just had poor leadership."

Jess nodded. "I understand. And are you thinking it'll be an independent group?"

"Probably not. The heyday of independent practices is clearly coming to an end. If they aren't totally turned off by the idea, given the circumstances, I'd love to see the possibility of a primary-care practice supported by Midwest Health." He looked at her closely to gauge her reaction.

"Well, you've done a lot of thinking over the past twenty-four hours. I can tell you're a natural leader, Adam." She paused. "I knew that before, actually." She smiled warmly at him. "Tell you what. Let me think about this. I'd like to confer with my colleagues, and then I can give you some advice on your ideas. Is that OK?"

"More than OK, Jess." They stood and walked out of the diner together. "By the way, the only time I lost patience with Personne when he came crying to me was when he started to attack you. Unbelievable how some guys always need a scapegoat. Anyway, thanks for meeting and thinking this through with me."

"Of course, Adam. And thanks for lunch." Jess smiled as they parted, and kept smiling until she got to her car. Could this be coming together? She pinched herself, then remembered that Larry Personne and his attorney were with Cindy at that very moment. She checked her phone. No text yet—maybe they were still meeting. Was that good or bad?

Chapter 46

◇◇◇◇◇◇◇◇◇◇◇◇◇◇◇◇◇◇◇◇◇◇◇◇◇

Jess slept in the next morning and, for the first time that week, awoke feeling relaxed and refreshed. She put on her running shoes and took a four-mile jog in her neighborhood. She stopped to grab a latte at a local coffee shop, then walked home leisurely, enjoying the rustle of a light breeze through the trees and the distinct fragrance of the last of the lilacs. The garden beckoned, but she wanted to get to the grocery store before the afternoon rush to shop for food for Sunday brunch. She planned an easy meal of cheese strata, fruit, and antipasti so they wouldn't be preoccupied with cooking while planning the prewedding festivities.

She drove to the grocery store with the windows rolled down, relishing the warm air on her face. Now that the Goodmoor situation was exposed and Personne was cooperating with legal counsel to guide him through the morass of reporting to the authorities, she could take a breath. She, Cindy, and Dan had already made a quiet overture to Dick Morrison on behalf of the physicians of the practice, and he had expressed interest in assisting them, although he had asked Jess to determine exactly how. She already had some ideas, but right now she was going to enjoy her weekend.

The neighborhood was alive with birds chirping, lawn mowers grinding, and joggers and moms with strollers making the most of the beautiful May Saturday. She realized how many of these people she knew and waved to as she drove. She picked up the mail when she got back from the store and hooted with pleasure to see a card from Tom.

Mom,

Like the picture? Gotta use these beautiful Italian postcards for someone special. Wanted to tell you that summer is set. I leave June 1 from here. I can store some of my stuff at school and will send some things home by UPS. I'll be home for two weeks in August. Expect great meals prepared by yours truly. So glad you supported this culinary summer for me. Thanks again, Mom.

Love you!
Tom

She sighed and sat down on the patio to read it again. Nothing was as satisfying as the happiness of one's own children, but she knew she'd miss him anyway.

She headed back to the car to unload her groceries and interrupted a florist deliveryman at her doorstep.

"Mrs. Lawson?" he asked politely.

"Nope. *Ms.* Lawson." She smiled at him. "Thank you." She took the flowers into the kitchen and began unwrapping them. She hadn't quite finished when she saw that they were the color complement of the spring flowers she had received six weeks earlier. She left the arrangement and put the groceries away. She picked up the card, went to the patio, breathed deeply a few times, and opened it: "Jess, I'm sorry. I'm not sure why I went at you that way. I guess it was fear. Please forgive me. Jim"

She pulled out her phone and drafted an e-mail—"I think it's time to take a step back. Thanks for the flowers. Enjoy the ball. Jess"—but decided to sleep on it.

She worked in the shade garden for a couple of hours, then washed up and was trying to decide between tea and her book or wine and cheese and crackers for dinner, when the phone rang. She hesitated before answering, wishing she had caller ID.

"Oh, Beth. What a lovely surprise to cap off my lovely day. How are you, honey?" Sweet relief as she curled up on the couch, preparing for the pure pleasure of a call from her daughter. And this one started on an interesting note: "Mom, I think I've met somebody special . . ."

Chapter 47

◇◇◇◇◇◇◇◇◇◇◇◇◇◇◇◇◇◇◇◇◇◇◇◇

First thing the next morning, Jess, clearheaded, reread her message to Jim twice before sending it.

She prepared food and walked outside to greet Claire as she drove up. They rescued PJ from his car seat and strolled around the garden. He went for the bright colors in the garden pots Jess had planted now that the frost warnings had passed. When Diane drove up, PJ recognized her and reached out immediately.

"Will you look at that? I'm already losing him to another woman." Claire laughed.

Diane took him from Claire. "He's getting so big. I can't believe he's already crawling."

"And getting into everything," Claire said as they entered the house.

"I thought of that. How about we set up in the great room and let him crawl around?" Jess carried the baby toys and diaper bag in from the car. In the kitchen, she took the strata from the oven and then carried it out and set it down with the food already on the great-room table. They all helped themselves and gathered around to watch PJ and do their planning.

An hour later, PJ was down for his nap and Jess had finished her to-do list for Diane's showers in both Goodrich and St. Louis. They carried dishes into the kitchen, and Claire zeroed in on the flowers on the table. "Those are lovely. What's the occasion, Jess?"

"From Jim. A long story there. Are you two up for that?" Jess started a fresh pot of coffee.

"Always." Diane filled the dishwasher. "You know that."

"Yes, please. What's up? Why aren't you going to his place for Memorial Day weekend?" Claire read the card with the flowers. "And why is he apologizing?"

"Well, he kinda went after me for doing my job the way it has to be done." Jess winced. "Seems he didn't like how it might turn out for a fellow doctor."

"A friend of his?" Claire asked.

"No. that's the odd thing. Jim doesn't really know this guy. There's been some bad stuff going on in this practice, so I had to call them on it. I think Jim just plain didn't like it."

"How do you feel about it? Seems like he's apologized." Diane found her coffee mug.

"Yes, he has." Jess scowled. "But, actually, it's a good time to take some time out."

"Because?"

"Well, the anger was surprising—and misplaced. That's the first thing. And I'm worried that we're moving too fast, or at least at different speeds." She paused to pour herself coffee too, and they headed back into the great room.

"I'm not sure we both want to get to the same place. My gut tells me that Jim is looking to get back into a married lifestyle and wants me to take on a traditional wife role."

"Why do you think that?" Claire asked.

"He's rushing me. 'Meet all my friends, come to the Symphony Ball, come to the lake and we'll do all of my lake things, meet my kids, host dinners with me, why are you going home, why not just stay here?'"

"Isn't that behavior consistent with being in love and wanting to share everything with someone?" Diane added cream to her coffee. "And you did introduce him to *your* friends."

"Yes, and that's why I'm not sure. That's why I want to take some time."

"How long have you been dating—two, three months? It's still new. What do you like about this dating thing?" Claire asked.

"Closer to four months now. Not that long, really, especially given that both of us are recently single. Anyway, the best part about being with Jim is that he's helped me realize how much I've missed the intimacy of a relationship—the sex, sure, but also the tender touch, the good-night calls, the intimacy of caring for someone. I love that." Jess looked up carefully.

Diane was smiling broadly at her. "Hey, that's totally healthy and a good thing for you. I bet you didn't have that with Arthur anytime recently, and I know you didn't see so much of it in your own family when we were growing up."

Claire piled on, "So maybe it's not Jim, but maybe Mr. Right is out there somewhere, waiting for you."

"I'm not sure. Maybe he is. Or maybe it *is* Jim." Jess paused and looked at each of her dear friends in turn. "Or is he just convenient because my kids are moving away from my orbit now? Tom is starting off toward being a chef, and Beth has a new boyfriend. Am I afraid to be alone?"

"Well, what *do* you want, Jess? The world awaits," Claire said, but Diane was leaning in for the answer.

"That's the problem—I really don't know what I want now. And it's frustrating!" Jess felt the scrutiny getting to her. She rose too quickly from the sofa and, in an attempt to avoid tripping on a baby toy, steadied herself on the console table, toppling a stack of books, which fell to the floor.

Claire helped Jess pick them up. "This is an unusual book. What is it?" She held it up, and as she did so, a photo fell out of the inner flap.

"Oh, that's the guest book from the lake place." Jess put her pile back on the table.

"It sure is!" Claire laughed. "Look at this pic! Lookin' good, girl!" She held the picture out to Jess. There she was—a younger, nude Jess, hair cascading over her face, backlit by firelight and lying on a plaid blanket.

"Oh my God!" Jess felt her face flush with embarrassment—and relief. "Unbelievable!"

Diane rushed over and exploded in giggles as she looked. The three of them laughed, pointed at Jess, and took turns with the picture until the ruckus woke PJ.

Claire brought her warm and fuzzy son out from Jess's bedroom to say goodbye and packed him up. They were still chuckling as they left—but not before they concluded that there are more mysteries in life than anyone can predict.

Acknowledgments

◇◇◇◇◇◇◇◇◇◇◇◇◇◇◇◇◇◇◇◇◇◇◇◇◇◇◇◇◇◇◇◇◇◇

My writing practice grew from years of hanging out at the Loft Literary Center in Minneapolis. I was an anonymous student in many a class, soaking up the ambience before I ever lifted pen to paper. Excellent teachers, talented fellow students, and intriguing class curricula finally gave me the courage to give it a go. Thanks to the Loft community for making it so.

Thank you to Mary Carroll Moore for your thoughtful and supportive teaching through my early drafts. I am a grateful student of your in-person and online classes, as well as your wonderful retreat at Tanque Verde Ranch. And to all of my classmates, thanks for your honest feedback—the only feedback worth getting.

During the writing and production of this book, I have learned so much from so many gifted professionals. Thanks to Annie Tucker, whose editorial chops and light touch coached this debut novelist to a better finished work. Thanks to Brooke Warner, Cait Levin, and everyone else at She Writes Press and BookSparks for your visionary leadership and steady guidance in keeping me on task and on pace during the production side of publishing.

Finally, to my early readers, Diamond, Lucy, Melpomeni, Sharon, Gabrielle, Kate, and Mary, I am so grateful for the gift of your time and valuable input when I needed it.

Last but not least, my book club, the steadfast No Guilt Book Club, never fails to keep my horizons fresh with appealing literary choices and always feeds my inner artist. Thank you!

About the Author

M aren Cooper grew up in the Midwest and now resides in Minnesota. During her long career as a health services executive, she led a number of organizations in their efforts to respond to the challenges of new, competitive business models, improve their operating systems, and optimize their governance structures. A lifelong reader, Cooper recently discovered the Loft Literary Center in Minneapolis, began taking classes, and slowly unearthed the aspiring writer inside her. She writes best on the shore of Lake Superior, where she retreats frequently to hike, watch the deer devour her hostas, and needlepoint.

For book club questions and to learn more, please visit: www.marencooper.com.

Author photo © Leslie Plesser

Selected Titles From She Writes Press

She Writes Press is an independent publishing company founded to serve women writers everywhere. Visit us at www.shewritespress.com.

Duck Pond Epiphany by Tracey Barnes Priestley. $16.95, 978-1-938314-24-7. When a mother of four delivers her last child to college, she has to decide what to do next—and her life takes a surprising turn.

Play for Me by Céline Keating. $16.95, 978-1-63152-972-6. Middle-aged Lily impulsively joins a touring folk-rock band, leaving her job and marriage behind in an attempt to find a second chance at life, passion, and art.

Shelter Us by Laura Diamond. $16.95, 978-1-63152-970-2. Lawyer-turned-stay-at-home-mom Sarah Shaw is still struggling to find a steady happiness after the death of her infant daughter when she meets a young homeless mother and toddler she can't get out of her mind—and becomes determined to rescue them.

Appetite by Sheila Grinell. $16.95, 978-1-63152-022-8. When twenty-five-year-old Jenn Adler brings home a guru fiancé from Bangalore, her parents must come to grips with the impending marriage—and its effect on their own relationship.

American Family by Catherine Marshall-Smith. $16.95, 978-1-63152-163-8. Partners Richard and Michael, recovering alcoholics, struggle to gain custody of their Richard's biological daughter from her grandparents after her mother's death only to discover they—and she—are fundamentalist Christians.

Again and Again by Ellen Bravo. $16.95, 978-1-63152-939-9. When the man who raped her roommate in college becomes a Senate candidate, women's rights leader Deborah Borenstein must make a choice—one that could determine control of the Senate, the course of a friendship, and the fate of a marriage.